W9-CRI-956

PRAISE FOR FOXBABY

"Delicious and sustaining . . . an anarchically ramshackle comedy of manners. . . . [Jolley's] fiction shines and shines and shines, like a good deed in a naughty world."
—Angela Carter, *New York Times Book Review,* front page

"An interspersed novel-within-a-novel. . . . This complex structure extends Jolley's range of satire and allows her the fullest play of her genius for creating characters who levitate off the page. There is no discomfort for the reader in moving from one imagined world into another, often within one page, sometimes within one paragraph, for all the worlds and the characters have equal validity and equal vitality. This mixture of fantasy and fact, this equivalence of the real and the imagined, is Elizabeth Jolley's theme, and she explores it with great wit, perceptiveness and joy. . . . Her narrator, Alma Porch, has one of the most entertaining imaginations in fiction, and thanks to her creator we can enter that imagination and enjoy."
—*St. Louis Post-Dispatch*

"Hilarious, wry, disturbing, and optimistic. . . . Jolley weaves together farce and satire to illuminate the endless, serious difficulties involved in being human."
—*Boston Globe*

"A raucous, sometimes raunchy tale . . . deliciously outrageous. . . . No matter how the reader takes Elizabeth Jolley's work—for its wit and devilish irony, or its profound darker message—it shimmers with a richness of place and character and dialogue that is breathtaking and rare."
—*San Diego Tribune*

"A witty, sophisticated novel."
Library Journal

ELIZABETH JOLLEY

Foxybaby

A Novel

A Karen and Michael Braziller Book

PERSEA BOOKS / NEW YORK

This book is offered as an expression of thanks to the Literature Board of the Australia Council and to the Western Australia Institute of Technology. The final draft of the book was completed this year during which I have been receiving a Literature Board Fellowship.

To the Western Australian Institute of Technology I am indebted for the continuing privilege of being with students and colleagues in the school of English and for the provision of a room in which to write. I would like, in particular, to thank Don Watts, Brian Dibble, and Don Grant.

ELIZABETH JOLLEY, DECEMBER 1984

First published in Australia by the University of Queensland Press, 1985.
First published in the United States of America by Viking Penguin, Inc., 1985.
Republished in North America and in the British Commonwealth by
Persea Books, Inc., New York, 2010.

Copyright © 1985 by Elizabeth Jolley

All rights reserved. No part of this publication may be reproduced or transmitted in any form or by any means, electronic or mechanical, including photocopy, recording, or any information storage and retrieval system without prior written permission from the publisher.

To request permission to reprint, make copies, and/or for other information, please write to the publisher:

Persea Books, Inc.
853 Broadway
New York, New York 10003

Library of Congress Cataloging-in-Publication Data
Jolley, Elizabeth, 1923-2007
    Foxbaby.
    1. Title.
PR9619.3.J68F6   1986   823   86-8102
ISBN 978-0-89255-363-1

Printed on acid-free, recycled paper in the United States of America by Kase Printing, Hudson, New Hampshire.

First printing

. . . To be conscious that the end of the dream is approaching, and yet has not absolutely come, is one of the most wearisome as well as the most curious stages along the course between the beginning of a passion and its end.

THOMAS HARDY

. . . Then I saw that there was a way to Hell, even from the Gates of Heaven, as well as from the City of Destruction. So I awoke, and behold it was a dream.

J. BUNYAN

FOXY BABY

The Towers
School for Girls
Broadbent
10 June

Miss Penelope Pencraft
The Director
Trinity House School
Cheathem East

Dear Miss Pencraft,

I am delighted to receive your charming letter inviting
me to participate in your January School. I shall be
quite free during those weeks mentioned in your letter
and shall be happy to arrive the day before the School
starts to, as you put it so well, settle in and get down to
the nitty gritty. . . . I have my own car, a Volkswagon,
and am quite able to make the journey comfortably. In
fact I am looking forward to the drive.

I hope to send off my submission of a title and an
outline of the course within the next few days. I note
that you wish me to encourage thought and discussion in
such a way that, through food for the mind, the individual will transcend the need for bodily nourishment.

Yours sincerely,
Alma Porch
(Tutor and writer)

The Towers
School for Girls
Broadbent
17 June

Miss Josephine Peycroft,
   Principal
Trinity College Private Bag
   Cheathem East

Dear Miss Peycroft,
   I am sorry I made a mistake with your name and your position and the name of your establishment. The fault of carelessness is entirely mine and I do hope sincerely that I have made the necessary corrections properly. As Teiresias, who made various pronouncements and at least one serious judgement on our lives, says, "No man alive is free from error . . ."
   Thank you for printing your corrections in block letters. I found them, the block letters, most helpful.

Yours sincerely,
Alma Porch
(Tutor and writer)

The Towers
School for Girls
Broadbent
20 June

Mr Miles
Suite 5
Trinity College
Cheathem East

Dear Mr Miles,
Thank you for your letter. I do not anticipate trouble
on the road or any difficulties of the kind you suggest
during my forthcoming journey but thank you, all the
same, for your kind offer. As for changing wheels and
repairing burst hoses, though I am not in the habit of
carrying out these tasks, I hope I shall be capable of
doing them should the need arise.
I shall not need to buy or hire equipment from you as
I shall bring with me all that I shall require both for the
School and for the journey.
I look forward to meeting you.

Yours sincerely,
Alma Porch

Miss Josephine Peycroft
   Principal Private Bag
Trinity College
   Cheathem East

Dear Miss Peycroft,
   I am sorry to be so long in supplying title and outline.
I do understand your impatience. Thank you for your
letter, by the way. I quite see that you need the material
for your brochure. I must point out, however, that a
novelist is expected to do something remarkable every
time with fresh landscape and with unexpected
characters in the drama of unusual situations. You
realize, of course, that an individual has only a limited
number of ideas, a limited number of phrases and
images and has to work, like a musician, within the
range of notes at his disposal — with what is available.
All this takes time, especially as, in complying with your
request, I am determined to be as topical and as contemporary and as inventive as possible.
   You will appreciate it is not possible to fling a title
together in a matter of moments. I need time to look
into the many ways in which writers can transform their
self-searching exploration and their deep awareness of
human feelings and lives into something which can be
familiar to us all.

I do not think you will regret the little extra time I need. I therefore beg a little patience. I hope to have the submission ready within the next few days.

Yours sincerely,
Alma Porch
(Tutor and writer)

P.S. Your request for absolutely unreserved student participation is noted.

The Towers
etc.
1 August

Ms Josephine Peycroft Private Bag
Principal
Trinity College
Cheathem East

Dear Madam,

No, I do not enjoy arguing about titles. I am always cautious of anyone who either writes or begins a sentence with "for the sake of argument". You say in your letter, "I do so enjoy an argument about titles, don't you?"

I will repeat I do not enjoy this sort of argument. I have too much to do.

What is your exact objection to Dr Johnson? Is it his comparison of the woman preacher and a dog on its hind legs? The reference is essential to my course and nothing derogatory towards women or their attempted liberation is intended.

Of course I realize it will be mainly people attending the course.

And why should people take exception to the words "water trough"? I know that piped water is now available to most places in the country districts. The reference to the water trough is not intended in any way to belittle the tremendous strides progress has made since the turn of the century.

Yours sincerely,
Alma Porch
(Writer and tutor)

P.S. I fully appreciate your water connection and your electrical ditto.

The Towers
etc.
15 August

Miss J. Peycroft
   Principal
Trinity College
   Private Bag. Cheathem East

Dear Miss Peycroft,
   Yes I am willing to shake hands, so to speak, across the miles, like you I feel we have stepped off on the wrong feet. Guides' Honour if you insist, though I never had the privilege.
   Pax too, double Pax, there, is that okay?
   I have made a rearrangement and please note, I went wrong with Samuel Johnson. I have corrected S.J.
   I'd like to explain that my reference to the Japanese

6

writer has absolutely nothing whatever to do with the price of beef or with the possibilities of selling beef or other commodities to that country. My course is entirely literary, concerned only with the drama of human conflict and the resolution of conflict and it has no commercial or political overtones. I am entirely ignorant of what is taking place in the export markets of the world. And, where I have written about a man hurting another man unnecessarily and deliberately, it has nothing whatever to do with homosexuals, politicians, governments, shire councils, education departments or the health scheme. And I can assure you, from the bottom of my heart, there will be nothing to offend "any people from any walk of life who will be kind enough to spend their dollars on enrolment" (your words). I fully understand your feelings of responsibility, indeed I share them. I am perfectly aware that we are concentrating on the nourishment of the mind to counteract the lamentable results of over-nourishment elsewhere.

Yours etc.
Alma Porch (Tutor etc)

Towers
For Girls
Broadbent

Ms J. Peycroft
  Principal
Trinity etc. Private

Dear Miss Peycroft,
    I am sorry you are uneasy. You say I am obsessed

with Samuel Johnson. I think this is an unfair criticism since you base your judgement simply on your knowledge of me through the submission of this title. I would like, however, to point out to you that it was Dr. Johnson in 1759 who made the following observation:

"He who has nothing external that can divert him, must find pleasure in his own thoughts, and must conceive himself what he is not. . . . He then expatiates in boundless futurity, and culls from all imaginable conditions that which for the present moment he should most desire, amuses his desire with impossible enjoyments. . . . The mind dances from scene to scene, unites all pleasures in all combinations, and riots in delights which nature and fortune, with all their bounty cannot bestow. . . . To indulge the power of fiction and send imagination out upon the wing. . . ."

Do not these fragments of quotation show you the ways in which I mean to offer the students the maximum of what you desire for them?

"There is a difference," says a Japanese writer, "between a man who offends because he is forced to and a man who hurts others unnecessarily and deliberately."

And the poet writes simply: "Someone was before me at my water trough . . . and I have something to expiate."

In my course, in the drama, an outline of which I enclose, I plan to look at the reverence for life and the responsibilities between human beings as the writer makes, through his own life and experience, the search into the unknown to reach some kind of blessing.

Miss Peycroft, if still unsuitable I'll take out something or put in something. I quite agree it is simply not feasible to submit a suggested reading list if books, other than those I bring with me, are not available.

Yours sincerely,
A. Porch

Towers
30 September

Miss J. Peycroft
   Principal
Trinity House
   Private Bag. Cheathem East

Dear Miss Peycroft,
   I am pleased to sign and return the contract you enclose. I note that all money owing to me will be paid on the last day of the School. I note that further discussion of the course will be held at Trinity College on my arrival there the day before the commencement of the School.
   A. Bientôt. Till January then, yrs,
Alma Porch

There is only one road going east from the township of Cheathem West and this road after approximately two hours of sedate driving (one hour for the reckless) becomes the main high street of Cheathem East.

There are scarcely any houses in Cheathem East as very few people live there. There is no hotel and no shop.

Scattered between the two Cheathems are a few lonely farms tucked and folded as if sewn neatly into the landscape for many years. In places, where the road rises, the dark seams of these farms can be seen in the distance. It is as if they are embroidered with rich green wool or silk on a golden background. In the design of the embroidery are a few trees and some silent houses and sheds. Narrow places, fenced off and watered sparingly, produce a little more of the dark-green effect in the picture.

At intervals, sometimes as if they do not belong to anyone in particular, there are unsupervised windmills turning and clicking with a kind of solemn and honest obedience.

On reaching Cheathem East the high street, after passing directly alongside the surprisingly unexpected windows and front door of a very large old house, very soon becomes a gravel track which, with many twists and turns through endless paddocks of wheat, turns finally and like a river without any water reaches the sea. This place where land and water meet is scattered with enormous rocks as if some enormous children, the sons and daughters of a pair of happily married giants, suddenly tiring of their playthings, have hurled them into the sea. The dark waves running and rising wash endlessly over the rocks from both sides giving an impression of two oceans meeting in conflict. Some of the rocks dropped by the little giants rest where they have fallen along the wide sandy bay.

Miss Alma Porch, snug in her battered Volkswagen, drove with pleasure through the peaceful surroundings. Enjoying the delightful feeling of escape she sang tunelessly, something operatic, and nodded her head in time to her own aria. She was on the way to Cheathem East. Occasionally she stopped singing to listen, from habit, with some anxiety to the rattle of her engine. This noise being sustained as usual she let her mind race ahead. She hoped Trinity College would live up to her expectations. She thought about sunflowers. Sunflowers with heads as big as dinner plates, golden sunflowers in the corners of old buildings and by crumbling walls. She hoped they would be growing in Cheathem East.

With failing confidence she thought of the death of Chekhov in her brief case and other unsuitable things remembered and stuffed in at the last moment. She wondered how the students would respond. Cheathem West, she reflected, was positively a forest of television aerials. The aerials were very tall, probably, she thought, because of some geographical and unchangeable error in the choice made by the first settlers who naturally would not have had television in mind when selecting and clearing their land. The thickets of these aerials, all the same, showed unmercifully the tastes of the community, especially as the antennae were possibly capable of picking up only the less desirable programmes.

Frowning, Miss Porch urged her noisy way between the paddocks of golden stubble now spreading on both sides of the road. The aerials, she told herself, were simply a dark wood through which she had passed. She was a little tired that was all. It was a very good thing, she thought, that she was travelling on this long unfamiliar road during daylight. It was still early in the afternoon. It would not get dark for several hours.

"Nel mezzo del cammin di nostra vita
mi ritrovai per una selva oscura . . .

"In the middle of the journey I came to myself in a dark wood where the straight way was lost . . . Alas!" Miss Porch sighed, "I can only misquote a translation made by someone else.

"I' non so ben ridir com . . . my pronounciation is so awful, really appalling! It's fortunate that I am travelling alone. Let me see, something like . . . I cannot rightly tell how I entered it. So full of sleep was I about the moment that I left the true way . . ."

Miss Porch's sturdy waggon approached the beginning of a long curve, the first in a very straight road. She was more than a little anxious to finish her journey before nightfall.

The first part of the drive had not been without incident. Foolishly driving through the city when everyone else was intent on getting to work she had been suddenly aware that she was being followed. In her rear mirror there appeared plainly a car exactly like her own with a greyish-green shabbiness and about the same number of dents. Whichever way Miss Porch went the other car followed. In the uneasiness of this she told herself that the driver had mistaken her for someone else. A hard-working wife had obviously left her cut lunch on a suburban kitchen table and the devoted husband was weaving in and out of the lanes of traffic trying to catch her. Perhaps a neat package would sail across the cars and drop into her lap. Miss Porch wondered whether to have her window open in readiness.

Later it became quite clear that the other car was actually, with curious leaps and jerks, following her car. Perhaps, she told herself, feeling indulgent, the two cars were, unknown to both drivers, acquainted. After all, they were roughly the same hideous colour and they looked almost the same age. Perhaps in some car yard they had endured months of waiting side by side, perhaps during a whole winter of endless rain. Or they might actually have followed each other on the same paths of the assembly line sharing the experience of being put together at exactly the same moment.

At some point on the edge of the city Miss Porch's car lost its follower and the rear mirror reflected only the lengths of empty road which gradually lost width as it became embedded in the apparent tranquillity of a more rural landscape.

She knew that what seemed like an incident had not really been one. She wondered whether machinery was capable of feeling excitement and then, of course, after excitement the possibility of disappointment. . . .

Using a little ordinary language Miss Porch told herself to pull herself together and to concentrate on the road.

There are strange things about driving alone on long lonely roads through the wheat. Old, grey, bent men and women wait indefinitely on green misleading corners, becoming part of the bushy roadside undergrowth as soon as the helpful traveller stops to investigate. Comfortable inviting tracks in the twilight, lined with soft sand and leaves, appear to lead off easily to the right as the main road curves to the left. And, as dusk advances, more gnarled old men march in formation, keeping up a remarkable speed, alongside, in the shadowy fringes of the saltbush. Occasionally a solitary driver pulls off on to the shoulder of the road to allow a ship to cross in front of him from one moonlit paddock to another.

Miss Porch had her foot flat to the floor. She sang with more fullness perhaps to urge her way with greater speed. She had been driving for several hours and seemed to be penetrating, as she said to herself, the back of beyond.

An ancient bus, once the property of a reputable boarding school for young ladies from good families, still bearing an uplifting motto and emblazoned with crests and colours, travelling in an easterly direction some distance ahead and, because of starting to round the long bend, out of sight, stopped to pick up an elderly woman who was proceeding slowly on foot in the same direction.

The woman, who was dressed in respectable black, Miss Porch thought in the briefest possible time for any thought, must have walked a tremendous distance to be in that remote and lonely place. As she was about to raise a heavy and obviously weary foot to the iron step, Miss Porch, reaching top G, took the first part of the bend in a style suitable for a *prima donna* and crashed into the substantial fender at the back of the bus.

Another phenomenon connected with travelling through the wheat is that motor vehicles remain spaced with considerable distances between them, thus causing the driver to feel he is the only person on a deserted road passing through an entirely empty landscape. Should it be necessary to stop, it becomes evident very quickly that other people are on the road too. An uncanny concertina-like closing of the long-distance spacing occurs. Cars in a hitherto unrealized succession pass the halted one if it is off the road. If the car is standing on the road, there is every chance that the next one, coming more quickly than expected, will run into it.

As soon as Miss Porch's chariot crumpled up on the back of the bus, a second car with a frantic yelping horn and an ineffectual squeal of brakes crashed into the back of Miss Porch. After a few moments a blue Mercedes, purring along on the bitumen, smoothly rounding the bend, crushed the second car. The Mercedes was unharmed. The same could not be said of the other two, sandwiched as they were between the greater strengths.

Miraculously, as if in anticipation of at least two prayers, a tow-truck manned by two muscular men emerged from the shade of the only trees along that part of the road. There was a convenient smooth patch of gravel beneath these trees. It was here the drivers gathered to inspect the damage, shake their heads and exchange names and addresses and insurance companies.

Fortunately, though the drivers were badly shocked and bruised, they were not seriously hurt. Perhaps relying on their shocked state, the bus driver stated simply and quickly that he was not insured and neither was his vehicle. He could, he told them, fully recommend Finch's Smash Repair Yard in Cheathem West, its excellence being out of this world. He would advise them to let the two lads here with the truck take their little problems in hand.

"In tow, I should say," he added wittily. He suggested that he would then drive them all to where they wanted to go.

"It's the least I can do for youse." He gave Miss Porch a wink which was startling in its suggestion of familiarity. She noticed his eyes were a clear china blue and very steady like the eyes of a white goose.

"Seeing as there's only the one place to go to along this route," he pronounced it rowt, "I shan't be goin' out of me way if I take youse all for a ride."

Gratefully the car drivers and the two passengers belonging to the second car climbed into the bus where the stout woman in black was sitting in an attitude of resigned patience, as if this sort of encounter was an everyday event in her life.

That the bus was there, they all agreed, was an incredible piece of good fortune.

One of the tow-truck men approached the driver of the Mercedes. "That's a great roo bar you've got there" — he indicated the solid ornament.

"Yes," the owner of the Mercedes said, "I like to think of it and this great big bonnet between me and the next man, especially if, inadvertently, I am driving the wrong way in a one-way street." The tow-truck man nodded in good-natured agreement and suggested that the Mercedes would benefit from a check up over in Finchy's Yard. "It's more'n likely," he said, "that with her being new, still wet behind the ears, so to speak, she'll need respringing for country driving. How's about we run her along with the other two while we're about it . . ."

"A perfectly splendid idea," the owner of the Mercedes boomed pleasantly. "I would simply love to finish my journey in good company. Oh! Yes, please do put my luggage, I'm afraid there's rather a lot of it, up on the racks there. Thank you so much."

16

The old bus rattled off along the road carrying the travellers and their boxes and bags and cases to Cheathem East.

Miss Porch, leaning her forehead against the cool window of the bus, felt sure she heard Mr Miles, he had told them he was called Miles, talking in a low voice to the woman in black. She heard him say quite distinctly, "We're in Business! What did I tell you! We're in Business. I'm telling you, three cars orf to the smash yard just in the one trip, not three trips but one. Yo'll get your share never youse worry, after all you done your bit 'anging about for the arternoon. You'll 'ave a nice lay-down soon as we get in. Could do with a kip meself." It seemed to Miss Porch that Mr Miles, yawning, leered at her. She suddenly felt extraordinarily tired. Sensibly she told herself she was suffering from shock.

During the warm afternoon Miss Porch, turning over on the narrow bed in the small room, knew she had not been asleep. A few bruises seemed to be aching and, as she said to herself, it is hard to actually rest and sleep in a strange place without unpacking and making some sort of territorial investigation and establishment. Usually on arrival in a new place she inspects the cupboards and makes a point of discovering as soon as possible the more strategically placed bathroom.

Half-sitting up she remembered that on one occasion

she had been forced to dust the window ledges before being able to feel comfortable. She had really no idea where in the College this room was.

"You'll be having arternoon tea with Miss Peycroft," Miles had said, "arternoon tea tit-a-tit with Miss Peycroft." Simply, after being conducted to the room with her luggage carried up by Miles, she first sat on the bed and later lay on it as if needing to recover from the journey. Shortly she would need to tidy herself. The thought of the tea was comforting. It was quite an ordeal to have to wait until the appointed hour for it.

There was a rustling and a whispering as if people were trampling on the dried-up herbaceous border immediately beneath her window. It was a gruff conversation, the voice being lowered almost to a growl.

"Of course Rennett, you understand, I am not able to offer you marriage. Naturally as we are, er, of the same sex we are not in a position to marry but I have been entertaining the idea for some time, ever since I met you for the first time, here, ten years ago wasn't it, that you should share all that I happen to have the good fortune to possess."

After a silence, quite brief and with a feeling of embarrassment transmitted through the quiet afternoon stillness, the gruffy talk continued. "I do hope you will consider my offer, Rennett." Another silence, and then in an even gruffer, almost inaudible tone: "I want you to know, Rennett, I do offer my sincerest apologies for my beastly behaviour when I arrived earlier today. I was and still am somewhat overwrought, you understand, the travelling — the mishap on the road and the excitement of being here at last, you know I look forward to it all tremendously — and then seeing you again, well, it was all too much. I hope you will shake hands, Rennett?

Please? You will? Oh thank you, you are a dear! A dear old sossidge.''

Miss Porch was conscious of another short silence and then the low growlings of half-spoken endearments, tinged with self-conscious noises of affection, floated upwards through the warm drowsy afternoon. The gruff voice, almost a hoarse whisper, said, "There's absolutely no need for you to make up your mind in a hurry, Rennett. I know you're settled for the time being. It's just that I'm a lonely old thing wanting to share the comforts I have. I'm thinking of you for later on, when you're ready. Do you see?"

Miss Porch, cautiously leaning over the cracking wood of her unpainted window sill, heard a remnant of a song, a deep throaty singing:

"Madam will you walk
Madam will you talk
Madam will you walk and talk with me . . ."

The words were soon lost in a droning humming sound. The singer and the object of the song appeared momentarily blocked solid in an unmagical meeting of denim and heather tweed supported on sturdy legs planted wide apart among the small weeds and flowers. Almost at once the vision disappeared and Miss Porch, leaning out a little farther, saw that a door leading into the house was under her window. She drew back into her room. She was too tired to rest. She supposed the lover and the beloved would be a part of the class, her class. Her heart sank. It rose too, for the voice was an excellent one, even if the figure was all wrong. Miss Peycroft had, in her initial letter stressed imagination and invention as being essential for creativity. Miss Porch felt sure she would be able to use this voice. . .

19

"This title's no good," Miss Josephine Peycroft said, "surely you could have seen that, Paisley. What do you think, Miss Porch? I mean you must realize that we cannot possibly use it. Sorry to be so negative."

"I've forgotten what it was." Miss Paisley blinked behind her round bifocals. Miss Porch thought she had the look of someone given to the furtive eating of biscuits, the crumbs collecting in the corner of her soft mouth . . .

"But we have just spoken of it," Miss Peycroft said as smoothly as she could in the presence of Miss Porch, whose recent arrival had caused a tarnished silver teapot to appear. That Miles had not polished the tea-service was yet another small annoyance, Miss Porch felt sure, in the back of Miss Peycroft's busy mind.

"I do like your theme immensely." Miss Peycroft, in flowered silk, turned her full attention to Miss Porch. She handed stained Queen Anne cups on chipped saucers. Miss Porch took hers gratefully and tried to drink slowly. It would look vulgar to reveal her thirst.

"Subject's a bit dicey," Miss Peycroft continued, "but it's so, how shall I say, up-to-the-minute topical. Also it's an unusual way of tackling a current problem in our society. Another aspect of the problem, seen from a different angle. Your written submission was, I must say, extraordinarily well prepared. I hope you had a good run today, a good journey?"

"Oh yes thank you. I'm afraid my car's a write off, though. Went straight into the back of a bus, so unexpected, the bus being there, I mean, luckily the driver . . ."

Miss Peycroft interrupted with some hurried noises of sympathy. "Have another cup," she said, standing up to refill the teacups with the aromatic pale liquid. "I hope you like our tea," she said, bending a hawk-like smile upon Miss Porch. "We make it ourselves from a dried weed which grows in profusion here. I believe it used to be known locally, when there were people in Cheathem East, as one of the stinkworts." She gave a laugh which ended in a sigh. "But we must get back to the title. Paze, old girl, I can't think why you didn't get on to Miss Porch about the title before." Miss Peycroft shuffled some papers. "Here it is," she said, "I'll read it again: *He gave no thought to how fearful it is to have to sit and have your ears assaulted by inadequate talent.*"

"I realize," Miss Peycroft said, "that it is from Goethe and therefore beautifully written but we can't, we simply cannot invite students, mature age students from the more — er — the more well-to-do suburbs, to come to The Better Body Through The Arts Course and throw that at them, especially not the music and drama students. In colloquial language, it's not on."

Miss Porch, to hide her annoyance, watched Miss Paisley who was making shorthand notes with a freshly sharpened pencil on a folded pad held over one knee.

Miss Peycroft frowned. "Oh Paze," she said, "there's no need to put all this down. You know perfectly well that you'll dump the whole lot in the wastepaper basket. For simply ages now you haven't been able to understand your own hieroglyphics. You did, I see," Miss Peycroft continued, turning towards Miss Porch once more, "you did offer us a choice of titles, this one from Brahms I do quite like in itself: *It is easy to compose but it is very difficult to let the superfluous notes fall under the table.* — But, bearing in mind our enrolments, that's rather insulting too." She glanced across at Miss Porch, her slender fingers holding the page at arm's length. "I'm thinking," she said, "of someone like Mrs Viggars. She's been coming to our School for years. She always enrols for music, composition of and appreciation of, and for the drama. She is intelligent enough to be offended by the title and we simply cannot afford to offend anyone — especially Mrs Viggars. As I said, it's not on!"

"Did you know," Miss Paisley interrupted, "that Brahms wrote twenty string quartets before he published one?"

"Yes, Paze," Miss Peycroft replied. Miss Porch noticed that Miss Peycroft seemed to treat Miss Paisley's muddled attempts at intellectual survival with the kind of gentleness which restrains impatience. "Yes of course I know. It was I who told you that." Her smile, in the direction of Miss Paisley's shorthand, exposed her bottom teeth. "I am not certain of the fact," she said, "so if you intend to use it for further quoting it would need to be verified. Clearly Paze," she continued, "I am amazed that you have remembered something! You must not," she turned quickly to Miss Porch, "you must not mind our amusing little quarrels. Anyway, Paze," she continued, "that little fact would not be suitable for a course title even if it happened to be true."

"I don't think Mrs Viggars would be put off by anything," Miss Paisley said quickly. "I mean, she loves coming. Remember last year." She giggled.

"Of course I remember." Miss Peycroft rummaged among the papers on her desk. "Oops! my tea! Must be more careful. I'll just find some of the photographs. Miss Paisley and I were just looking at them when you arrived. Ah! Here we are, we were reliving last year's School." She held out some pictures to Miss Porch who took them carefully between respectful fingertips.

"That's Mrs Viggars," Miss Peycroft said, "the one sitting in the cardboard-box, rather a squeeze but she managed it ultimately. Luckily Miles found something big enough, a console television carton or was it a double-door refrigerator . . ."

"Whatever is that on her head?" Miss Porch, in her curiosity, forgot good manners and interrupted Miss Peycroft, who did not seem to mind.

"Oh that. That's a cushion," she said. "It was hilarious. They all wore cushions on their heads and rocked across the courtyard in the boxes. Great fun! We offered Basic Self Expression as an Extra d'you see. Mrs Viggars loves to take part in everything and will do anything she is asked to do." Miss Peycroft shuffled the papers and the photographs. "By the way," she said, "I'm very glad to have this word with you in private, it's about Mrs Viggars. She must, at all costs, be given the leading rôle in the drama. But more of that later. Just now we must concentrate on the title . . ."

"What about *Food For Thought*," Miss Paisley said suddenly. Miss Porch was surprised at the neatness of this and was about to say so when Miss Peycroft remarked not unkindly,

"It's a terrible cliché, Paze," she seemed to be considering it for a moment, "*Art and The Human Body. Food For Thought*. It is utterly banal." She smiled at Miss Porch and at Miss Paisley. "But then that is what people understand and like. We'll simply put the course up on the board under the heading of:

CREATIVE MUSIC AND DRAMA WITH AMAZING
OPPORTUNITIES AND RESULTS

Caps please, Paze, and a note about weighing in and weighing out. Got that down Paze? Will you see to that as soon as poss? Some of the tutors and students are here already. Meanwhile I will take Miss Porch on a little tour of reconnaissance. And Paze," Miss Peycroft raised her voice slightly "Paze, when you go downstairs, look in and see if Miles is back. He was thinking of taking the bus out again. Remind him about the service this evening."

She turned to Miss Porch. "Do please come this way," she said, moving swiftly across the floorboards; her slippers were, Miss Porch noticed, embroidered in a medieval design and made no sound. "I am so glad," she said glancing back at Miss Porch with a mixture of approval and doubt, "that you seem to be a twinset-and-pearls sort of person, so reliable. I don't mean at this time of the year of course," she added, "naturally it would be too warm for such clothing now — though it does get fearfully cold here at night even in the summer. I was afraid," she gave a musical laugh, "I was afraid that being an authoress and perhaps something of a feminist you'd wear hob-nailed boots and a man's hat pulled down over your eyes. Why is it" — she paused as if thinking aloud — "why is it that Wimmins Libbers keep those terribly ugly hats on all the time, even at mealtimes?"

Miss Porch tried to step lightly in spite of her heavy shoes. she would have like to take off her hat but even if she did this surreptitiously, Miss Peycroft would be sure to notice. It would be best, she thought, to try and look as if she had not noticed the comments on clothes.

At the top of the stairs Miss Peycroft put her hand lightly on the smooth curving bannister and, leaning forward, she called downstairs: "Don't forget, Paze! Don't forget to remind Miles that he is taking the service tonight."

Leading the way Miss Peycroft took Miss Porch along

the upper passages of the house. "As you see," she said, "Miss Paisley and I have these rooms over the chapel. The rooms along the passage here are for the School. The open doors await the students. Closed doors mean that those rooms are taken. The attics are for the men," she explained, "and these ladders, one at either end, are for access to the attics. The bathrooms are in the middle."

Together they walked down the polished stairs and crossed a well-proportioned hall in which were various cabinets of Art Work.

"All presented by grateful students over the years." Miss Peycroft waved her loose sleeves to the left and to the right as they passed woven mats, patchwork quilts, stained-glass lampshades, paintings of sunsets and bowls of fruit. "The ceramics," Miss Peycroft said, "are particularly interesting, the tiles and vases and basins in that rather gritty grey are produced from our own local clay, quite a speciality, and believe it or not, the goblets and candlesticks are carved from the golden wood of our cape lilacs. The students, for some reason, do not wish to take their work away."

Miss Porch made a small noise of what she hoped would sound like enthusiastic appreciation. She had not been at the College an hour and she was wishing she could drive on somewhere else. This was not a new feeling. She had experienced many times before the pleasure of arrival in some country township being followed immediately by a wish to continue driving to yet another place which, holding in its position of distance some magical quality waiting to be discovered by the traveller, remained forever on an unreachable horizon. She knew, with slight feelings of panic, that she was not able to drive anywhere. Because of the state of her car, unless that Mr Miles would take her away in his bus, she had no means of escape. She tried to listen to Miss Peycroft who simply did not seem to know how to stop talking.

"This chair" — Miss Peycroft indicated an ornamental chair which occupied a central position so that any one passing through the hall either had to fall over it or walk round it. "This chair," Miss Peycroft said, "was also a gift from a student, perhaps more a gift from the grateful relative of a simply enormous student who died shortly after completing his seventeenth course at the College. I suppose," she said, "it could be looked upon as a sort of monument, a paying of homage. At the time I tried various purrings of suitable suggestions about the possibility of his dying in any case, you know, death occurring *not* from his being here at Trinity, but the giver of the chair would not, under any circumstances change her mind. 'He died here,' she insisted, 'after taking your course. He would have liked you to have it.' Even though I protested she was adamant. 'You've got to have it,' she said, 'after all he did make it here.' She really accused, you know, and she kept on, 'and I do have a very small flat, so small, you have no idea, I haven't got room for even ordinary chairs let alone this, this monster. I insist that you do have it.' " Miss Peycroft gave Miss Porch a little smile of helplessness. "Have you ever," she asked, "been in the painful and unfortunate position of having to receive, for example, empty jam-jars as a gift from someone who is clearing out cupboards and, even if you declare you never have made and never will make jam, is determined to give them to you?"

Miss Porch tried to recollect if she had been the receiver of empty jars but her mind refused to bring any such memory forward.

"I don't think. ...." she began, but Miss Peycroft, not waiting for an answer continued: "It's the most uncomfortable chair, and so heavy no one can move it. Sometimes I sit in it here opposite the front door when I am waiting for new tutors to come. The uneasiness of the chair is even worse than the sense of uneasiness which accompanies the arrival of new staff. It's an ancient practice, medical of course, a counter-irritant, if you understand what I mean, present company excepted of course."

"Thank you," Miss Porch said, trying to keep up.

"The house," Miss Peycroft said, "is a long house with a double row of windows facing the absolutely deserted street on one side and on the other side the windows look over the courtyard. There are two short wings at either end. You will like the charming verandas, rather derelict but that is a part of the charm, don't you think? At the far end is the music room. I'll take you there later, it opens on to a sort of decrepit terrace. A good place to sit and think. Oh, and by the way," she went on as she struggled with the bolt on the front door, "talking of music we shall be having a quartet in residence during our Easter School. I hope you'll be able to whizz back for it during your hols. I can give you exact dates. They've promised us opus a hundred and eleven." She paused as if after a large, well-formed exclamation mark.

Miss Porch, feeling the exclamation mark, nodded. Her lips were drawn thirstily back over her teeth in what she hoped was a smile of musical appreciation and knowledge. She gulped, wondering whose one hundred and eleventh. It would be possible, she thought, racing in her mind, to inquire in the public library, in the non-fiction section of course. Perhaps she would be able to check all the opus scores available for public scrutiny. . . .

The front door was opened and they stepped out together on to the pavement.

"I like," Miss Peycroft said, "to think of this brass plate on the wall as some kind of inherited blessing. The name on the plate in itself has no significance, for one thing it is impossible to read. In quiet moments," she said, "between Schools — it is scarcely a week since our previous course, Multi-racial Tolerance Through Fasting and Meditation, finished — I like to think about the man or woman whose name is now invisible in that worn, rather dull metal. Perhaps it was a writer," she mused, not seeming to notice Miss Porch, "or a painter or a silversmith. Perhaps it was an historian or a chiropodist or someone giving music lessons. Or," she added with her charming smile, "the plate might have, at one time, announced the presence of a doctor or a gynaecologist or even an obscure order of nuns."

Miss Porch looked across the empty street to the partly ruined buildings. One looked like a house, another could have been a shop.

"Once there was a shop there." Miss Peycroft seemed to echo Miss Porch's thought. "It was possible," she said, "without moving your feet at all, to buy anything from bolts of cloth, harness, saddles and drums of linseed oil to groceries, baby clothes, sweets, postcards and toothbrushes. There was an hotel too here in Cheathem East." She waved her arm in the direction of a faded sign. "It was," she said, "as you see, called *The Good Shepherd*. Though the building has gone and the people have forgotten Him — there is His name still creaking to and fro in the wind. You must admit He has a commanding view in both directions." Miss Peycroft laughed.

Miss Porch shivered; the wind blowing, as it does across the wheat stubble, was cold in spite of the season. Drab sheep, straying in radiating lines like a fan opened over the paddock, were feeding in the stubble.

"This wheat," Miss Peycroft explained, "is only a very narrow tributary to much wider paddocks. Of course we see the wheat in all the glory of growing and ripening; you, on arrival, are simply presented with the stubble. But," she said turning with a kind of rapture to Miss Porch, "even the stubble stained with thunderstorm showers has a peaceful loveliness which cannot be ignored. You must excuse me if I get poetical in the evenings about the beauty and the usefulness of wheat. I am sorry we have no river as they have in Cheathem West and we are a considerable distance from the sea but if Miles can strip down the bus and make her more roadworthy we shall have our usual expedition to the coast during the Course. Now," she said, "come through and have a look at the courtyard where you will have your classes. It is paved and partly walled. There is the orchard over there and, as you see, we have an abundance of weeds and some flowers. There is a carpark behind the East Wing, if any cars get here. And we have an assortment of sheds." Miss Peycroft drew breath. "Play with it," she said.

"I beg your pardon!" Miss Porch stared at Miss Peycroft.

"What I say," Miss Peycroft said, "play with the whole place. You are absolutely free! You have *carte blanche* to go where you like. Arrange things as you wish them to be. Simply roam wither thou willest, or words to that effect."

They stood in the middle of the courtyard. Miss Porch tried to look as if she was planning something to fit into the spaciousness.

"Come up to my room again," Miss Peycroft said suddenly. "I must let you get on with your unpacking but there are one or two more things to discuss."

Upstairs Miss Peycroft poured out the rest of the now cold tea. She seemed excited. "About your theme," she said, "I see the whole thing as a series of *Tableaux Vivants*. That's it. A splendid idea! *Tableaux Vivants* accompanied by the dramatic reading which, I gather, you will do yourself — and suitable music which I, of course, am only too pleased to supply. The recorder you know, and Miss Paisley will be only too pleased to perform on the tapping sticks. It is possible too that we may get a pianist or a harpist among the enrolments. By tomorrow they will all be here and we can see what instruments we can have."

"Yes, of course." Miss Porch hoped that Miss Peycroft would not notice her lack of interest. The idea of the *Tableaux Vivants* had given her a shock. All energy seemed to drain away and she had an incredible longing to yawn, to relax in a deep bath of warm water and to sink into bed.

"The students," Miss Peycroft continued, "have all paid through the nose. It is an expensive Course so it simply must succeed. I am relying absolutely on your story breakdown and on the video. The mime," she said, "can all be put on video and we can have a replay in the evenings thus making the symposium more satisfactory. By the way, we don't dress for the evening meal. We don't even sit down for it and we just wear something simple, you know, the little silk dress, perhaps one little ornament and something woolly to slip on if it's cold."

"Oh thank you," Miss Porch said, searching her luggage, in her head, with a frantic despairing wish for a suitable frock. Something with berries on it would be attractive she thought. In her mind she raked through the few clothes she possessed.

"I think the students will rise to it," Miss Peycroft, unaware of Miss Porch's mental unpacking, went on. "It all depends on how you present the treatment of the story. The storyline's the thing. Give that well and it'll succeed. I like very much," she said, "your idea of the elderly man and the young girl and a baby holed up, as it were, in a dreary motel unit. Also, *a propos* the scene of desolate passion between the two prisoner officers, I notice while dealing in detail with women you don't attempt to, how shall I put it, explore male homosexual relationships?" Miss Peycroft paused as if waiting for an answer but, before Miss Porch was able to utter some kind of a reply, she continued with a low-voiced earnestness, "I believe, with men, some kind of explosion takes place. Might be worth looking into some day. In any case, I must say you'll certainly send the students on their way after this School with their Thinking Caps on and, I hope, having lost considerable *avoirdupois*. Goody! Jolly Good for you, Alma. May I call you Alma?"

"Oh but of course," Miss Porch tried a well-bred murmur.

Miss Peycroft, having finished her tea, played a few notes on a handsome treble recorder. "Thank you Alma, it is a very nice name, not heard very often these days. This tune," she continued, "is part of a little thing I call my *Wagner in the Wheat*, a sort of *Folly Piccolo*. A little dance." She played the tune, nodding at Miss Porch and, since her lips were busy, her smile came twinkling through her eyes.

Miss Porch, worrying about the mime, was not able to appreciate the expressive music and smile. She looked past Miss Peycroft to the window trying to imagine this entirely new idea, the mime, in practical detail.

Miss Peycroft stopped playing. "Do you know Cyril Scott's *Water Wagtail?*" she asked.

"No, I don't think so." Miss Porch gave a little sigh of regret.

"Oh what a pity," Miss Peycroft said, "do you mean to say that no one, but no one, played *Water Wagtail* for you when you were a little child?"

"No, I don't think they ever did." Miss Porch bit her lip with a suitable display of acute misery and loss.

"I shall play it for you now." Miss Peycroft was firm.

"Oh thank you," Miss Porch said.

"I must confess," Miss Peycroft said when the music had been suitably applauded, "that I suffer from an annoyance, a frustration."

"Oh?" Alma Porch, in spite of her exhaustion, tried to look intelligent and sympathetic.

"Yes." Miss Peycroft opened the recorder case, it was lined with soft red silk. "Can you imagine the downright absolute frustration of not being able to play the cello and the double bass — at once, I mean — simultaneously?"

"The idea has never occurred to me," Miss Porch said. "I can see there would be difficulties.

"Difficulties!" Miss Peycroft laughed her rich laugh. "The music lover's laugh, Alma," she said, "to be stored forever in delicately curved brackets in your mind! Difficulties! My dear Alma. Impossibilities. Just imagine! It would be like trying to be raped by two men simultaneously. One after the other, yes, but both at once, absolutely no. That is how I am, Miss Porch, unable, absolutely unable to produce the cello notes and the double bass notes at the same time. I suppose one cannot be a musical hermaphrodite . . . but I must be quiet about myself. I just wanted to ask one other thing. I wanted to ask . . ." Miss Peycroft fondled her recorder.

Miss Porch, aching with boredom and bruises, yawned out of the corner of her mouth. She would die, she thought, if she could not escape from this woman.

"I wanted to ask," Miss Peycroft was suddenly shy, "I — well, we are very fortunate in having the poet Xerxes Kolynosodes with us for this School. He has come from Europe with Miss Harrow . . ."

"Ah yes," Miss Porch said, "I met him briefly on the road. They travelled in the bus with . . ."

"It would be wonderful," Miss Peycroft's words rode over Miss Porch's, "if you and Xerxes could have some flesh and eyeball contact in the next few days. Traditional Greek chorus in the yard would be super. Really splendid. The music, that characteristic dying fall of the melodic line . . ."

"Mine," Miss Porch said stiffly, "is definitely solid rock, punk rock and disco."

"Oh yes, of course," Miss Peycroft stood up quickly. "You will find Mr Miles, our outside man, downstairs," she said, "he is the person to see about your stage arrangements. She accompanied Miss Porch to the top of the stairs in such a manner that Miss Porch felt she was being dismissed.

In the morning, she thought, she would leave this shabby College — house — whatever it was. She wished she had not come. This Miss Peycroft, Josephine Peycroft, was impossible. She thought of the students and wondered whether they would be impossible too. How could the drama she had written have anything to do with the students of the school losing weight? The whole thing was absurd. And then the idea of the mime. . . .

The soft rustle of silk behind her on the stairs caused her to turn round. Miss Peycroft was beside her. "My dear!" she said, "I am having an existential crisis." She paused, they were about halfway on the stairs, neither up nor down. As Miss Porch did not reply, Miss Peycroft ended her pause with a sigh. "Alma dear," she said, "there is one other thing." She laid a slender hand on Miss Porch's freckled arm. "I am so excited," she said, "but do you think you can have some sort of performance of your musicale, er, your operetta *Foxcubs* or whatever it's called ready for the School break-up party? There will be a grand weighing session on the last day and, I hope, an exhibition of the Waste Not Want Not Art Sculptures also some Cottage Industry, an ongoing thing really. We have the sculptor Vladimir Lefftov . . ."

"Yes," Miss Porch said, "I . . ."

"I hope you will enjoy meeting him," Miss Peycroft interrupted. "I believe he doesn't speak a word of English. Neither does Xerxes. Such a nuisance really. I do feel most strongly that our language is the most satisfactory for all communication. After all, we all speak it, why can't they. But about the Break-up Party, I think your play would draw the whole School together, something for every one to work towards. I do hope you agree, Alma, I am tremendously keen on the idea. You do have three whole weeks in which, as they say these days, to get it all together. And if it doesn't come off we can always fall back on a dramatic reading with recorder and tapping sticks. And there's always the cloakroom piano. Miles, though not the best, can usually be relied upon." She arched her fine eyebrows and smiled her most handsome smile. "I shall be supervising the diets myself," she added, "with the assistance, I hope, of two village maidens imported from Cheathem West and occasionally Mrs Miles, of course. And, I must remind you," she squeezed Miss Porch's thick arm, "I have spoken to you about Mrs Viggars. It is imperative, for reasons which I will not go into now, that she is given an important rôle in the play. You will find her very agreeable. Mrs Viggars," Miss Peycroft said, "would take off, if asked to, all her clothes and immerse herself in the Trinity College Pond, even though it has not been dredged or cleaned in any way for years, on the understanding, naturally, that the request was a part of the Course. Furthermore she has a fine voice. As usual I have spoken too much. Amen, Alma. From now on I shall be silent!"

Miss Porch found Mr Miles in a room next to the kitchens. There was not much in his room and everything that was there seemed to be for sale. Trying to make an effort to alter her ideas about her class, keeping the shocking suggestion of the mime in mind, Miss Porch asked him about benches and things which could be used for scenery. While she looked about the room with private misgivings Miles tried to sell her a battered electric fan. The blades, in motion, constantly slipped sideways till, resting on the floor, they made feeble hollow rattling sounds.

"It don't stay on too long," Miles explained, "saves you from catching noomoany while youse kippin' — very dangerous a fan is if it don't turn hitself off." He straightened the fan once more and stood back to watch it sink.

"No thank you, Mr Miles, not just now thank you. Yes, I know it gets hot and all that." Miss Porch paused and tried to collect her thoughts as though she knew what it was she wanted. "I shall be needing some coloured lights," she said, "for the disco, and, oh yes! A spotlight for the prison yard scenes." She moved away trying to avoid his next offer.

"What about a nice tranny," he said, "look at this nice tranny here, only needs a small part to make it go. It's a gift at twenty dollars . . . nineteen ninety-five to you, a steal!"

"I hope you will see to the lights and things." Miss Porch felt that her voice was ineffectual in the face of the renewed agony of the fan. She left the room quickly. Her feelings of hopelessness and exhaustion were worse than ever.

As she crossed the hall to go upstairs she met Miss Paisley armed with pins and notices for the board.

"Oh! I am glad of a chance for a chat," Miss Paisley said. "How do you like Miss Peycroft?" She put the notices on a chair. "Do you think she is a lesbian?"

"Good heavens!" Miss Porch said, "I'm sure I don't know. I don't really think — I mean, I don't agree with putting labels on people. And in any case, I've only just arrived."

"You wouldn't think, would you," Miss Paisley continued, "that Miss Peycroft is only thirty-four, I mean she seems much older — don't you think? I mean being in her position and all that."

"Oh, I haven't any idea," Miss Porch said, "I am hopeless at guessing ages."

Miss Paisley, undaunted, tried again. Did Miss Porch know that the Principal was reputed to be a one-time Prioress, "till she jumped off a wall." She seemed pleased to be able to impart this information.

"Jumped over the wall you mean," Miss Porch corrected.

"No, I have it straight from Miles," Miss Paisley insisted, "that she jumped off a wall and broke both her ankles. Just imagine! Miles carried her home. That was before my time," she added.

"Good heavens!" Miss Porch tried to raise one eyebrow in what she hoped would be an approved Trinity College style.

"I've got so many notices to put up," Miss Paisley said, fussing over her pieces of paper. "Miss Peycroft," she dropped her voice, "found something not quite nice in the orchard yesterday."

"Oh?" Miss Porch tried to send her eyebrow higher.

"Yes," Miss Paisley said, "a used one. She wants me to put up a notice about that too. I'm finding the wording difficult. By the way" — she darted to another subject as if to detain Miss Porch. "In case you are wondering why your room is in the passage where all the students are — Miss Peycroft likes the School to mix. After all you're not exactly one of us are you, not one of the real staff of the college. Miss Peycroft thinks it is cosier this way — tutors and students all in together. The men, of course, are up in the attics. You will see the little windows in the gables when you are in the garden. Miss Peycroft and I are in the rooms at the west end of the passage should you want either of us." Miss Paisley blinked and went on without breathing, it seemed: "Miss Harrow has brought two gorgeous young men from Europe, not that I go for men at all, one is . . ."

"Yes, I met . . ."

"How d'you spell 'contraceptive'?" Miss Paisley's quick pencil was hovering over one of her sheets of paper. "We have fifty-seven rooms," she continued without waiting for Miss Porch to imagine the word in readiness for spelling it. "The School's packed." She scratched out a notice and wrote another. "Some of the rooms are shared," she said. "I hope I don't have to put someone in with you. But you never know, do you. Miss Peycroft and I are moving in together to make more space."

"Well if you'll excuse . . . I've a few things . . ." Miss Porch paused on the first step of the stairs. She wondered whether to say outright that on no account would she share her room with anyone.

Miss Paisley, with her mouth full of pins, started to put up her notices. "It's exciting isn't it?" She almost swallowed a pin. She turned to Miss Porch. "Listen to this," she said, spitting out the pins, "this is a — let-it-all-hang-out — a first day get-our-act-together lecture by Miss Peycroft. She's speaking on some movement of Agapanthus in the Wheat accompanied by three hundred and fifty-two slides and a bush ramble. Isn't that great!" Miss Paisley's eyes shone. Before Miss Porch could think of an enthusiastic response Miss Paisley said, "I expect you'd like to know who you've got in your group. Wait on! I'll tell you." She flipped over several pages of a large pad.

Miss Porch confronted with the skills of administration felt incapable and inexperienced. "Thank you," she said in a meek voice.

Miss Paisley began to read some names. "You've got a huge class," she said. Miss Porch, gratified, smiled. "Oh! Wait on! Wrong class, that list's the Pop Art with Count Vladimir Lefftov. Everyone, but everyone wanted to join his class! The idea of a Count is so romantic isn't it. Ah! here we are." The new page had very few names. Miss Porch began to feel acutely ashamed.

"Let me see" — Miss Paisley ran her sharp pencil

down the little list, "you've got Mrs Viggars, old Mrs Crisp and Miss Crisp — used to be a gym teacher, was at school with Josephine, I mean Miss Peycroft. You've got Mr Robinson and Miss Maggs, you'll know them, you'll have seen them . . . No? They won the ballroom-dancing trophy on T.V. Oh hang on! They switched. They switched to chicken-wire weaving." She scratched out their names on the flopping pad. "Pity," she said, "they're a lovely couple. You've got Mrs Castle and Christobel Selby — possibly Miss Harrow and — blast! I've lost a page! But Miss Rennett's with you and Anna Brown. She practically lives here now and her kids have different uncles every time she comes. Josephine is sure she's preggers again. It's quite hard on Josephine. She realizes that her brother — I suppose you know she has a brother, he's not here at the moment. He comes and goes. Anyway, Josephine realizes that he has to have his sex life somewhere. Sex is such a strong emotion isn't it . . ."

"You really must excuse me." Miss Porch tried to make her voice louder. "I really do have a few things I must . . ."

"Oh yes of course," Miss Paisley said cheerfully, "I must just say I am so looking forward to your play."

"It's not a play exactly, it's a treatment."

"Oh never mind what it is, I've read the outline. I'm dying to know everything that happens. Also, it's going to be on video, just think a film every night!"

"Yes." Miss Porch frowned gently. She was pleased about Miss Paisley's enthusiasm but in her mind she could not see the possibility of video. "I'd better go and do some work to be ready," she said and made her way up the bare but still noble staircase. Entering the bathroom she waited for the lavatory. The door opened after a noisy flush and a handsome woman with flamboyant nonchalance shook her skirts rapidly into place. "Ah!" she said, "as you see, the largest and most prudent virgin got here first!"

Miss Porch, safely in her room once more with the door closed surveyed, with a new satisfaction, its simplicity. During her previous visit to the room she had scarcely noticed its qualities. Now she saw, with pleasure, the white cotton quilt on the bed. A small wooden chair, a small chest of drawers and a narrow pinewood cupboard, like a coffin standing on end, completed the furnishings. After hanging up her spare frock she pushed her suitcase under the bed.

The chair stood close to the narrow window which had the bottom half of the sash pushed up. The open window and the unpainted wood of the sill pleased her. She sat down and gazed at the honey colour of the old floor boards. She felt a great need to rest. She could not remember ever in her life feeling so tired. There was some work she must prepare for the morning but instead of taking out her notebooks she began to go over, in her mind, the events of the day.

The drive to Trinity College was a very long one and the last part from Cheathem West had seemed endless. The surrounding golden paddocks, though exciting to the imagination, were lonelier and emptier than she expected. The remembered details of the crash kept coming into her thoughts. The bus suddenly being there in front of her on the road was so vivid now that she found herself putting her foot forward to an imaginary brake more quickly and more firmly than she did at the time. The toe of her shoe knocked the wall below her window several times. The image of her smashed car became distorted and she tried to tell herself that the damage was not so great as it now appeared, in her mind, to be.

It was strange too that someone should be walking on that stretch of road at a place so far from both Cheathems. In her shocked state at the time Miss Porch paid very little attention to the other people who, because of the accident, were forced to become passengers in the bus. Obviously they were at the School too; the woman in the bathroom, Miss Porch remembered now, was a Miss Harrow travelling with two young men in the car immediately behind her. Doubtless she would see her and the others again. She told herself to 'get over the whole thing and get on with some work.' The thought of her manuscript was soothing. She pulled the case from under the bed.

Pressing images of Miss Peycroft interrupted her thoughts. Miss Peycroft, she supposed, was a sort of pinnacle of the Trinity with Miss Paisley on one side and Mr Miles on the other. Miss Peycroft, she thought, did not write either words or music. She was a performer with a delicate appreciation of both literature and music and was impressive with her treble recorder, the cello, the double bass and a fund of literary quotation. Miss Porch yawned and scratched her pen without much success on some sheets of paper.

Almost at once she was disturbed by a gentle knocking.

"May I come in Alma dear?" Miss Peycroft opened the door. "Alma dear," she said, "I'm sorry to bother you but I have a few more thoughts to share with you."

Before Miss Porch could offer her the chair Miss Peycroft sank onto the bed. "I have this idea, a wonderful idea," she said, "that your musicale — when we get it off the ground — should be narrated, chanted, in a sense, alto, you know and accompanied by the cello or the double bass — rather like that part of Smetana's *Bartered Bride* where the wonderful bass voice is so beautifully sustained by an exquisite obligato — the cello speaking in a human voice, don't you agree? As you know, I play the cello and I thought . . ."

"As I told you before, it's definitely punk rock, solid rock and disco." Miss Porch felt even more tired. "If possible," she added, surprised at the harshness of her voice, "some of my characters should wear leather and spikes and metal studs."

"Ah! Yes. Yes. Of course, I do know." Miss Peycroft sighed. "I must not intrude. I have to keep reminding myself. But," she wagged an elegant finger at Miss Porch, "you will be sure, won't you, to get full creative participation from your group, writing, acting, singing, dancing, mime — " She gave a bleat of pleasure. "Oh! My dear Alma! The superb opportunities for Body Language!" She jumped up like an excited schoolgirl. "But I must let you get on," she said, "you haven't even had time to unpack your corded bales — sorry, slight misquotation from Matthew Arnold. And," she added, "don't forget the service in the chapel, eight o'clock. Supper will be late as Miles is inclined to run on. Oh, and before I forget, I must tell you that Mrs Viggars is definitely one of your enrolments."

Miss Peycroft, having opened the door, stood

gracefully poised as if about to make an arabesque either into the room and on through Miss Porch's narrow window or out of the room and into the passage. The passage, Miss Porch thought, would be very uncomfortable being so narrow, unless the door immediately opposite was open. For a moment she wondered whether to duck under the flowing drapery and fling open that other door to allow for the generous leap. On the other hand Miss Peycroft might make the jump in the first direction and dash out her brains on the uneven flags of the courtyard below. Even then some damage might occur in transit, the window being very narrow and only partly open . . .

"As I was saying," Miss Peycroft's voice put an end to Miss Porch's problem, "last year, after the cardboard-box jaunt, my dear, the entire Self Expression Course, who were also into Basic Self Discovery, were hosed down by Miles out there in the yard and then they had to speak for ten minutes on How I Managed To Get Round The Library, The Music Room and The Dining Hall Without Touching The Floor. Mrs Viggars and Miss Rennett, I do recall, had overcome the problem of the hall by walking on each other. Such a successful Course!" Miss Peycroft laughed. "But seriously, my dear Alma, it is most important that Mrs Viggars, who is dreadfully keen to lose weight, gets what she wants. I have no doubt, creatively, you will offer her everything she needs." She paused. "Take me!" she said suddenly holding out her arms.

"I beg your pardon." Miss Porch was immediately ashamed of uttering such banal words. How could she have let "I beg your pardon," the language of a bourgeois housewife, a commonplace remark, fall from her lips in a place like Trinity College, in front of Miss

Peycroft of all people. Just when she wanted to impress.

"Use me!" Miss Peycroft had not noticed the lame phrase.

"What d'you mean?" Miss Porch was aware painfully of her poor quality accent. She forgot to raise one eyebrow.

"Use me!" Miss Peycroft cried in ringing tones. "I am absolutely ready. Pure, so to speak, and unsullied, ready and waiting to be the heroine of your next novel."

"Oh I see," Miss Porch said. "Thank you. Thank you very much."

Miss Porch knew she had no beauty in her voice. Neither had she any instrument. Sometimes she wished that her pen had holes in it like a flute. Sometimes she wished that she or the pen could sing. A singing pen to hold in the hand; quite often her pen did not seem able to write words, let alone be musical with them.

She sat down again at her window-sill with her pages and, taking her pen, she wrote a heading neatly:

FOXYBABY PAGE ONE: THE TREATMENT
We shall be using the courtyard, and the windows into the kitchen will represent the window of a cafe in a small seaside town. Loud music with a heavy beat throbs from the cafe. It screams and moans and it sighs and shrieks, it sings and laughs. Flashing green and blue and red and yellow lights are part of the scene. The breakdown of the story is roughly that Doctor Steadman, an eminent scholar and writer, has a terrible problem.

Miss Porch wondered whether to put that sentence in parentheses as a note purely for herself. She left it as written and wrote another note in brackets:

(Tell the person who is playing Steadman to creep up to the window as if he is peering into the disco cafe. Remind that it is dark — being late at night.)

Miss Porch, not knowing her students, tried to imagine an unknown voice speaking the opening monologue. "Steadman," she wrote,

turns away from the window after the first three and a half lines. He says, "That's my daughter in there in that cheap cafe with all those half-naked people. She doesn't know I'm waiting for her. She doesn't know I'm outside the cafe looking in. I'll wait all night if I have to."

Miss Porch read through Steadman's monologue and made a note that the class should feel free to discuss whether Steadman should continue in monologue (first person interior monologue) or whether, in the absence of anyone to talk to, he should address his remarks to God, perhaps apologizing because until something has gone badly wrong in his life he has never spoken to God either to ask Him for something or to thank Him. She added another preparatory note to the effect that it might be better, before suggesting discussion of any kind, to see what sort of people turned up in the classes. For some people, she realized from experience, the term 'discussion' might suggest an animated exchange of recipes or anecdotes about operations or intestinal troubles while travelling. There too the ever-present dangers of politics and religion.

Being bored while drinking tea was perhaps the best way to have a rest. Miss Porch carried the mug of black tea, which proved to be the only item provided for supper, carefully to her room. She wondered how much could be in a person's mind in short intervals of time. She felt crowded with confused thoughts, the long sermon adding more discomfort after a curiously uncomfortable day. Her knees, too, which were badly bruised, were no better for the prolonged kneelings necessary during Miles' wandering prayers.

"I simply must sort myself out," she said to herself in the sanctuary of the small room. She looked anxiously at the other little bed in the room as if it could show that someone else had been given possession. A quick glance into the coffin cupboard revealed only her own frock hanging there in its dismal shapelessness.

With relief at the prospect of not being disturbed Miss Porch listened, contentedly sipping her tea, to the crashings from the kitchens immediately below, the courtyard making an admirable sounding-board for these noises. She sighed deeply, hearing animated reunions and new friendships as students going to and fro in the long passage indulged themselves.

She took happy little sips. Noise did not trouble her unless she was in some way involved. She hoped no one would come to her door. A residential school had disadvantages in that one was never completely free. Tireless students could pursue their tutors at any hour of the day or night.

Still sipping Miss Porch continued with her unpacking. She took a fox fur from her case where it had been flattened between her books and manuscript. As she handled the red-brown pelt her movements became delicate and solemn and reverent.

The golden eyes of the fox were bright still, frightened and cunning. They held in their glassiness a knowledge of things not found in a spinster's luggage. It was as though the ways of the fox and his one-time energy, his swift movements, his thoughts and his freedom were held forever somewhere inside a heart sewn up in the smooth bronzed silk of his lining. The fox reposed on the white cotton quilt. It was the repose of an outward lifelessness only. He was ancient now and thin. It was not for him now to lie on the creamy neck and plump white shoulders of a concert-going woman.

The fox was perhaps the only autobiographical detail in the fiction of Miss Porch. Scarcely making acknowledgement she stroke the worn reddish fur. She picked up the useless remnants of the little legs one by one, feeling between thumb and finger the little feet with the tender awe of a child who has been allowed to dress up for five minutes before being sent off to bed.

Two thin gold chains and a broken clasp dangled from a patched little piece of the lining. From the fur there was a slight but unmistakable perfume, not a scent of fox but something womanly. Something heavy and aromatic with the rich overpowering sweetness of an older charm, an experienced passion accompanying the strength and the determination and the sadness of the ageing huntress.

The fox was one of the few props for her performance. Miss Porch, with foresight, had brought everything with her even the music. Miss Peycroft's suggestions were unexpected but, she reasoned, she had come with her own ideas to the School. Miss Peycroft would have to play her tunes on some other occasion. Quickly she worked out something on a piece of paper:

A Recital will be held
Starring Miss Josephine Peycroft
On the cello and the double bass . . .

But the fox. The eyes of the fox were full of secrets.

Whenever Miss Porch fondled the fox she thought of some lines from Rilke, not about a fox but there was a matching. The words went round in her head:

> *Just now and then the pupil's noiseless shutter*
> *is lifted. Then an image will indart,*
> *down through the limbs intensive stillness flutter*
> *and end its being in the heart.*

She regretted in a conventional way that, though she had learned several languages, she had not mastered any one of them well enough to appreciate fully a poet in his own language. Her half-made apology, in silence only, echoed all the unmeant apologies people make about their inabilities.

Perhaps an early night would be wise. Early was hardly possible in the true sense, so much of the evening being spent. Gently Miss Porch put the fox in the bottom of the cupboard.

The bed, when she lay down at last, was more comfortable than she thought it would be.

She had first seen the girl on the sands when the sea, no longer at high tide, was still coming in up the sloping beach in lines of dark choppy waves, one line after another with tumultuous energy and, at the same time, was receding as if being sucked back with that strange boiling quality suggesting an unwillingness to give up. It was as if a great force was being held in an unseen restraint. The perpetual sound of the sea and a few bird cries in the wind filled any possible silence of loneliness.

The girl looked about twelve years old though her mincing, hip-twisting, head-tossing walk suggested the awakened movements of a much older girl. She was walking alongside the restless foaming water. Moving her small, slightly formed body seductively, she kept her head turned so that she looked endlessly out to sea where the surfboard riders, remaining as if for ever far out between the shores and the distant horizon, crested the waves as the waters built up and turned over with a roar which, as it dissipated, became a part of the long-drawn-out sighing of the sea.

The eyes of the girl were narrowed with looking. They were like slits in her white face. She had pale freckles, a scattering on the whiteness, an inheritance from the red-gold hair which she wore piled on her small head and secured by three brilliant tortoise-shell combs.

As the girl and Miss Porch advanced towards each other, the girl kept her head still turned towards the sea and did not look at Miss Porch. As they passed each other the girl opened her eyes very slightly and, though the glance was directed towards the heroes of the surf, Miss Porch caught the shining look briefly. The girl's eyes shone cool with the amber-glass brilliance of the eyes of a foxcub, a she-cub, a foxybaby cub, a vixen.

There was something about the glance which Miss Porch was not quite able to define. The girl seemed experienced beyond her years. Perhaps somewhere in a darkly curtained motel room a man was waiting, a much older man. . . .

"Mrs Finch? Where are you, Mrs Finch? Daisy? Daisy Finch?" it was distinctly the voice of Miss Peycroft, so close it could have been in the room. Miss Porch raised herself sleepily on one elbow. Light from the kitchen door, opening into the courtyard below, reflected on her ceiling.

"Ah! There you are Mrs Finch, a devoted resident of Cheathem West, who has so gracefully consented to move into the little pad prepared for her in the West End Corridor. I want to thank you, Mrs Finch, for coming so readily to assist us here at Trinity College. As you know we have the biggest School ever about to go off into full swing . . ." Miss Peycroft's voice came like a fanfare on the night breeze. Miss Porch, wishing to be asleep, listened unwillingly.

"Mrs Finch," Miss Peycroft continued, (did the woman never sleep, Miss Porch wondered crossly). "Mrs Finch, I shall require you and your sister village maiden Mrs May to . . ."

"Lawks!" Daisy Finch broke in with a gravelly noise like a laugh. "Maiden is it? I'll have you know Miss P I'm goin' on fifty and maiden I am not as Mr Miles here will tell you me having raised four kiddies and just carrying me change of life. Also Dolly May ain't no chicken neither . . ."

"Well, that's as may be." Miss Peycroft was patient. "These are my arrangements, Mrs Finch. I shall require you to be in charge of the long passage and, with the help of Mr Miles here, you will sweep out the rooms daily while the students are in classes. You will come downstairs to serve our simple meals. Also I would like you to keep an eye on the bathrooms and the attics . . ."

"She'll do that orright!" said a voice which could only belong to Mr Miles.

"I gather, Mrs Finch" — Miss Peycroft ignored the interruption — "I gather that you are, together with others, the Finch Cheathem West Smash Repair and Wrecking?"

"She is too," Miles said proudly. "Me and Mrs Miles here was only saying last night — in bed wasn't it love — we was saying you can't beat Finchy here, 'er and 'er lads. You've got to 'and it to her. It's a synch, eh Finchy? Really we was only just saying three for the price of one, we was saying, it's been a while since we've took three off the road at one go. Very quiet the road to Cheathem E from Cheathem W as a rule. A real lucky strike . . ."

"Get up Miles orf yor arse when you're speakin' to quality," another voice said. "Will you take some tea Madam?" the same voice asked in more refined tones.

"No thank you, not just now thank you, Mrs Miles," Miss Peycroft said. "It is beautiful cosy in your kitchen but I can't stop. I've heaps to do before bedders. About the crash Miles, I just want to stipulate that the bus must be parked farther on to give people more time to go round the bend. As you know, I'm perfectly willing to go all the way with you, Miles," Miss Peycroft's voice was rising, "but this time you've gone too far. You realize of course we shall not have a potter for the School. It's a bit steep, Miles! Miss Porch seems all right, though heaven knows if she's hiding something painful. But the potter, Miles, has two shattered kneecaps, a broken collar bone and a broken nose, also her false teeth have not been found. Dr Black thinks she might have swallowed them. Such a nuisance really. Dr Black is admitting her to the Cheathem District Hospital probably at this very minute.

"Also, Miles, while I am here, Vladimir Lefftov, our

sculptor, is not at all satisfied with the materials you have provided for his students. He says, quite rightly that they smell. I think I told you Miles, quite plainly, to get metal pieces from the wreckers' yard. I told you I wanted the real thing, not the Cheathem West dustbins and certainly not the contents of dustbins containing discarded fish bait. And, I ask you, what am I going to do without a potter? Half the School at least have come for pottery . . ."

"Aw!" Daisy Finch allowed her sympathy to over-flow. "Aw! What a shame!"

"I'll have to make the best of it I suppose." Miss Peycroft sounded tearful. "I mean," she said, "a small well-organized crash is one thing but not to have a potter is a major disaster. I shall have to ask the other tutors if the pottery people can be spread, a few to drama, a few to sculpting and so forth. And Miles!" Miss Peycroft seemed to choke, "one other thing, your sermon this evening. How could you! That dreadful crude joke! Words fail me — how could you!"

"Madam," a soothing voice interrupted, "you go on up, just you go on up to your room Madam, and Miles will bring up some nice hot tea. There, there and there Mad-dam I'll make a nice fresh pot — up you go now."

"Oh thank you Mrs Miles, it is most kind of you. I think I am rather tired. It has been a long day. Goodnight, Mrs Miles, goodnight, Mrs Finch."

Thankful for the silence which was so abrupt it was in-credible Miss Porch thumped her pillow and turned over. She was really comfortable in spite of the little hard bed. The girl, the foxybaby, could just as well pick her way through the wheat stubble. The faint roar of the wind rushing across the paddocks was like the sound of the sea. The loneliness of the seashore and the movement of the waves could find a parallel — the girl could step, mincing, between the wheat stubble stalks. . . .

"Got a kiss for me then?" The voice was at the end of her bed. "Go on, Finchy. Got a kiss for us, love? Just a goodnight peck my lovey dovey, that's all I'm not asking for your all." A loud smacking kissing noise followed.

Miss Porch sat up. "Who's there?" she called in a thin wavering voice. The room was empty. A slight scuffle beneath her window was brought to an abrupt end. Suddenly the silence was broken by a raucous voice which echoed across the courtyard: "Miles, you disgusting crab! Take this tray of tea upstairs at once, Miles! I don't hot up my water to let it go cold."

"Coming, ducks. Just helping Finchy off with her corsets."

"What! Out there in the apple trees?"

"Yep, you'll never guess — she's give me a apple."

Miss Porch lay back as a squall of laughter burst, it seemed, above her head. She pulled the pillow up to both ears as she tried not to listen to the succession of squeals and the pounding of middle-aged feet.

"Aw! Don't you dare!"

"Aw! Come on! Come on then!" More screams of laughter.

"Aw Gawd, Miles, you are awful! They do say blue eyes is oversexed." — Mrs Finch, immediately under the window, was gasping for breath. Even Mrs Miles seemed to be laughing, Miss Porch was sure she recognised her voice: "Oh now I've been and gone and never come. I've split myself, that's what I've been and done."

"Can't catch me!"

"Oh can't I, Daisy Finch, my pretty bird."

"Quick Dais. Run!" Mrs Miles shouted. "Oh!" she wailed, "I'l wet myself next. Oh Gawd's sake! There's Miss Peycroft's tray gone. Whatever next!"

Clearly Miles was off again chasing both ladies through the yard and into the orchard.

Miss Porch put on the light telling herself to keep calm but resolving to make a complaint. Outside her room the long passage, dimly lighted, was deserted. The house seemed quiet and empty. There seemed to be a musty smell as if the house was uninhabited. Miss Porch retreated quickly and closing her door climbed back into her bed. It was almost midnight and she was not asleep. It was easy to panic when unable to sleep, especially with the prospect of new work in a strange place. She must succeed, she told herself. So much depended on success. Leaning over she pulled her case from under the bed and took up her manuscript.

There was a little tap at her door.

"Who's there? Who is it?" Miss Porch, in spite of herself, was nervous.

The door opened. "It's only me. Jonquil Castle. Mind if I come in? I saw your light. I was just paying my last thing at night call — you know, to the bathroom. It's long past my usual bedtime but I suppose it's the excitement of being here, but it's not only that. Would you mind awfully if I moved in here with you? You see, I can't bear the room they've given me, well it's not the room exactly . . . I . . . I'll explain . . ."

"Oh?" Miss Porch raised her eyebrow satisfactorily.

"Yes, I'll tell you later, it's something I can't talk about easily but it's too dreadful . . . I had to leave. I don't want to disturb you but I noticed earlier, when your door was open, that you had two beds. I feel awful asking but I simply can't stay in that other room. Tomorrow I'll speak to someone and ask for a room change. I feel awfully sorry, really I do, asking you because of your being the Tutor."

"Of course, go ahead." Miss Porch tried to make her voice sound friendly. She pulled her substantial nightdress up on to her shoulder and fastened the button at the neck.

"Don't take any notice of little old me," Jonquil said, "I'll be as quiet as a little mouse and just slip into bed."

Miss Porch put down her pen.

"Oh, don't stop writing just because of me," Jonquil said. "I suppose you writers write all night if the inspiration comes to you. At home," she said, "I go to bed early. I tell my grandchildren, 'Nana's skin is so beautiful, darlings, because she goes to bed with the dicky birds and wakes up early with lovely rosy cheeks.' "

Miss Porch picked up her pen.

Jonquil Castle, with deft fingers, adjusted one of her rollers and patted her tangerine headscarf into place. She sat on the empty bed. "I've been preparing my folder for the first class," she said. "I wrote a fragment, a poetic fragment which includes the phrase, 'filled with beauty in the eye of the beholder.' I penned it on impulse." Jonquil smiled at Miss Porch. "I also wrote a little thing called 'Trinity College, my first impressions' just in case you asked for something like that. I also have some pages of the cute things my grandchildren have said from birth to the present time, so I am all prepared," she said happily, "if I am asked to read aloud."

Miss Porch put down her pen once more. She wondered what it was that made Mrs Castle leave her own room. "Are you sharing a room?" she asked.

"Well, I suppose so," Jonquil replied, "but not any more." She shaded some sketched vine leaves with her biro on the cover of her file. "My son-in-law Boris — he's an itinerant magistrate," she explained, "he enrolled me for the course and, I am certain, would have wanted me to have a single room. He asked me if I would prefer the Pop Art Sculpture or the Contemporary Drama. I told him the drama and of course there's the Early Rising Health and Beauty Plan to go with it. I'm really looking forward to it though I believe we start early at dawn with some extraordinary physical culture."

Miss Porch studied her own programme. "Ah yes," she said, "I see it."

"It's not that I'm tremendously overweight or anything," Jonquil went on, "but I am quite pleased really to try the lettuce and lemon diet, even if it is a little stark. It is important don't you think, to keep the figure trim. Being a widow," she gave a sigh which was partly a self-conscious shudder, "all my widowed friends agree, one misses the boudoir exercise." She sighed a second time. "Boris of course," she added, "does not joke or make remarks about my appearance."

Miss Porch, stifling a yawn, thought a son-in-law would have to be very fond of Mrs Castle to make remarks or jokes about her appearance. Troubled by a second yawn she tried the square mouth and taut neck method of stopping it. The result was a painful cramp in her shoulders.

"Boris gave me the choice," Jonquil said with her tangerine head prettily on one side, "and I chose the mind-over-matter side of things." She paused. "My friends tell me I write very good letters," she added.

Miss Porch knew only too well the dull courageous letters Mrs Castle would exchange with her friends, none of the letter writers revealing their unhappiness or their loneliness. Most of them widows, they would rather die, Miss Porch guessed, than disclose to one another their feelings of hurt in connection with their sons and daughters. Daughters mainly and the husbands of daughters; the letters being chiefly about the families of the daughters but never describing the feelings of exclusion experienced daily.

"What are you looking for?" Miss Porch asked.

"The mirror," Jonquil said, "my room had a little mirror in it. You don't seem to have one and funnily enough the one that was in my room earlier disappeared. It was not there this evening. I must say I like a mirror," she continued, "it's company, isn't it."

"Oh I see," Miss Porch said. She thought that there had been a mirror in her room, possibly on the nail up there in the window-frame. She couldn't be sure, she said, she was trying to remember. In any case, it was not there now.

Mrs Castle, she understood at once, would be sure to need to look, smiling at herself, in a mirror frequently, patting her hair with plump fingers and tidying up the smudged corners of her lipstick. She would be accustomed to repeated smilings at her own reflection. The brief smile being for her a pretty expression of tender understanding. An exchange which Jonquil Castle would need often.

"Yes, I am sure there was a mirror here too," Miss

Porch said entering the quest with sympathy, "rather small and oval and dreadfully tarnished so that one could never really look one's best," she added, hopeful that this thought could soothe Mrs Castle.

"I always feel strange in a new place," Jonquil confided, "as if it isn't really clean. I must say," she lowered her voice, "I am glad the men are in the attic rooms. It would be so embarrassing wouldn't it to actually meet one coming out of the toilet. I think I heard Miss Peycroft announcing at supper that there would be a men's toilet erection behind the barn. Did you meet Miss Harrow?" Mrs Castle gave one of her self-conscious shudders. "I believe there is some trouble about her grandsons, one of them doesn't speak English. I don't believe," she said with an edge in her voice, "that they are really her grandsons, they don't look at all like her and, oh well I shouldn't say it but Miss Harrow is — well, there's something — "

"I don't think," Miss Porch said putting aside her paper and pen, "that the young men are related to Miss Harrow."

"Oh silly little me!" said Jonquil, "I just imagined they were. Perhaps because I am missing my own little grandchildren Jonathon, Bristow and Annabel." She sighed. "Don't let me disturb you. You get on with your writing, I have some letters to write. I don't feel at all able to sleep, it's the excitement and the awful thing that happened just now."

"You mean out there in the orchard?" Miss Porch shrugged. "That wasn't anything more than silly noise," she said.

"I don't know anything about the orchard." Mrs Castle's tone implied that there could be nothing of importance connected with the orchard. "Look! I'll be as quiet as a mouse and just sit here and write my letter.

I like to start a letter with something a bit special, you know, a tiny patch of purple on the first page. Sometimes if I close my eyes I can try to remember a particularly lovely cloud or a graceful tree, just a little something stored, over the years, in memory lane.''

As Mrs Castle was quiet with her pen poised above her writing-pad, Miss Porch took up her own pen only to put it down at once. A glance at her watch brought back the feeling of panic. It was after one o'clock.

"I must tell you," Mrs Castle said, "you might be able to bring them into something, a story or a poem. I must tell you about Boris' cats. There are four, Siamese, real personalities all with different points, a lilac, a tabby, a chocolate and a seal. The chocolate is the mother of the lilac, the father being a lilac tom. They are beautiful, priceless really but so spiteful you have no idea. You have no idea how nasty they can be. I suppose they're no different from people when you come to think about it. The chocolate never stops complaining, she complains at Daphne the whole time! I don't know how Daphne will manage while I am away. Heaven knows she already has far too much to do with the children. I suppose Boris needs all these expensive animals, he has other creatures, Muscovy ducks, they never stop eating, and all sorts of exotic fish which have to be fed — you see he is away such a lot and all the work falls on Daphne. Cleaning an aquarium is, well, it is an extra. That's why I feel more than the weeniest bit guilty coming away like this even though Boris does have several weeks holiday just now. He has been so generous paying all the fees and the travelling expenses for me to come to this wonderful School. But I will hand it to myself, before I left I did manage to run up some curtains in the boys' rooms and I made matching bedspreads for them and then I knocked up some little runabout cottons for Daphne and Annabel. No, I'm a liar! I did the sewing for Daphne and Annabel before the boys' curtains and spreads. Oh my! My memory is shocking these days . . ."

Surprisingly Miss Porch seemed to see the magistrate's family at breakfast. Just on an ordinary day, quite haphazard, pleasantly wealthy, comfortable, deliciously untidy. An early morning scene came clearly into her mind.

Daphne in a blue housecoat accusing: "Oh Mumsie, there you are, we started breakfast without you . . ." It was not an accusation really, Miss Porch understood, it was simply a statement which falls on Jonquil Castle's ears daily for, Miss Porch was sure, she comes late to breakfast on purpose making a smiling, neatly dressed, apologetic entrance into the messy family room. Miss Porch was sure Jonquil would be honest with herself, well partly honest with herself about her lateness at breakfast. She would really know, but not quite acknowledge, that she makes a point of being late, of noticing aloud that they have started the meal without her and of apologizing elaborately for being late. "I'm not very late am I? Perhaps a teeny two minutes at the latest?" Miss Porch was sure that Jonquil knows that every day this irritates Daphne and yet she continues, even in the presence of her son-in-law, with the habit. Miss Porch was sure too that Mrs Castle addresses them all in turn with a pleasant smiling, "Good morning Bristy, good morning Jonty," simply adoring them, eating them with her white dentured smile and her hungry eyes, implying with that smile that she has a place in the household to be held on to. She even greets the newspaper defence, held high as it is against her: "Good morning, Boris."

Miss Porch began to hate Mrs Castle and to feel deeply sorry for her at the same time. She imagined easily how this little performance everyday annoys the daughter, especially the way the mother has of making pet names from the children's real names. Easily imagined too is the reason, it is something inside Mrs Castle which insists.

"Oh Mother!" Miss Porch knew the kind of voice with tension mounting. "How often have I told you the children can't possibly call you Jonquilly, it's too utterly ridiculous. And surely Mother, you must see that you simply can't make a similar endearment out of Annabel so please don't go on trying. Also, the children do say 'good morning' when you come in, so please, don't for heaven's sake keep trying to get them all to say it to you in turn. It doesn't work Mumsie, really, please don't get upset, don't cry, I'm only trying — Oh Mumsie darling, please don't cry."

With an incredible snorting end to a snore Miss Porch was suddenly awake, ashamed, realizing she must have been dozing. Mrs Castle, on the edge of the other bed, was having a quiet little cry over her writing-pad. She patted her eyes with a tissue being careful about her cold cream.

"Oh please don't mind me, Miss Porch," she said with a brave smile. "I'll finish my letter later. You'll be wanting the light off. This letter can wait, there might even be a gorgeous sunset tomorrow for my first page, and by tomorrow night I'll have more news."

"What time is it?" Miss Porch shook her watch. It had stopped. She understood completely that Mrs Castle knew only too well why Boris had been so generous though she would never reveal this. Miss Porch allowed herself a few moments with the itinerant magistrate as he enjoyed the weeks of freedom celebrating the absence of his mother-in-law by spending whole days in the bath drinking brandy and walking about the house without any clothes on.

"My son-in-law," Mrs Castle said, still catching her breath with a restrained sob, "is a most generous man. We get on like a house on fire really. We share the same interests and jokes. I have lived with them ever since I sold my home and they were able to buy a bigger house. We really are one Big Happy Family."

"Oh yes, I'm sure you are," Miss Porch, reprimanded, said as Mrs Castle folded back the quilt and slipped neatly into the other bed.

Miss Porch leaned out of her bed and, reaching up, switched off the light.

"There might even be picture postcards to send to the children." Mrs Castle's voice came across the small dark room. "I'll write to them first so that they don't forget their Jonquilly." She seemed to start crying all over again.

"Cheer up!" Miss Porch said, trying to adopt the voice of her one time gym teacher. She shook her pillow, annoyed and yet filled with pity, and tried to curl up in her own narrow bed.

"Tomorrow," Mrs Castle said, "I shall throw myself into the physical and I shall try to meet as many of the students as I can. I shall learn all the names." She gave one of her noisy little shudders of excitement which Miss Porch understood to be pretended excitement, understanding too that the pretence for Jonquil Castle was so habitual it had become, for her, very real.

In the morning, Miss Porch told herself in her head, she would see Miss Paisley first thing and insist that she have the room to herself or else she would leave the School. "It is essential that I have a room to myself" —

she began the necessary phrases in her thoughts. She had no idea why Mrs Castle was so adamant about not spending the night in her own room. She nearly asked Mrs Castle to give some kind of explanation but the other bed was shrouded in silence, perhaps she was asleep. The silence now that it had come was too precious to be surrendered.

"I am cold," Miss Porch said to herself in an attempt to make some sort of diagnosis. The bed was reasonable, quite comfortable. There was no noise. Mrs Castle, in the other bed, was so quiet in her sleep that it would be unrealistic now to blame her for her own inability to sleep.

The nights in the wheat are cold. Miss Porch had been warned, Miss Peycroft's sixteen page letter had not left out any advice: '. . . warm knickers and your warmest ever nightie because it's absolutely freezing here at night even during the hot weather and bring a torch in case the power goes — our generators are of the more unreliable sort.'

Miss Porch's nightgown was good-natured and very warm. It was of a soft brushed-up material, frilled and ruffled and covered with little pink flowers. She did not usually wear such garments; it had been purchased especially.

A hot bath might bring desired sleep. She wondered if the water would be hot. Cautiously she left her bed and made her way along the dimly lighted passage to the bathroom. Some other sleepless person must have had the same idea, for at this extraordinary hour of three o'clock in the morning the bath on the other side of the wooden partition was being filled. Someone was splashing and swishing the water as it was running.

Miss Porch, not quite at ease in the spaciousness of an ancient upstairs veranda converted into bathrooms, surveyed the large rough bath with suspicion. Steam appearing at floor level from the next cubicle encouraged her. She adjusted the huge plug and turned on the taps. The warmth was almost too much as she eased her chilly body into it. Gradually she felt able to lie back in the hot water. A point in favour of the place, she thought, was the hot water at all hours. She relaxed.

"It's all right for you," a subdued but angry voice said, "it's all right for you, Mabel."

"Oh, don't please, Anders, say my name, Mabel, like that when you can, if you wish to, say it quite different-ly, you know how you can say it in your French — well — imitation French accent which is so sweet. You know, your *Maybelle*, you know how you can say it."

Miss Porch, shocked to be inadvertently eavesdropp-ing, lay very still in her own bath. The steam coming in from the other side of the partition was laden with a scent. A bath oil, perhaps violet or jasmine. Miss Porch, having only a limited experience of such things, could only guess. There was a sound of water slapping as if a body moved in the other bath and then more hot water was added and more curls of steam came under the hem of the partition. With her foot Miss Porch managed to turn on her own tap and added more hot water to her own bath. Quickly she turned it off as she heard the first voice speak again in complaining tones.

"It's perfectly all right for women." He sounded near to tears.

"Oh don't Anders, please! I have a headache." From the voice Miss Porch envisaged a limp wet hand held with its back to the offending forehead.

"It's perfectly all right for women," Anders said again, "you don't have to pretend anything, you can be as you are, Miss Harrow, you don't have to pretend to be married, I mean actually to get married. It is very unfair."

"Miss Harrow? Miss Harrow? Anders, what is this? Why not *Maybelle*?" There were more sounds of a body moving in the bathwater. Or was it two bodies. Miss Porch wondered. The bath she was in was quite big enough for two. She supposed three children could bathe simultaneously quite comfortably. She considered, for a moment, how much water a family, for the sake of argument with nine children, could save over a number of years, providing, of course, that the children, in groups of three, were quite close to each other in age . . .

"Oh Anders, don't shudder like that." Miss Harrow's voice interrupted Miss Porch's water-saving calculations. "It's so affected Anders, you know I cannot bear affectation of any sort — especially not from you. And please, Anders, don't cry."

From her voice Miss Porch deduced that Miss Harrow found the tears genuine enough.

"You know I am helpless when you cry," Miss Harrow said with more gentleness, "and I am not going to ask you — I never have asked that you should marry me."

"Heaven forbid! *Ma tante ma tante tante* Mabel!"

Miss Porch did not need to imagine the scorn and distaste the young man would be showing. His voice carried his tossed head and his curling lip. This scorn, she knew, would not even be hidden in his expression as he looked with slightly bulging, usually devoted and obedient eyes upon the wrinkled, grey-haired companion of the bath.

"What I mean is," Anders said, "women can please themselves — with men — with women — or by themselves and no one expects from them the conventional — the performance — the expected — you know what I mean."

"Well," Miss Harrow's impatience was reflected in an agitation of bath water, "well, Anders," she said, "you can always marry, I've always maintained this. There are plenty of nice girls. I have made several introductions, all of them very chic. And then, suitably married, you are perfectly free to follow your own wishes. I mean, Anders, it is not impossible for you to father a child, or even two, is it?"

The silence which followed this question was so intense Miss Porch began to wonder if anyone was still there. She felt that Miss Harrow was on dangerous ground, "Or should I say in deep water," she growled to herself, her chin submerged comfortably. Miss Harrow, she felt, must have been deeply hurt and so could not resist hurting back.

The silence was broken by the increased breathing of someone crying, trying to cry without noise. Miss Porch pictured the distorted face and the tears welling and overflowing from eyes carrying all the hurts humans inflict on each other.

"Oh don't, Mabel!" Anders sobbed. "How can you say such things!"

" 'He who takes delight in deceiving others must not complain when he is deceived himself' — and I quote," Miss Harrow said lightly.

Probably, Miss Porch thought, she is caressing the young man's golden head. She began a complicated unravelling of the possibilities when lying or sitting in a bath full of water, without too much effort and without drowning, of one individual stroking the head of another also in the bath . . .

"Don't cry, Anders." Miss Harrow's voice cut across Miss Porch's attack on the problem of the intricate design of waterlogged human bodies. "For God's sake Anders, don't cry," Miss Harrow repeated, "someone will hear you. These walls are very thin. I had no idea when I arranged to come here that the place would be like this. It's awful here. Really. So draughty and uncomfortable, completely off the map as far as shops are concerned. This bathroom's positively barbaric. Crude. I never though I'd have to share a room either. That idea went out with the Ark. I came here to take the Cure, the Diet as you know. I never expected to be boxed up in a hideously small room with a demented suburban widow who literally can't stop bleating about her grandchildren. As soon as the car's fixed — such a damned nuisance having that prang on the way — as soon as the car's fixed we'll leave."

There was a splashing of water as if Miss Harrow was raising herself up in the bath. "You realize of course, Anders," she said, "that I am on the plug end, it's very uncomfortable but that's beside the point. What I really want to say is, and I mean this, give him up, Anders. Give him up! And we'll go back to Europe at once to that nice little hotel in Paris, the one with the pretty brass bedsteads and that lovely healthy *femme de chambre*, remember? She who waited on us so deliciously bringing us that fragrant bouillon and those crusty white rolls with butter and ham. Such service! Give him up, Anders! You have deceived me, Anders, and, as Cervantes says, you must not complain if Xerxes deceives you. Give him up! He can't even speak to you, not having any English or even any French.''

"But *ma tante*, he does speak, in other ways.'' Anders paused. "In other ways'' — he seemed to savour the words — "his Body Language, Mabel, is out of this world. It is superb!''

Sudden splashing movement sent a deluge of storm-water over both ends of the bath. Water trickled under the partition and made rivulets on the green painted boards in Miss Porch's cubicle. Her own bath was decidedly chilly. She hoped to be able to climb out under cover of the noise of what seemed like a water fight next door and quietly dry herself a little before heading off down the passage to the now simple little room; simple in spite of the complication of it being a chosen nest for Mrs Castle.

"I should have known, Anders'' — Miss Harrow was speaking again. Miss Porch stood with one leg in her bath and one on the floor not daring to move towards her wished-for towel. "I should have known, Anders,'' Miss Harrow persisted, "that your way was to jilt suddenly, cruelly for no reason other than someone better turning up. When I look back and remember your last breakfast with that poor Yotta or whatever his name was, that Mr Kalchi; the sight of him so nicely dressed in his business suit — complete with white shirt and collar and the subdued tie; his hair combed in those terrifyingly sad neat strands, almost white that hair on that pink head, I can't forget the look of hurt devotion in his eyes!''

"Oh *Maybelle*. Pussychatte, please don't! Moosseychatte!"

Miss Harrow was ruthless. "Anders, you left him at the breakfast table, in the hotel. I was at my table in the corner. I was watching you yawning and looking around, examining your nails, playing with your croissant and taking not the slightest notice of poor Yotta begging you not to leave, promising you all kinds of presents, and while he still had his miserable plate all piled up in front of him you came, how shall I put it, sauntering across to me and joked and laughed at his expense."

"You laughed too *ma tante*." Anders' voice was low.

"Is that what you do now, Anders?" Miss Harrow raised her voice, "with Xerxes? Joke about me? It is too much! Especially as we are here so far from everywhere and quite unable to get away."

"You were laughing too, *ma tante*, that morning." Anders sounded sulky. "You laughed at Kalchi. You said he resembled a lovesick but neatly dressed hippopotamus."

"That's enough, Anders," Miss Harrow hissed in anger, "I will just remind you that Xerxes is utterly common, he's banal. I mean he eats chips with everything, but everything!"

"That's because he is homesick." Anders rose to the defence. Miss Harrow evidently made some sort of gesture of exasperation which sent another flood of water under the partition. Miss Porch, able to move during the noise of the splash, was just too late to save her bath towel.

"Listen *Maybelle*, Pussychatte," Anders pleaded, "there must be some other arrangement. I cannot stand this set-up." His voice changed. "He isn't deceiving me is he!? Xerxes? He can't be. Have you noticed something? Anything? You would tell me at once, wouldn't you."

"Your arrangements, as you call them," Miss Harrow said in chilling tones, "cost money, Anders. My money. Now, if you will, I am quite ready to be helped out of this bath. You may, if you wish, come to my room. As you know I now have it to myself. And, Anders, I do not intend to go on listening endlessly to your troubles, and I certainly have no intention of pouring out mine. That is not what our relationship is. If you will be more cheerful I promise not to be a bore

and like a whore unpack my heart with words
and fall a-cursing like a very drab

— that's from *Hamlet* but I do not expect you to know Shakespeare. And this time don't pretend you don't know the room number. It's written in biro on your wrist. And, Anders, if, and I say, if you are going to Him now, do not consider for one moment that you may afterwards come to me. I have an utter distaste for wilting or dying flowers.

Leaving the now entirely silent and apparently deserted bathrooms Miss Porch, partly dry, crept along the passage and entered her room sliding a little from the well-worn polished linoleum of the passage on to the floorboards. It was idiotic to have to be so quiet. If only that Mrs Castle had stayed in her own room she would have quite happily given herself up to the sleepless night. She often wrote during the night.

"Anders?" Miss Harrow moved slightly in the narrow bed, "have you brought my boots? I thought you weren't — "

"Oh sorry! Sorry!" Miss Porch jumped back in fright. "Oh sorry!" she said again, "I must have come back to the wrong room. Pardon me! I'll just — "

"Oh no," Miss Harrow said, sitting up quickly, "don't go. Switch on the light. I know you. We were together in that dreadful bus. That awful man, the one with the bus, d'you know what he said to me, he said: 'D'you make a habit of driving round the countryside running into the backs of other vehicles,' his very words, so impertinent don't you think?"

"I really think I should go to bed," Miss Porch said, "I'm sorry I came into your room by mistake."

"All these beastly little rooms look alike." Miss Harrow gave a discontented snort. "But don't go, sit down for a bit. I do badly need company. I had a bad journey apart from the accident, I had those two together in the back as well as all the luggage. Anders knew beforehand that I did not want him to bring that Greek and there they were holding hands and God knows what else in the back seat." She paused. "I'm an actress you know, used to late nights. Creative people never sleep."

"But it must be about four," Miss Porch said.

"Wait while I consult my elegant wristwatch." Miss Harrow dived under her pillow. "Spot on!" she said. "But do please just sit down and stay for a little while. I can't offer you a drink or even a cup of tea. I never imagined for one moment that I was coming to a place with absolutely no facilities and no service. It's ghastly here isn't it. I'm afraid I'm very poor company, positively embroiled in troubles, Anders and Xerxes, d'you see. I would so love a little chat with a mature and sensible person. My nerves, every single one of them, are all on edge."

Miss Porch sat down on the edge of the other bed, presumably the one intended for Mrs Castle. Miss Harrow smiled a quick nervous smile.

"That's Anders," she said, "he always does that to beds." She slipped her elderly but still beautiful legs out from under her covers and reached for her dressing-gown. "But Anders!" she continued, "one of the really amusing things about Anders is the way, possibly because of his youth and his energy . . ." Miss Porch noticed how Miss Harrow relished the word 'energy'. "Because of his energy," Miss Harrow said, "he can make a room or a bed or a person, for that matter, look as if there has been a recent disaster, an earthquake or an explosion. His complete lack of concern about his unwashed clothes left in little heaps round the room is a part of his charm." Miss Harrow started to pick up clothes. "I am tidy myself to a point of obsession," she said, "but only in a superficial way." She dropped the clothes in the bottom of the cupboard, a replica of the one in Miss Porch's room. "In here," Miss Harrow pointed to her own head, "all is utter chaos! Do you mind if I prattle?"

"Of course not." Miss Porch could not think of a reason for leaving. If only a telephone would ring calling her away, but who would telephone at four a.m. The only telephone was a public one on the landing and possibly one in Miss Peycroft's private apartment. It was remarkable, a sign of progress, she reflected, that the telephone penetrated the lonelier regions. She wondered if she could present some other reason for leaving . . . "Excuse me, I think there's someone at the door," but where was the door in this house, and who would come by, alongside that worn brass plate, to ring the bell at this hour? And in any case, as a guest, it would be bad manners to answer the door. Miss Porch, for the first time in twenty years, regretted the untimely death of her mother. Had her mother been alive she could have instructed her to phone with an urgent message. The problem being of course, when would her mother know, if she were alive still, the right time to telephone her daughter.

"I really feel as if I want to leave at once." Miss Porch was shocked at the echo of her own feelings in Miss Harrow's reopening of the conversation. "But the drama you are offering interests me immensely. Also I think I would benefit from the diet. I have had some conversation with Miss Peycroft about it all. It is my ambition to play Brünnhilde but I realize she would hardly be a part of your script. But really," Miss Harrow lowered her voice, "my main concern is how on earth I can get Anders away from that dangerous Greek." She paused. "Perhaps he isn't even a Greek," she said, "but something quite common and ordinary like an American. All sorts of people," she seemed to be thinking aloud, "all sorts of people come from America. One cannot be too careful." She turned to Miss Porch. "Tell me what I should do," she said, "you are a writer, I am sorry I haven't read your work, but as a writer you could tell me what to do."

Miss Porch felt sure Miss Harrow was displaying her shapely legs; she wondered if she should pay them some kind of compliment: "Black really suits you both. Legs! Black is your shade. Perhaps not black but something more bronzed — something metallic." The compliment should fit whatever it was the legs had on them. Miss Porch was not certain of the colour . . .

"D'you know," Miss Harrow said before Miss Porch had composed a suitable sentence. "I published a book, my autobiography, some years ago. It's rather like childbirth, I imagine. A child of the brain? A brain child. Well, I took the publisher and his editor or whatever you call them — '' Miss Porch, who had great respect in this direction, flinched, but Miss Harrow, not noticing, continued: "I took them both out to luncheon. And, in order to encourage my guests, the meal was a sort of 'thank you', you see, I ordered all sorts of things — you know, soup of the day, a ravishing minestrone, paté with fairy toast, an entrée sea food — baramundi, I think it was, panfried in butter, and on to Chateaubriand, rare, and chocolate mousse for dessert with devilled kidneys as a savoury. I ordered wines too." Miss Harrow paused while Miss Porch tried to control, without success, a deep rumbling of hunger somewhere inside her. "Ditto!" said Miss Harrow patting her own substantial waist. "Well," she continued, "to make a long story short, they being slender young men, runners into the bargain, believe it or not, asked simply for plain yoghourt and a green salad. And then *quelle horreur! ma vielle*, after a very short time, when they had finished their small meal they said they had to get back for a meeting or something. Can you imagine how I felt! It was so uncomfortable sitting there all alone, my guests having departed, while I waded on through all that food. Imagine my humiliation. Oh!" she cried, "Why! Why, when I am so low about Anders do I have to remember things like that frightful meal with two absolutely commonplace men, completely uncivilized, uneducated and without any manners at all."

Miss Harrow, diving into her cupboard, pulled out a pleated skirt, very short, and a tank top in white crochet. "I must change the subject," she said, putting her face close to Miss Porch's face, "Do you think, these will be suitable for the early morning knees full-bend exercises?"

Miss Porch, edging towards the door, said she could not think of anything more attractive and suitable.

"I shall find Anders and Xerxes in the morning," Miss Harrow said. "Well, it is the morning now, but as soon as it is light I shall make them come to the exercises. After all I am paying for them." She paused. "But did you," she lowered her voice, "did you notice the tow-truck man?"

"There were two if I remember clearly," Miss Porch said. "I mean the chestnut one," Miss Harrow said, "he had chestnut curls. His being so capable was the only pleasant thing about the whole dreadful day. I tried to be well-bred. 'I'm an intellectual,' I told him, 'academics are hopeless about the day-to-day trials and tribulations of life,' and he said all I had to do was to give him my name and my insurance company and he would do the rest. D'you know he'd even made a neat little diagram of how we all crashed. I'm sure he'll do everything properly. I told him I was an actress and he seemed very impressed. I ask you, why couldn't Anders wish for him? I am sure he's wholesome, d'you see, much safer than that sly foreigner, the so-called Greek. I am sure he is not a true Greek, he's not even an American. I do happen to know some lovely people who are Americans."

Miss Porch felt a glow of relief at the reprieve of the Americans. The Relief of New York, it could be a title she felt sure, a scene in downtown New York, an innocent American family at breakfast . . .

"As I was saying," Miss Harrow said, "I am sure Xerxes is not a true Greek. He does not seem to have the quality of *metos* or whatever it is called, or perhaps he does have the evil side of skill and cunning without the intelligence. Anyway he is not at all noble." She paused.

"No, he can't be a Greek. Xerxes was a Persian Emperor who conquered the Greeks. No self-respecting Greek would ever call his son Xerxes. Can you imagine a Frenchman calling his son Wellington?" She paused again but did not wait for Miss Porch to take a quick look through the door of a hastily imagined nursery, heavily decorated in blue, where an argument, in French of course, was going on about suitable names for newly born French triplets, boys, the family being in the dilemma of not having any more names, nine sons already having caused a serious shortage. The irate little father stamping first one foot and then the other, the mother, too soon out of childbed, sobbing helplessly as she tries to share two breasts between three hungry little mouths . . . "I tell you zere are no more apellations. Zey 'ave to be Wellingtons! *Wellingtons!*"

"That tow-truck man," Miss Harrow continued, "he looked very healthy. I am certain he would not have any kind of disease. One cannot be at all sure about Xerxes. After all, who can know what his background is — where he has been during his life and all that. Also," Miss Harrow said, "it was amazing wasn't it that they, the tow-truck men, were there on that lonely stretch of road. It was fortunate!"

Miss Porch agreed and, more than halfway out into the passage, said she was sure she would see Miss Harrow later on.

"I shall look forward to it very much," Miss Harrow said graciously. "By the way," she added, "I do know that Mrs Castle will be wearing a crushed-strawberry bikini, a two-piece with a halter top. She showed me her entire wardrobe. She described in detail the complete history of every garment. I suppose she, er, told you what I did. I couldn't help myself! It was all those terrible hours yawning like great holes ahead of me — filled with her voice and her clothes and her daughter and her clothes and the grandchildren and their clothes — hours and hours of it. Of course I am deeply sorry now. Deeply sorry.''

Daylight, like a twilight of dusk, came suddenly, filled with the sweetness of an unexpected scatter of fine rain across the stubbled paddocks. Miss Porch, sitting at her window, saw the darkness change to light with relief. It was like waiting for a pain to go away. For some hours she had been like a sick and anxious person waiting for the morning. The innocent country beyond the orchard was sinister and frightening during the night. Miss Porch had never seen such an intense darkness. The first streaks of light reaching along the far horizon were beautiful, she thought. It was surprising to see how quickly the blackest shadows were transformed into the simple and natural buildings and trees of the previous day.

A flock of rosy-breasted birds flew by, screaming, skimming the last grey mists from the orchard and the sheds before disappearing into the pink sky above the rising sun.

Ten minutes in the fresh air is worth an hour of sleep. Miss Porch, after her sleepless night, remembered this consolation and hung her head as far as she could out of the window. She ignored Mrs Castle's meticulous preparations for a quick and quiet journey to the bathroom. She listened instead to the softly-spoken doves and watched the long-legged hens racing to and fro across the yard. Sometimes they disappeared into the long dry grass and weeds of the ancient orchard. The almond and apricot trees were neglected, overgrown with gnarled and twisted branches. The doves paced along the gutters and on the edges of the roof. Sometimes doves venturing to the ground flew up suddenly, their wings making a tiny clapping, a sound of applause.

Miss Porch closed her eyes listening to the early morning sounds in the country. There was a subdued but continual rushing of wind. Roosters, still in the sheds, crowed. A second flock of birds, this time black cockatoos, screaming, showing flashes of red in their ragged wings, flew swooping across the stained stubble.

Leaning out of her window, Miss Porch studied the courtyard trying to work out, from above, how she could arrange the opening scene in which Steadman waits for his daughter to emerge from the punk rock and disco cafe.

Already a few people were beginning to appear from different parts of the house. Some were men treading the orchard weeds, anxiously engaged in silent searching for the hidden toilets. A podgy young girl, Christobel, was one of the first to come out of doors. Miss Porch had fitted her to her name the night before at the serving of the black tea. She watched the plump girl as she joined the little group of students who were gathering to start their exercises with the knees full-bend.

The courtyard scene presented, Miss Porch thought, a natural *tableau vivant* with the mingling of the brightly coloured clothes chosen by the fat people, who were surprisingly gentle and graceful in their movements. Miss Porch looked along the far veranda searching for the young woman she had in mind to play Sandy, Dr Steadman's daughter. She had seen this woman the evening before. She thought she must be the mother of the two little boys who spent their time running in widening circles round the yard. The woman was pale and thin; she wore a black caftan and stood apart from the others. As Miss Porch searched she saw her standing in the same place again. Her expression, so entirely remote from the noise and colour of the excited students, pleased Miss Porch. She wondered if Anna Brown would agree to play the part. For the black caftan a sunburned skin would have been attractive, but the thin, pale face, the expression in her eyes as if she was gazing, not at her children, but sadly at some distant place, at an event perhaps belonging to some other time, was most suitable for Sandy.

The two little boys ran endlessly on bent legs between the orchard trees. They circled the ever-growing groups of students who were coming out bobbing and curtsying, sometimes falling over, in their obedient performance of the knees full-bend exercise.

From somewhere immediately below the window there was the smell and the crackling noise of frying eggs and bacon and a man's voice, surprisingly close, said through a mouthful, "When I'm through with this lot I'm off upstairs to hose out them bathrooms and toilets." A woman's voice, Miss Porch thought she recognized the melodious chimes of Mrs Miles, said, "I tode her straight. It's cereals. Cereals to start off with and cereals to finish. 'put the diets on two clorths,' she sed, 'the yaller for the cereals and the green for the lettuce, then,' she sed, 'they can't make no mistake.'

'I'm not frying,' I sed, 'I'm not fryin' myself for sixty-odd I tode her, I'm not fryin' myself for sixty odd. . . .' "

Alma Porch thought, with longing, of the fine fragrance of bacon and waited for her students. It was strange to feel so weak at the beginning of the day. She attributed this weak feeling to the lack of a proper breakfast. She was not remotely interested in lettuce or cereals.

Anna, occupied with her secret sorrow, ignoring her surroundings, still stood at the edge of the veranda. The thin children continued to chase each other.

"Good morning Miss Porch, KFB." Christobel folded up in front of Miss Porch.

"KFB? KFB?" Miss Porch was bewildered.

"Oh sorry," Christobel laughed, "we thought of the abbreviation, it's knees full-bend, remember? Miss Peycroft wants us to use the exercise as a greeting instead of saying 'good morning'. Remember?"

"Ah yes, Of course." Miss Porch, with two swollen knees, was unable to do more than stiffly bend her head forward.

"Is this all you have written?" Christobel asked.

"What d'you mean?"

"I mean where you've got the marker in your folder, is that as much as you've written?" Christobel's eyes, set wide-apart in her childish pink-and-white face, looked earnestly at Miss Porch. Standing very close to Miss Porch she gave the red marker a tweak.

"Heavens no!" Miss Porch, understanding, did not want to reveal that the question annoyed her. "This is just for today's class. Don't pull the marker out, please."

"Is it published?"

"Is what published."

"That. Is that published?"

"No, not yet." Miss Porch tried to look past Christobel's large good-natured face to see who else was approaching.

"I started writing some novels," Christobel confided, "years ago when I was in year ten. I've got heaps of material. I'm going to be a novelist. Mummy said I should ask you to recommend some publishers." She turned her own notebook over. "Oh!" she said, "I've brought down the wrong book. I'll go up and get the other, don't start without me please."

"What a delicious girl that is." Mrs Viggars was beside Miss Porch who recognized the voice from the flower-bed conservation the evening before. "I said to Rennett, 'What a delicious girl,' but Rennett's in a bit of a huff this morning. Oomph. Hasn't slept well." Mrs Viggars laughed. "There's a lot going on, isn't there."

"Yes." Miss Porch, with her back to the house, surveyed the activity in the courtyard. The weavers had already nailed up a screen of chicken-wire at the side of the barn and were busily threading dry grasses, leaves and sticks through it, standing back to admire from time to time with little excited exclamations of delight.

In the double doorway of the shed the sculptors were gathered in a half-circle of reverence listening to Vladimir Lefftov the defected Russian Scrap Iron and Pop Art Sculptor. Miss Porch could hear Vladimir, whose quaint English was attractive, telling them that, like Mussorgsky, he wanted his characters to speak on the stage as they would in real life yet to make a performance which was artistic. The sculpting, he said, should be a mixture of real life, a cry from the soul of a real person but with the weight of Thought and the beauty of Art. Miss Porch felt she would like to be part of this; she wished to be not a tutor but a participant. She felt she would like to handle something from the heap at the side of the shed and make from it something which could reveal more than its immediate appearance of being ugly, spoiled and discarded.

The sculptors disappeared inside the shed and Miss Porch heard Vladimir's music, *A Night on the Bald Mountain*, she thought she recognized it. She could hear the hammer strokes and wished to be able to watch Vladimir's initial demonstration. She waited for her students and for Miss Peycroft.

Miss Peycroft's voice came clearly, a dangerous contralto, through the kitchen window beside which Miss Porch had taken up her position.

"Miles," Miss Peycroft was saying, "I see that you have confiscated the mirrors again. Please see that they are put back in the rooms at once."

"Fifty-seven mirrors is fifty-seven mirrors, Miss." It was obviously a repeated conversation.

"Undoubtedly, Miles," Miss Peycroft said, "but kindly replace all the unsold ones immediately. And Miles, before you go, I must have a word about that dreadful sermon. Whatever possessed you! It was perfectly in order for you to spout from *Proverbs*:

> *Who can find a virtuous woman?*
> *For her price is above rubies*
> *The heart of her husband doth safely trust in her* . . .

but to say all those commonplace and disgusting things and to repeat that crude joke in that language was, how shall I put it, quite beyond the pale. And what did your opinion about Women's Prisons have to do with any of it? If I hear you say once more that the women's prison is too small and that more women, especially the middle-aged and elderly, should be locked up — I'll — never mind what I'll do. I will just remind you once more that if transport was available most of the students would be leaving today. How could you, Miles! We could have lost this whole School before it got off the ground. And why — going back to the sermon, if you can call it that, how could you bring it all to the subjective in the way that you did by singing and I repeat singing, 'Mrs Miles, she did not buy a vineyard, Mrs Miles, she did not buy a vineyard' *ad infinitum*, that's my phrase, I do not expect you to understand it. I must remind you that Mrs Miles has not yet bought this house.''

Miss Porch, hearing Miss Peycroft's voice break with indignation, moved away from the open window. A group of students, including Mrs Castle, Christobel and Mrs Viggars, were waiting. Miss Peycroft came out of the kitchen door unruffled except for a reddening of her eager nose. Miss Porch had hardly time to ponder on the thought, the possibility of Mrs Miles becoming the owner of Trinity College, of the House. Perhaps the House would become disreputable, a place of low repute and Mrs Miles a Madam. But who, Miss Porch wondered, would visit the House so far away from . . .

''Gratters! Josephine, mother and I want to say how much we enjoyed your opening lecture.'' Miss Porch's ramblings were interrupted by the ex-teacher of gymnastics, Miss Crisp. Mrs Crisp, leaning on Miss Crisp's reliable arm, took her place in the semi-circle of hopeful students.

''Oh thank you, Yvonne,'' Miss Peycroft said, ''it was nothing really. I simply used some notes from the old school days, Lower Third. Remember when we did

Hedgerow Research, Seed Dispersal and Sanitary Landfill? Fascinating! So glad you enjoyed my little rehash. Now! Knees Full-Bend, Class. Down and Up and Down and Up. Not too far the first time Mrs Crisp and Mrs Viggars. Gently! Gently! Down and Up and Down and Up. All set Miss Porch? For the breakdown? For the breakdown of the scenes? The Foxybaby Treatment? We call it a Treatment,'' she explained to the students who were regaining their balance as gracefully as possible.

"All set," Miss Porch said unwillingly. She had not supposed that Miss Peycroft would be present. The whole idea of her class was, it seemed, slipping out of her hands. She would have to do her best to ignore Miss Peycroft if ignoring was possible.

Mrs Viggars, wearing white flared slacks and a portly blue blazer was delighted to be cast as Doctor Steadman. "I've brought my boots," she said, "you never know in advance what you're going to be asked to do." Her heavy jowls quivered and her eyes behind the thick-lensed spectacles bulged. "I'll just trot off and get my boots." Her growling voice betrayed her pleasure.

She returned quickly with the immaculate trouser legs folded and pushed into the tops of the boots.

"Well, Rennett," she said, rubbing her hands together, "have you been cast yet? Oh I see you're to be a prison wardress, a screw it's called or rather a screwess I suppose you'd say, eh? What? Oomph?"

Anna showed no emotion at being asked to play Sandy, Steadman's daughter, though Miss Porch noticed that the pale skin of her neck and throat flushed slightly. It was pleasing too to notice an area of roughness and a few spots about the chin. A lip sore, she thought, would have been acceptable, but she was pleased with Anna's hair. Beneath an apparent sheen of a greenish colour on the top of the head, the hair underneath was sun-dried, pale with traces of old dye and had the stringlike quality of the hair of a sick person. Her feet too were thin with revealingly uncertain bones. Timid feet, Miss Porch thought with increasing pleasure. The girl's knuckles too, they whitened as she clenched her fist; nervous and irritable, Miss Porch hoped. "Excellent!" Miss Porch said to herself. She felt there was a blossoming of the right kind of ugliness necessary for the part of Sandy. She glanced quickly at the top page of her notes. The file was heavy on her arm. She knew that her own bones were frail.

"We must," Miss Peycroft announced in her loud voice, "accept and acknowledge the truth of limitation and prepare to be condemned. We must dismiss," she continued, "what we feel to be sparse provision and have confidence. Thank you."

The courtyard was freshly watered. The drama class waited for the treatment.

"All ready to start the breakdown of the storyline?" Miss Peycroft asked. Miss Porch nodded.

Rock music with a heavy disco beat pounded from the kitchen.

"Mrs Viggars," Miss Porch said, faith in her own voice fading as she tried to raise her voice. It was as if she heard her own voice in some sort of dream from which she might wake at any moment. "Mrs Viggars, you will speak your lines in first-person interior monologue. Here is your copy of the script . . ."

"Excuse me! I am not quite certain," Jonquil Castle interrupted breathlessly, having been upstairs to change from her little lemon silk into the chocolate cotton, it being more suitable for the part of the nursing sister.

"I'm not quite clear," she said, "about first-person interior monologue. Is it the same as rivers of conscience?" With her head charmingly bobbing, tilted to one side and fluttering her carefully tinted eyelids she smiled at Miss Porch and at the assembled group.

"Stream of consciousness," Miss Porch said. "No, it is not the same thing at all. A discussion now," she turned to Miss Peycroft, "would hold things up terribly. I think," she said, trying to sound firm, "we must try to get started."

"Yes of course. Rather!" Miss Peycroft frowned slightly and looked thoughtful. "We should be held up till lunch time," she said.

"Mrs Viggars," Miss Porch said, ignoring Mrs Castle, "as Dr Steadman . . ."

"Yes, Mrs Viggars" — Miss Peycroft stepped forward briskly. "You are the lead. You are Dr Walter Steadman, an eminent professor and a scholar, burdened with one of the heaviest problems life can offer."

Mrs Viggars nodded, puffing her good-natured flabby cheeks and her solid breast.

"As you walk," Miss Peycroft continued, "show in your demeanour that you are bearing something unbearable." Miss Porch was about to explain more to Mrs Viggars but, before she could say anything, Miss Peycroft took up a hurricane lamp rented at enormous cost by Miss Porch from Miles and gave it to Miss Paisley. "Wave this to and fro," she said, "this will indicate the flashing lights of the disco joint, I know it's only one colour but . . ."

Mrs Viggars, holding her script high in front of her face, paced towards the kitchen window. The other students stood in an obedient semi-circle watching.

"Foxybaby Treatment," Miss Peycroft said,

"Foxybaby beat one, beat two, beat three. Take one, okay! 'That's my daughter,' that's where you start okay! Okay!"

"That's my daughter." Mrs Viggars cleared her throat and continued, "that's my daughter in there with all those people. She's dancing in there. She's been dancing for hours, she's almost naked. All of them — naked — dancing non-stop, practically naked."

"The flashing lights, blue and green, red and orange are all a part of the dance," Miss Porch, trying not to be self-conscious, read aloud, "the music has a heavy beat. It throbs and pulses. It screams and moans and beats . . ."

"Just a moment!" Miss Peycroft interrupted, "turn the volume up in there please," she called towards the kitchen, "turn it up!" She turned to Miss Porch. "Viggars, Steadman next?" she asked. Miss Porch nodded. "Okay, Steadman," Miss Peycroft said, "okay Steadman, your lines. Give them all you've got!"

"This music," Mrs Viggars said, "just now, this music is everything to her. She doesn't know that I'm here. I'll wait. I'll wait for her all night if I have to. She is completely given up to the dance."

"Turns from the window," Miss Porch said in a low voice, "pauses — and now keep going with the first-person interior monologue."

"Perhaps," Mrs Viggars gave her pages a brisk shake, "perhaps," she said, "we looked forward to the birth of the child with too much hope. Perhaps I was too hopeful. It's impossible to know what she hoped. I've always known that it is wrong to pin hopes on to a child but this is what people do. In my life this is the second time . . .

"No one in this little town recognizes me in spite of

my work and my television programmes. I am utterly alone and unknown. No one, not one friend knows that at this moment I'm standing outside this cheap noisy cafe in this dirty street. She doesn't know that I'm here. She thinks, if she thinks at all, that I'm in that empty restaurant where she left me.

"We haven't been here long, two days. Perhaps I expected too much. She, when she spoke in one of her better moments, seemed to think that the holiday would do her good. I think I hoped for a miracle. Perhaps I am still hoping.

"During the journey I longed to tell her how much I loved her. Her baby too, I love him. He's ill with her illness. I couldn't find the right words. Any words I thought of were pompous or self-conscious. Perhaps, in reality, it has always been like that with me . . ."

"Fade out," Miss Porch said, "fade in, continue, Viggars. You cut to the scene in the car now. Pause and continue."

"The shadows lengthen across the paddocks, it is nearly dark," Mrs Viggars read, "we still have a long way to travel. The baby is unusually tranquil, sleeping in his cradle in the back of the car . . ."

"A little more emphatic, Steadman, please." Miss Porch, surprised at herself, was animated. She waved her papers. "Go back to — 'I longed to tell her . . .' Do that bit again."

Mrs Viggars nodded and, clearing her throat, read, "I longed to tell her how much I loved her . . ."

"Good! Goo-ood!" Miss Porch encouraged. Mrs Viggars smiled over the top of her script as she read on.

"Fade out Steadman. Bring up Sandy," Miss Porch said, "starting with 'My baby'. Anna, you're in the car . . . Steadman has looked back. Flashback to 'My baby'."

"My baby." Anna's thin fingers rustled like dry feathers on her sheets of manuscript. "My baby. My baby's rotten like me. Even his mouth. He can't suck. The pain's awful. I never thought it would be like this. I wanted him born and now it feels like I don't want him. And this bloody journey, it's like it's never going to end. It's getting dark and we're not anywhere.

" 'Look at the cows. Look at the freesias,' He says. He's always on about something. How can I look at anything? He parrots on and on.

"I really thought everything would come right when I got my baby. Like Hell! Shit! I feel cold. Cold all the way inside I'm cold. I want to be warm. I'm cold. Cold. Cold.

"My hair! It's one goddam mess. I hate my hair! 'Stop scratching,' He tells me. 'Stop scratching, there's a good girl.' He says it like I was a little girl again. His little girl, that's what he calls me. I can't be that again never ever. I'm no one's. 'There's sure to be a hair-dressing shop,' He says. Big deal! Hairdresser in this dump, this goddam place, a shithouse paddock. That's all it is."

"Good," Miss Porch said in a low voice. "Steadman, your next line."

Mrs Viggars cleared her throat, smiled quickly at Miss Porch and spoke: " 'Wait till we reach the town,' I want to tell her, *There is a town*, I want to console her with these lines, *There is a town by the rocks where the sea meets another sea*, but how can she be comforted by Sophocles? Instead I tell her that it's better to wait to have her hair done, 'not too soon after childbirth,' I say. My voice is too emotional, I know that my voice gives me away.

"Her hair is a knotted mass. I can't help my feelings

of horror about the state of her skin. Her mouth is hidden in sores, infected eruptions. I keep hoping that the holiday will bring about a miracle . . ."

"Cut!" Miss Porch said. "Excellent! Thank you Steadman, Mrs Viggars."

The music was suddenly louder.

"When's this noise leaving my kitching?" Mrs Miles, resplendent in new black satin, marched into the court-yard carrying the transistor. "I can't hear myself think in there," she said to Miss Porch, "I can't hear nothing of what's in my own head. It's past mawnin teas, I can't keep on the boil all day and I don't care to be stared at in me own kitching."

"Oh sorry," Miss Porch said, "thank you Mrs Miles." She took the transistor and switched it off. "We'll have a ten-minute break," she said to the students, "and then straight back here. Right? For the next *tableau vivant*, Sandy — that's you, Anna — will need to slip from the cafe to the bench over there. This will be for the scene set in the hospital ward. I shall read in the third person present tense for the treatment. Ten minutes break then." Miss Porch felt her trembling would be noticed; she seemed to shake from head to foot.

"How d'you do it! It's great!" A little group sur-rounded Mrs Viggars.

"Oh, Mrs Viggars, let me get your tea for you!" Christobel was flushed with excitement.

Mrs Viggars seemed perplexed. She held her paper beaker of black tea as if she did not understand why it was in her hand.

Miss Porch noticed, with shy pleasure, that Anna was paler and that her hair was positively awful. She seemed to have stopped staring into a vague distance and she took absolutely no notice of her two little boys.

"I fear your Mussorgsky will drown our cello!" Miss Porch, surprised at her own boldness, called across the yard to Vladimir who was waving the steaming stinkwort to and fro in the doorway of the barn. "I turn down," he called in reply. "Too hot!" he tapped the beaker. His smile, in her direction, made Miss Porch feel quite pretty.

"On location!" she raised a whistle to her lips. "Come along Drama!" She blew the whistle and the students came hurrying back from all over the courtyard.

Miles, doffing his cap, limped round the broken edge of the orchard wall.

"Oh goody, Miles! You've got the video all set up." Miss Peycroft, with her cello, took her place on a chair near Miss Porch.

"I must just tell you, Alma," she said in a low voice, "don't expect too much this morning. Anna's a perfect zombi today. I'm told she's stuffed herself with valium. She's not exactly with us — "

Miss Porch, with a suitable expression of understanding, nodded. "Steadman," she said, "Steadman — Mrs Viggars," she looked from her page across to Mrs Viggars. "Anna," she said, "you are Sandy and and Mrs Castle, you will be the nursing sister . . ."

"Excuse me one moment, if I may." Miss Peycroft jumped up. "Miss Porch will read and the characters will mime the action. Miss Porch and I would like you," she said, "to observe the effect of mime on the human individual. We shall discuss the performance which will be on video this evening. Please, Miss Porch, do go on, sorry for the interruption."

"Miss Rennett and Miss Harrow," Miss Porch said, trying to form a picture in anticipation of the effect of mime on the human individual. She began, in her mind, to see a large circle of people of various shapes and sizes (the individual) walking slowly round and round, each person with a hand delicately placed (mime) on the shoulder of the person in front. "Miss Rennett and Miss Harrow," she said again, "please will you take up your positions on the other side of the wire fence. That's right. I know it is a poultry pen but for the prison scene the effect will be admirable."

"One more little thing." Miss Peycroft sprang up once more, the cello perilously balanced. "For the purpose of the *tableau vivant*" — she surveyed the group of students "if you like to split up you may also take part in the mime and the camera will include some long shots which should give a mirror-like effect of the action. I hope this idea appeals?" She looked at Miss Porch with her eyebrows raised.

"Oh quite, thank you," Miss Porch replied. "Right!" she said, "music please."

Miss Peycroft played the phrase she had composed before breakfast. Miss Porch stepped forward. She gave her manuscript a glance and a shake. "Everybody ready?" she asked, and began to read: "When Steadman visits his daughter in hospital, he sits at some distance from her bed. She does not speak to him until it is time for him to leave. She tells him then that the nurses do not like her." Miss Porch paused and then continued: "the nurse comes to take the baby as if for rites which may only be performed beyond the reach of relatives. She returns him quickly, replacing him in the wire basket. Steadman notices that the baby has an expression of dismay and that the small head is suffused with a dull red rush of anger.

"The nurse mistakes Steadman for the baby's father

and is embarrassed when she notices Steadman's fleshy cheeks and shining silver hair smoothed back on his temples. Nervously he fingers the gardenia in his buttonhole.

"The disturbed baby is fretful and the nurse explains that he has to be treated for the same symptoms as his mother has. 'The apple does not fall far from the tree,' she says.

" 'That's the one who doesn't like me,' Sandy says when the nurse has gone, 'more than the others that one hates me. You heard what she said. You heard. She's an old cow!'

"Steadman does not know what to say. He wants to speak about the unblemished valiant little shoulder he saw — this, by the way," Miss Porch said, "as with other details would be shown in production, in close-ups in a film and in written detail in a novel. He stands," she continued to read, "by the cot and with one finger strokes the baby's head. An expression of renewed and unbelievable tenderness crosses his face as he feels the crumpled edge of an ear and the softness of the not quite rounded cheek. He plays gently with the delicately curled little fingers, one hand having been left free of the binding blue cloth. He looks from the baby's hand to Sandy's hand as if recalling her baby hands years ago.

"She lies with her head turned away from him. He looks at his own hands. They do not seem to belong anywhere in the changing colour of the baby's round bald head or in the half-relaxed grip of the transparent blameless fingers. One of Sandy's hands is gripping the sheet pulling it taut towards her chin. As he looks Steadman wonders what has happened to change the once confiding soft little hand into an unreachable bony claw.

"He tells her that he has managed to arrange for her to come home to him with her baby instead of having to go back to the prison. She does not answer. He leaves the hospital room quietly without looking back.

"The next scene," Miss Porch rearranged her papers, "will be in the form of a flashback. Fade out the hospital. Fade up the journey to the prison . . ."

There was a wave of movement and colour in the courtyard as the students left their positions and gathered in a circle for the next reading. Gradually they separated again into little groups to take part in the mime.

"The first time Steadman visits Sandy in prison," Miss Porch read, "he loses his way and comes upon the place as if by accident. At nightfall, with heavy clouds low in the sky, the prison seems to cling to the sides of a hollow in desolate scrub-covered dunes. It is like a huge cage of shining, ringing cyclone and barbed-wire. The wind moans there. He is bewildered by the slow unlocking and locking of gates and doors as he is taken through the buildings and the yards.

"The interview, his first after not seeing her for some years, in the presence of a prison officer is not satisfactory. Sandy does not appear to listen to him and she does not speak. Feeling helpless he leaves after ten minutes.

"He waits for the gate-keeper. A bright clean moon is racing up the sky. From where he stands he can see the watchman in his well-lit office. There is a board of keys on the wall behind him. The man does not hurry to come out. Steadman waits.

"A short distance from Steadman on the other side of an inner fence there is a smooth well-cared for lawn. Two women in prison officers' uniforms are walking slowly to and fro, their heavy flat-heeled shoes making no sound on the grass. One of the officers has her tunic unbuttoned. Not seeing Steadman while he waits in shadow they come towards him and, stopping by the fence, clasp each other close in an embrace which lasts several minutes. They are just outside the arc of light which comes from the watchtower of the prison and they are close enough for Steadman to hear them. Suddenly the shorter of the two women, the one who is unbuttoned, turns away from the other one. 'I can't stand it any more!' she sobs and Steadman can see, in the moonlight, her dishevelled hair and her face which is swollen and twisted with crying. 'I can't stand it. Oh, I can't,' she moans, 'I think I'm going mad!' The taller of the two women puts her arm round the other one's shoulders. Steadman cannot help overhearing. 'That girl, that girl, Stella you know the one I mean, that red-headed vixen, she torments me. She's tearing me to bits. What shall I do, Stella! Oh, what shall I do? You'll help me won't you — you will, won't you?'

"The taller of the two, Steadman can see, is a very handsome and neat woman. He hears her soft, tender voice trying to console this inexplicable suffering.

"As he drives away he looks back at the deceptively tremulous cage. He sees the dark shapes of the two women leaning towards one another behind the moon-silvered wires.

" 'I'm as useless and vulnerable as they are,' Steadman thinks. 'I can't help wondering if the girl is my girl — I must be ill myself to imagine such a thing. There are a great many girls in there and there could be several with red hair and any of them, because of changes in their personalities, could be capable of what I've just heard. I've got to get her away from there as quickly as I can. This girl, this vixen did she say, is not my Sandy but I've got to hurry. She's so changed. She'll get worse if she stays there. I must get her home. Must do all I can to get her home . . .' Cut!" Miss Porch smiled at Mrs Viggars. "Well done!" she said. "The story will come together," she explained, "from these fragments. This is how a story is made, from little scenes and the thoughts and feelings of people, their ideas and their wishes." Miss Porch paused. Glancing sideways she could see Miss Peycroft patting and steadying people in the various poses they had taken up in the mime. "Steadman," Miss Porch continued, "sets out now to try to reclaim his daughter from the unknown quality of life which has claimed her."

Slowly the students relaxed and began to move away, some to the orchard and others into the house.

The supper tables were laden with small thick-skinned oranges and several bowls of a particularly tasteless variety of yellow plum. To replace the pleasure and comfort of a well-cooked, flesh-producing meal it was announced that the video of the story so far would be shown followed by a discussion.

"Zzz I shall speak French at meals," Mrs Viggars said, "*en pensant à, que veux-je dire zzz,*" she said, "*zzz que veux-je dire — en cherchant le mot juste, je reussis à ne pas penser à la nourriture.*" She gave a comfortable laugh. Little heaps of orange-peel and plum stones erupted on the scrubbed boards of the tables.

"*La sensation de maigrir,*" Mrs Viggars said. "The slimming sensation. What a beautiful idea! Food for Thought. Excellent. Let me see now, *la nourriture spirituelle!*" She leaned attentively towards the young Greek, Xerxes, who said something Mrs Viggars could not understand. She turned to Miss Porch for help. Miss Porch, her mouth puckered with sour orange, shook her head.

"They do say," Mrs Viggars said, "that your poet," she nodded towards Xerxes, "your poet, Herakleitos, has said it is not possible to step in the same river twice. To me this has more than the literal meaning, what do you think? Ah!" Mrs Viggars raised one hand. "Ah!" she said again, "you are saved from having to answer my question, dear boy. You are utterly saved! Miss Peycroft is about to say something."

Miss Peycroft, standing on the end of one of the tables, announced that for the purposes of compiling a report, students were requested to fetch paper and pencils in order to supply, anonymously, opinions after the film. "Miss Porch will collect the information," she said, "and tomorrow with our lemon juice and lettuce leaves there will be a detailed account of all your remarks. In this way," Miss Peycroft laughed, her voice plunging down the scale in a succession of well thought out consecutive major fifths, "in this way," she said, "we shall be able to iron out our teething troubles. Quite frankly," she added, "I am really excited about the whole thing."

There followed a general movement of students racing off to fetch writing materials. Miss Peycroft remained standing on the end of the table waiting while they returned quickly to their places.

"Just to give you an idea," Miss Peycroft continued as the overall breathlessness subsided and papers and notebooks began a businesslike rustling, "Miss Porch and I do want you to be perfectly frank about this, for example, if you think the cello playing was ghastly do not hesitate to say so. Alternatively if, on the other hand, you think the music was stunningly well-conceived you can say that. Mr Miles has already put forward an opinion. I'll read it. It takes the form of an objection: 'My objection by M Miles I object to the words dirty street when I am just thoroughly hosed down.' He is of course," Miss Peycroft said, "referring to the opening scene. Remember? The disco cafe in the dirty street? So now, ignoring our orange-peel and our plum stones — will someone — perhaps you, Christobel — please turn off the lights. All right, Miles? Let her roll!" Miss Peycroft leapt, lightly for her size, off the table.

The film with a series of flutters and jerks stuck at the scene where the two prison wardresses were walking intimately. An entirely new voice speaking patiently and evenly made the statement that it was now known that blood-pressure pills could cause superfluous body hair to disappear. If they cared to examine, the voice continued, the patient on the left, it could be noted that there was scarcely any pubic hair. This staggering information offered in a purely clinical and uninvolved way was received in silence.

"Miles," Miss Peycroft said, "we will wait while you unwind or whatever it is you have to do."

"Take the bull by the horns, though I do say so myself." Mrs Viggars leaned forward slightly to make her point in a voice somewhat louder than the hum of well-mannered conversation characteristic of an audience waiting for someone who is putting something right.

"Taking the bull by the horns as I was saying," Mrs Viggars made a second attempt, "that was, in spite of being out of context, a very interesting fact about the treatment of blood pressure. Miss Rennett here — you don't mind my mentioning this do you, Rennett old girl?"

Miss Rennett, who was crouched over a picture of a glossy chocolate blancmange, did not seem to hear Mrs Viggars.

"Miss Rennett," Mrs Viggars continued with an indulgent smile directed towards Miss Rennett's rounded back, "is on blood-pressure pills and she has indeed lost all her body hair. She literally has none. I, for one, naturally do not think that this matters in the slightest. I have always looked upon my own body hair with considerable distaste, especially since it turned white and took on a different consistency, quality is perhaps a better word, becoming quite rough and unmanageable, I would say like a cheap but durable hearthrug."

"I don't think that women," Christobel said, her large creamy face flushing slightly, "I mean — to have those two women in the prison scene like that, I mean, one of them had her blouse unbuttoned. I mean — it's a bit — well it's not — quite right — is it. Did you really write that, Miss Porch?"

"Take it or leave it, dear girl," Miss Crisp said before Miss Porch could think of a reply. "It does, after all, have to be women in a women's prison."

"You certainly don't get a man in a women's prison," Miss Harrow said, "except perhaps the gatekeeper and he wouldn't exactly turn you on! If one cannot get satisfaction," Miss Harrow paused and then, making her English sound like a Frenchwoman speaking, said, "after all, if no man — then a woman, and if no woman — what is the harm in looking after oneself? *Alors!*"

"Oh!" Christobel looked at Miss Harrow, "but what I mean is Two Women! I ask you!"

"A bit grainy. But after all Art is Art," Miss Harrow said.

"But women!" Christobel persisted, "two women!"

Miss Harrow shrugged. "Child," she said, "in a few years time — "

"I seem to remember," Mrs Crisp joined in the conversation, "it all comes back to me now. Girls in our times were like this, only in those days it wasn't drug addiction, at least I don't think so. At the time," she added, "I was president of the wives' club."

"Whose wives?" Christobel asked.

"Our husbands' wives," Mrs Crisp replied. "We were all married in those days, dear. Everyone was a wife and we had wives' clubs. We made jam, dear, and knickers for the children of the poor . . ."

"Oh I see." Christobel did not wait for Mrs Crisp to finish her half-remembered memory. "But I still don't see how women can . . ."

"We had vanishing morning-coffee parties." Mrs Crisp smiled at Christobel. "We managed beautifully. I seem to remember that the knickers were made," she explained, "for the Under Developed — you know, dear, the more Backward Regions . . ."

"Later," Mrs Viggars said to Christobel, "you will understand." She cleared her throat. "Unnatural surroundings," she said, "extra feelings, loss of balance, give and take, large extent" — she spoke like a telegram. "One can," she turned to Miss Porch, "one can condone incest for the same reasons," she said, "not condone exactly, it is not *le mot juste*." She waited for Miss Porch to supply a word and then continued, "one can see how it happens. Loneliness," she said, "lack of what we understand as love, followed by opportunity — followed by habit. But first there is the giving way, the succumbing," she said, "and where there is no opposition . . .? What is the general opinion on this?"

"She's right!" Miles called out "She's apples! If one of youse ladies will switch orf them lights again we'll let her roll."

In the sudden darkness all eyes were turned to the screen. There was no need to supply an answer for Mrs Viggars.

Miss Porch, sitting by her narrow window, looked across the deserted courtyard. The sky of the summer evening was pink and mauve between the dark twisted shapes of the apple and quince trees. Because of the light the roof of the barn looked as if snow lay on it. The scene was one of complete stillness. As the light faded Miss Porch was reminded of her own idea of what it must have been like in the Garden of Gethsemane. The pale patches of sky were drained of their delicate colours as the sun, on the other side of the house, sank somewhere beyond the distant rim of the wheat stubble. It was a time for solitude. It was not possible, Miss Porch thought, to exist without it.

All the students, or most of them, were in their own rooms to write an account of their first-day impressions in readiness for a reading arranged for the following day. Xerxes and Anders, oblivious to rules, were wrestling on the bank above the agapanthus.

Scattered on Miss Porch's pin-striped lap were the pieces of paper from which she must make her report. She reflected that if she had a room farther along the passage and on the ground floor she would be able to look right into the starved hibiscus and lantana bushes. She would be able to watch the tiny birds darting in and out of the dusty leaves. She knew she needed some sort of relaxation.

The other bed was neatly covered with its white quilt. Mrs Castle's things were no longer in the room. Perhaps she had been given another room for herself. Miss Porch hoped so. She sighed with relief at being alone. As she fingered the scraps of paper she peered at the writing, trying to guess who could have written each one. The more she tried to guess the more hopeless her report writing seemed. A quotation from Goethe came into her mind:

> *Experience had taught him that human opinion is much too varied to be unanimous on so much as a single point even in regard to the most reasonable proposition. . .*

She seized upon the remembered words with delight. What better way, she thought, than to start her report with this expression of the difficulty she faced when reading through all the collected fragments.

There were other problems on her mind. Not the least being that the class had been quite different from what she had planned. Miss Paisley, too; during the whole film Miss Paisley was in the foreground still swinging the hurricane lamp with its flashing red-and-yellow light. She was still there flashing all through the hospital scene and on to the visit in the prison scene and she was still there when Steadman had supposedly driven off — this being the end of that scene.

The flashing lights belonged only to the disco dancing in the opening scene, which was very brief. Miss Paisley, most of the time, was blocking the action as she had placed herself between the actors and the cameras. The memory of her silly pleased expression and the entirely unrhythmic movements she made irritated Miss Porch.

She picked up the notes and began to read them. Some she saw were in fact signed.

I am very much moved by it all.

Signed Meridian Viggars.

A second note stated that as Steadman Mrs Viggars should have more to say. This one was signed by Meridian Viggars too. A third note read,

I would like to continue in first-person monologue throughout please.

Signed Meridian Viggars.

Another was written on deckle-edged notepaper in a refined spidery hand.

Cut the crap. Shithouse crap. Never heard so much bull ever. When are we getting on to the good stuff. A bit of meat. The sex line. Fuck. Where's the Grab.

Miss Porch studied the handwriting. It was clearly that of an elderly person. She sniffed the paper. It was scented, Ashes of Violets, she tried to remember whose perfume — or was it bath salts?

She took up another note. She felt timid.

I'm trying to get an opera off the ground, a sort of documentary. I've done some interviews and set my deadline. I've brought it with me. I'll need a grant of about fifty thousand dollars. Can you tell me where to go.

The next note was brief.

The cello playing was ghastly the music stunningly well-conceived.

Someone simply writing down Miss Peycroft's own words. Miss Porch reminded herself, not for the first time, how important it was not to put opinion of oneself into other people's minds.

Someone else had written,

The Nurse should not have kept saying Wah and Aw and Ah all through the reading quite drove me round the bend.

A further fragment read:

Couldn't the camera give a close up of the dear little babby? The little ears? The little fingers? God's very own creation I like them "blameless" and the tiny little etc.

The pieces of paper filled Miss Porch's lap.

I am not at all keen on the name Steadman. Would it be possible for me to be called Roderick after my late husband?

signed M. Viggars.

'Oh Lord!' Miss Porch groaned over an illegible scrawl. It seemed to be a note to Anders in violet ink. Miss Porch felt a prickly blush on her own neck as she made out some of the words of passion

. . . from your very own Maybelle your Pussychatte.

She let that note fall with the others back into her lap. She groaned again. It was not possible to have a c.u. of the baby. There was not even a need for an explanation. Jonquil Castle, during the performance, tripped over an uneven flagstone in the yard and dropped the baby which was a smallish bundle of washing hastily put together at the last moment. Actions were not synchronized with the reading. Jonquil was supposed to be saying, "Oh you are like your Daddy," when she had scattered the bits of the baby all over the courtyard and was trying to get her heel out from between the broken pieces of paving stone. Also, Miles was seen quite plainly several times on film, at least twice fastening the front of his own trousers, and repeatedly putting a tattered geranium into the buttonhole of Mrs Viggars' blue blazer. This occurred even when Mrs Viggars, as Steadman, was standing near the cot in the hospital ward. Miss Porch made a note in severe printing in her own file.

THE BUTTONHOLES SHOULD BE FIXED BEFORE COMING ON LOCATION ALSO DRESS ADJUSTED.

Another fragment of well-founded criticism read:

The nurse overacts or over reacts to her mistake when she thinks the Grand-daddy is the daddy there is no need to burst out crying like she did anyone can make a mistake and it all comes right in the wash or the ironing anyway.

Miss Porch made a second note, calmly, to the effect that Jonquil missed her cue to leave the stage and was still present in her chocolate cotton, being the nurse, outside the prison fence, watching the two prison officers struggling in their tragic embrace. Fortunately Steadman ignored her completely.

Miss Porch added a reminder that, if the scene is run through again, a gate-keeper, to lock and unlock, would be needed.

The final note made tears come to her eyes, it read:

Is Alma Porch so moved by her own writing that she is, in places, overcome and unable to read?

This was painful because there was truth in it. Miss Porch did not know who had written the note but she knew that, in fiction, a writer should be objective and should not reveal personal emotional involvement in the writing. She reflected spitefully for a few moments on the number of writers she had seen who smiled with pleasure over their own descriptions and who nearly killed themselves laughing at their really quite unamusing attempts at humour. Turning the discomfort to spite helped to take away the pain. She reprimanded herself, knowing that it is right to feel pain. She tried not to think of Mrs Viggars. There was the real danger that in seeing this representative of money and middle-class security and comfort her own vision of Steadman would fade.

There was a soft knock on the door. "May I come in?" Miss Peycroft did not wait to be invited. "Mind if I sit down?" She flopped on the narrow bed. "It was an excellent beginning, Alma, Excellent. A few teething troubles, naturally. Any good comments?" She took the papers from Miss Porch, one at a time. "Good! Good!" she said, reading them quickly. "The music?" · she asked, "was it all right?"

"Perfectly, thank you," Miss Porch replied.

"Oh thank God for that." Relief and pleasure mingled in Miss Peycroft's face. "Sorry about Paisley," she said. 'She simply is an Egg and that's all there is to it. My dear! Can you imagine what I go through day after day, year after year with that woman's mistakes. Can't get rid of her, though. She's passionately in love — but I suppose you've noticed. No?" Miss Peycroft smiled and then stopped smiling. "When I saw her in the film I wanted to scream and pull her out by the ankles, the hair, anything to get her out of the picture. Sometimes, you know, I have this great wish to hold her dangling by the scruff of the neck over a cauldron of something, nothing too painful, but absolutely deadly. I actually visualize the scene and see her horrible little legs kicking helplessly over the morass. But they don't make cauldrons these days, do they. Now where was I? Oh yes! There she was, my dear, you will have seen her too, the Whole Time in Every Scene. Her stupid expression — face to the camera of course. It was frightful. I actually felt embarrassed.''

"Well," Miss Porch tried to hide a yawn, "it was only the treatment or what is sometimes called the breakdown of the opening scenes of the story. We could not expect perfection." She had pins-and-needles in both feet. She would have liked to stamp round the small room but was afraid that Miss Peycroft would not understand.

"I suppose I am too much of a perfectionist — always has been my trouble," Miss Peycroft said. She held out a dirty piece of paper. "I have a note here from Mrs Miles," she said. "To start with just look at her handwriting! It's the handwriting of an uneducated cook. But it appears that she wants danger money while the disco and the punk rock are in her kitchen. I mean, I ask you, what a perfect nerve!"

"But," Miss Porch felt as if she was trying to fight to the surface in a bad dream, "there was no one there, in the kitchen. The singers," she almost choked, "the singers are all on cassette. The music's all on cassette.''

"Exactly!" Miss Peycroft leaned back with her eyes closed. She leaned forward, opening her eyes. "What I suggest is that, just temporarily of course, you offer Mrs Miles a small fee for the use of the kitchen. A donation of perhaps a hundred dollars? We could arrange to take it off your pay. That way we would be all right. She'd accept the hundred and be happy and we'd be able . . .''

"But," Miss Porch interrupted, "we shall not be using the kitchen again." A great weariness spreading over her tired body made her unable to talk. She smiled with the weakness of fatigue which leads to acquiescence. "Only one person went in the kitchen," she managed to say, "just to set up the cassette player."

"Yes, I know," Miss Peycroft said, "and I believe Mrs Miles got her to clean the stove before letting her leave." She sighed. There was a silence of the kind which follows the recognition by two people of impossible behaviour in a third person who is not present at the time of the recognizing.

How do these Miles people have such power in the College, Miss Porch wondered. Perhaps there were family connections. Blood is thicker than water, she reflected, surprised at herself for being able to think of such a profound platitude. It might be possible to see a family likeness if she concentrated her observation. Within the family, though she had none herself, Miss Porch knew that people would go to any lengths to support or to protect. The mixture of servility and cold calculation in the clear blue eyes of Miles bore no resemblance whatever to the earnest expression in Miss Peycroft's brown eyes. Try as she might she failed to find anything in looks or demeanour which might reveal that they were related.

It then occurred to her that Miles might know something. Miles and Mrs Miles, now there was a strength. They, the two of them, could be blackmailing Miss Peycroft. Perhaps it was something to do with the secret of Miss Peycroft's brother. Miss Paisley had hinted that he was emotional. "My brother Edward" — Miss Porch easily imagined the once loving pride in Miss Peycroft's voice. A poet, a musician — a flautist, of course, and with a fine singing voice, a tenor, that would be it. Miss Porch had him walking pensively in the courtyard and wandering with musical notes stirring in his head through the enchanted orchard. With misgivings and sorrow Miss Porch imprisoned Mr Edward Peycroft, something dreadful to do with a woman, or was it — she quickened — to do with a child. An inability to come to terms with reality and with his own artistic nature — a kind of battle of sexuality versus innocence. In her excitement Miss Porch was able to overlook the phrase used often in literature classes at Towers, "come to terms with," she ignored it and incarcerated Edward Peycroft for life knowing that Miles knew about it, knew the crime, knew also Miss Peycroft's part in it and kept his lips forever sealed (Miss Porch did flinch a little here) but only at a price . . . She began, in some panic, to plan in her mind some way of getting free, of leaving. In her tiredness the plans were not realistic. She knew she could not hit Miles on the head, tie him up behind the barn and set off for the other Cheathem in his bus. For one thing where were the gears and the ignition in a bus. Her head ached.

She agreed to give, temporarily she hoped, the hundred dollars though quite unable to accept, in her own mind, the ludicrous idea.

"Rennett and Harrow were excellent as the prison officers," Miss Peycroft smiled, "don't you think? Especially Harrow. She is a very handsome woman. Good idea having a flashback scene," she said. "Oh! before I forget," she continued, "there were a couple of other quite minor things. Now what were they?" She consulted a list. "Ah! Yes! Mr Miles, such a nuisance, wants his hurricane lamp back as he thinks he's found a buyer for it."

"But I've rented it from him. I paid . . ."

"Yes Alma dear, I know." Miss Peycroft was patient. "But the buyer is Xerxes and he is apparently through Miss Harrow, horribly rich. He has taken a fancy to the lamp and really wants it. I simply cannot let Miles miss an advantageous sale."

Miss Porch, shrugging her heavy shoulders, hoped that the anger she felt did not show. The pulses in her neck seemed to throb and the throbbing pounded in her head.

"I am sorry about this other thing too," Miss Peycroft continued, leaning forward smiling like a crow presiding over roadside carrion, undisturbed. "Could you have a word with Mrs Castle as soon as possible. Apparently she is offended because her question this morning was brushed aside."

Miss Porch, unable to remember, frowned.

"You remember, Alma," Miss Peycroft said, "could you bring up stream of consciousness?"

"Oh good heavens! Yes, of course."

"Thank you so much, Alma." Miss Peycroft stood up, shaking down her skirts with the satisfaction seen in hens who have recently enjoyed a good deep dust-bath. "Would you," she asked lightly, "care to join Paisley and self in an orgy shortly?"

Miss Porch stood up slowly. Her legs were stiff and aching.

"Ah! I see you're too tired," Miss Peycroft's voice was soft with sympathy. "If, however, you feel rested later and change your mind, slip into something comfortable and pop along. You know where we are. In the meantime Knees Full Bend etc. Cheerio!"

Miss Porch rubbed her aching knees. She was glad to be alone in her little room. Her head was heavy and she was tired and hungry. She did not try for long to imagine what scene of debauchery could take place in Miss Peycroft's room along the passage. While preparing her material for the dramatic reading she had neglected to study some of the details in Miss Peycroft's letters. It now occurred to her, too late, that she should have brought some simple provisions with her. She saw, hovering out of reach in an attractive memory, the casual arrangement of a simple cheese board and some broken pieces of a crusty white loaf. Especially she thought of a camembert cheese of the right age melting to a delicious flavour and an inviting consistency. In her mind she added a hard green apple and the possibilities of an inexpensive red wine.

She leaned on the ancient window-sill. Outside the night was dark. She could hear the wind rushing. She imagined the lonely blackness of the wheat paddocks and the wind tearing across searching out the bleak corners. It was strange to be in a place where there was no ocean and no stream.

Miss Porch, living near a river, spent a great deal of her time standing or walking or sitting on a wooden jetty in the middle of an expanse of water which flowed and rippled with a life and energy of its own.

There was no shore in Cheathem East. She missed the leisurely wide river bay, though she supposed the wheat paddocks had the same endlessness. There was nowhere to walk in the wheat; nowhere to take a walk. It was inconceivable, the idea of setting out across the wheat stubble, a marathon, reaching forever towards an always distant horizon. If a person walked here, she thought, concerned dogs from unseen houses would be sure to question noisily. Farmers in shabby useful trucks would stop and reverse and offer unwanted lifts. People in places where there were no people would appear and ask where her car was. "Where did you break down?" "Where did you leave the car?"

If she could escape from this place and get back home she would feel better at once. She knew now that it was a mistake to take on something so demanding during the holidays. Her work at The Towers took all her energy throughout the year. She should be resting now.

She thought with longing of her own small house, set back from a quiet road, with the sandy shore of the river reaching through her garden almost to the edge of the veranda. The small house could be so many things, a nest, a platform, a stepping-stone. It was a tunnel of secret hiding-places closed against harm. And, at times, the bosom of the house rested in sweet-smelling grass and was a sort of summer bower; the windows and doors open on all sides, in tranquility, to the fresh warm air scented with garden flowers and the not unattractive sharp fragrance of weeds.

While she was away her house, in perpetual darkness, would wither. This was not the first time she had left her house. For a time she had lived in at The Towers, this being part of the agreement for a junior mistress, as she was then, to supervise the evening activities of the boarders and then to be on what was called bedroom duty. Once during this ordeal, for the residential life in a girls' boarding school was something of an ordeal for Miss Porch, she had, after arranging with Miss Marks to change duties with her, slipped away for an evening. On reaching her little house at dusk it was as if she had come upon it by surprise, finding the place locked up, naturally as she had left it. But, in addition, it was secretive and deeply closed as if already asleep for the night and not wishing to be disturbed. Trespassing, she walked with small rapid steps round the inside of the dark hedges and over the grassy plots. The garden, like the house, was as if folded up on itself, not having any recognizable features and not having any recognition for her. There was the impression that, by some curious mistake, she was in the wrong garden. Intruding still, she ate, in one hurried mouthful, a chicken sandwich at the edge of the porch.

A red rose, full-blown and sweetly scented, attracted her attention. As hers, she thought to pick it. The single rose refused to be parted easily from the bush and a large thorn pricked her arm causing intense pain. She was surprised, at the time, to see the drops of blood stain her blouse.

It was possible that even if she had the chance to get away from Trinity College she would not find comfort on returning home. Perhaps this partly had something to do with the wearisome feeling which accompanies the failure to achieve what has been attempted. A kind of disappointment with self which often leads to illness and the early onset of old age, manifest in the weakening of muscles and the feeling that flesh has actually fallen away from the face in the realization of failure. Mainly it was that if a place, a house, was left then it was left and, as if for the period of being left, it took on qualities of remoteness and mystery which prevented any kind of return or recapture before the appointed time.

Miss Porch began to sink in random thoughts. Momentarily it was a comfort to allow herself feelings of gladness that Christmas was over. She had come to dislike Christmas. It always seemed too quiet now with the streets and the small number of houses empty for the holiday. No one knocked on her door and, as she had no telephone, it could not ring. There was a public telephone a short distance away but Miss Porch never used it to have friendly talks with people. If often crossed her mind that if she had a heart attack she would not be able to reach that telephone nor a telephone in the house if she had one installed. Living alone, she often told herself, was only possible if one did not try to guard against possibilities.

Sadly she reflected that nothing of her mother's house remained. She did not want to visit that clean house and her mother, but up until her mother's death there had always been the possibility of re-entering the familiar. This no longer existed. The thought of returning now to the house but being a stranger to whoever lived in it was not bearable. Unbearable too was the idea of actually seeing the place and not being able to reach out a hand to the once present well-known shapes and fragrances.

All that had any meaning for her in Christmas was the church, the midnight mass and the singing. Her mother's present was always stockings. Six pairs, very good quality. Her father's imagination had stopped at lace handkerchiefs. The stockings were all worn out long ago but the handkerchiefs were still in a drawer somewhere. They were never used. They were simply pretty and not useful.

Sometimes she remembered things about her father or her mother. Both had been story-telling people. They described objects and the uses of objects or the way to get to some place, a shop perhaps, in detail so that the thing being described became tremendously useful or precious and the journey to a shop turned into an adventure.

She remembered being in a pushchair, her mother taking slow walks every morning moving slowly along the footpath as if encouraging Miss Porch, sitting with her legs stuck out in front of her, dressed in her little hat and matching clean frock, to look closely at stones — twigs — pavement — hedge — earth — flowers — tufts of grass — gate-posts and scatterings of gravel. All at a very slow pace, as if gently presenting the tenderness of the world, at her own level, every speck of which would gradually become familiar and describable.

Miss Porch felt it was a memory but she wondered, at times, whether it was something she had been told by Mrs Porch: "Alma, this is where I used to take you for little walks in your pushchair. You had dear little dresses with matching bonnets. You used to shout at the birds, you couldn't talk then but you clapped your hands and waved . . ."

As for the church, Miss Porch never thought about it now. She had not lost her faith; it had ebbed away very early. All that remained was an angry contempt for the religious trappings of Christmas, worse even than the mad last-minute Christmas shopping for unnecessary presents to symbolize non-existent relationships. Carols and hymns and Bible readings on the radio fell on the deaf ears of families contentedly chewing . . .

Lord what would they say
If this Lord Jesus came their way.

Tired with the end of term and hating Christmas, Miss Porch had looked forward to the January School. It suggested change and freedom but now other depressing thoughts followed in close succession. She remembered that at the end of the last lesson in one of her classes she had confused Rilke's death with the death of Heinrich von Kleist. . .

The fragrance of frying onions drifted on the night air. The frying onions suggested a panful of little squares of neatly cut steak and kidney. In the kitchen, immediately below, Mrs Miles must be cooking. Miss Porch was not, she felt, on the right side of Mrs Miles. When Mrs Miles looked at her she was aware of her own ugliness; the clumsiness of her bare feet in lace-up shoes, the drab shapelessness of her dress which was of an unfashionable length and the hat, which she never took off, all made an image of ugliness. She knew she was caught up in the originally self-chosen idea of ugliness with which she faced the world. She knew, because she was always honest with herself, that it was a kind of defence. Even her voice was not as harsh as she made it. She was not short-sighted at all but wore spectacles because she felt undressed, especially with men, without them.

Miss Porch wept silently on the window-sill. She took off her glasses and cleaned them on her dress, making them more smeary as the material did not have the soft absorbent quality needed for polishing.

This depression over personal appearance, she knew, was because of being tired and hungry. She was not longing for her parents. She knew that she had not really been able to love them and she had read somewhere if you don't love yourself and your parents the chances are that you will not be able to love anyone. Perhaps she longed for the imagined comfort of the household to which she could at one time always return.

She knew too that this profound despair was a part of the loneliness which accompanied writing. Added to this was the emotional stress of offering a partly-written work to a group of people who were concerned chiefly with losing weight. She was afraid that they would not want to think about and discuss her theme. She told herself that she knew this when she accepted the invitation and during the time of the letter-writing and the signing of the contract. Then the idea of the holiday work had appealed to her. Miss Peycroft, in her letters, had created an excitement in Miss Porch's dull existence. There was too an ever-present need to accept offered work because of the very real possibility of not having work.

While she searched hopelessly through her shabby handbag to see if, by any chance, she had a boiled sweet or a toffee a piece of paper was pushed under the door. It slid with a faint sigh across the honey-coloured boards. On the paper, scrawled in a generous hand, were the words,

I feel as Steadman I am being ennobled.

Viggars

There were no sweets in Miss Porch's luggage. The note made her feel better. She read it several times. She took out her notebook. She prowled up and down the small room. She sat down by the window. She stood up and took the few steps the space allowed. It was an act of the will. A savage preparation.

She opened the notebook and turned towards the empty pages where there was a pencilled note. All her movements, the bending of the head forward, the placing of the fingertips of her left hand on the open page and the hunching of the shoulders were a resignation towards the work of writing. The excitement spread through her as she read the note.

Foxybaby Note: For opening sequence —
Suburban Streets. Quiet with trees.
Quiet houses. Blinds drawn.
Well-grown gardens. Roses.
Lawns. Flowering shrubs.
Colour and Fragrance. More Roses.
Grass in ridges between paving slabs.

It is early morning
It is dusk.
Sprinklers. A mist of water spray.
Magpies.
No people.
Steadman walking
Turning corners walking and walking
The Foxybaby running running and running
Turning corners running.
Walking early morning — getting lighter
Running. Dusk — getting darker
Steadman disappears in water mist
Foxybaby comes round corner
Foxybaby disappears in water mist
Steadman reappears round corner
Walking/Running round corners every corner like
the one before. Walking/Running never meeting
Grass trees hedges fences garden flowers paths
movements of turning seeming to come towards
each other but never meeting. Fade into water mist

Miss Porch crossed a t and put in a full-stop. She could not write from the note. There was only the panic of being unable to rest and sleep. She lay down to sleep but the days ahead weighed too heavily. She thought again of how she might leave. Apart from the excitement of travelling to a new place for a different kind of work she needed the money. She knew that the need to earn her living would keep her for most of her life in places where she did not particularly want to be. All the same, she made up her mind, she would leave this impossible place and the impossible people.

The smell of the cooking made her even more restless. She, though poor, had never been without adequate food and had never before realized the lack of its regularity.

She opened her door cautiously. The long passage was deserted. From the far end came the muffled sound of what, she realized, must be the Peycroft-Paisley Orgy. She paused to listen and recognized Dryden's Ode for St Cecilia being adapted for the cello, the double bass and the tapping sticks.

Miss Porch, avoiding that end of the passage, turned to the back stairs and went down them like a thief. Perhaps a little walk in the courtyard, even though it was dark, would induce sleep.

As she passed the open kitchen door she saw the ennobled Mrs Viggars sitting up close to the kitchen table, a white napkin tucked under her chin and a knife and fork held at the ready in practised hands. The kitchen was light and warm and full of that comfort which accompanies the preparation of food. Mrs Viggars called out from behind a serious-looking plateful:

"Hallo there! Porch!" adding in a rumbling moist voice, "Come along in, Porch. Have you met Rennett? A very dear friend of mine. Oh yes. Of course you have! Miles! Serve Miss Porch, please. She is my guest. Glass of wine, Porch?"

"I don't mind if I do." Miss Porch revealed her background, making it even more commonplace by asking "What about Miss Peycroft?" She seemed unable to prevent the unwanted question from rising to her lips.

She sat down on the offered chair with mounting anticipation. There was a piece of old blackboard, Miss Porch had not noticed it before, propped at the side of the dresser. Beneath the amazing list of possibilities which included pregnant mare cubes, mineral licks, grow more calf pellets and golden-yolk layer mash was the chalked offering:

FRYING TONITE
SHATTO BIRAND STAKES
Vegies or Salad Trays Extra

Miles put a knife and fork in front of Miss Porch and busily polished a glass for her.

"Missis Peycroft's got 'ers also Miss Paisley. I've took 'em up a tray not halfhour ago. Vegables or salad, Miss?"

"My advice," Mrs Viggars leaned forward across the table towards Miss Porch, "my advice," she said juicily, "is to have both. The zucchini simply melt in the mouth and Miles makes an American salad which is out of this world. Also," she lowered her voice as if to utter something profound, a confidence for the ears of Miss Porch alone, "oomph, this meat, my dear, I am certain of it, is not a *Chateaubriant* at all. It is my earnest belief that it is venison."

With an enormous helping steaming in front of her, Miss Porch tried not to be unrestrained. She felt better already. The little carrots were positively artistic.

"What d'you fancy, Porch? Oomph?" Mrs Viggars offered Miss Porch wine. "Red or white? I'm a red wine man myself but I always think white is lighter on the stomach during the night. There's a good Riesling — or do you prefer a Moselle? Rennett here goes for the Sauternes. Laps them up. Would like to bath in Sauterne oomph? Rennett? Rennett old girl! By Gad! You're looking cheeky tonight. Rennett, oomph!" Mrs Viggars laughed somewhere down inside her generous trouser suit and stifled, by tucking in her chins, an inclination to bring up wind. "Now this Traminer Riesling," she continued, "I can thoroughly recommend. And for when we have our strawberries and cream, Miles has obtained an excellent Spätlese, quite a lively little wine with naughty thighs and a cheeky nose."

Miss Porch chose the Traminer Riesling and Miss Rennett, who had not looked up from her plate, pushed one of her glasses towards Mrs Viggars whose pouring was more generous than accurate. "Oomph! Oops. Rennett, sorry old dear, your dress. Miles! Have you a sponge handy? Rennett, old girl, I know for a fact that this Sauterne simply does not stain. All you have to do is to soak yourself in cold water, overnight preferably. Miles! This is Miss Alma Porch, a writer of books."

Miles touched his cap with a show of hitherto unseen respect in his bearing. "Evening, Missis Porch, I'm sorry to say I could never read a book. Give me a book and halfway down the page I'm orf snoring me 'ead orf. Mrs Miles, she don't let me read a book for that very reason."

For a time, as they worked their way into the food, no one spoke. Miss Porch noticed that Miles was actually smiling. Feeling comforted she confided in Mrs Viggars, telling her the mistake she made in the last class at school.

"Rilke had leukaemia," she said, "he didn't commit suicide at all, that was Kleist. I can't think how I came to make a mistake like that. Only think! I've spread terri ble confusion."

"I shouldn't worry at all," Mrs Viggars consoled, "it's more than likely that not one of those young gels will give either of the two men a moment's thought. C'est la vie. Have another glass of wine. Memories like that are an indication that you have not looked upon the grape sufficiently." With a quick tilt of the chin Mrs Viggars caught the beginnings of a rivulet of gravy. She filled their glasses. "All schools have midnight feasts," she said, "possibly there will be a larger gathering tomorrow, oomph, Miles?"

"Very possibly Miss," Miles said.

"The only thing," Mrs Viggars laughed and rumbled, shaking her heavy cheeks, "the only thing which will have lost weight after this school, Sensational Slimming or whatever it's called, is my portable cellar!"

For a time they ate and drank in harmony as if completely accustomed to each other's eating habits.

"Come on, Porch!" Mrs Viggars said after a few particularly succulent mouthfuls. "Come on, Porch, spill the beans. Why's that gel been in prison? And who the devil is the father of the baby? Why doesn't he show up and visit her in the hospital? I want to know, Porch, what's happened and what is going to happen. And what or who the hell is Foxybaby. I am, to say the least, absolutely intrigued. So is Rennett, oomph? Rennett?"

"Oh!" Miss Porch made her mouth as prim as a generous forkful of french fried potatoes would allow, "I never like to tell my ideas before they're born . . ."

"Oh, I like that. I do like that," Mrs Viggars cried, "fill up her glass, Miles," she called, "and have another bottle yourself."

"The truth is," Miss Porch suddenly felt even more able to confide, "the truth is that I am extraordinarily sensitive to insensitive criticism, especially if I feel the person being critical does not really know what he is talking about . . . I mean, I just can't write or anything. . ."

"Say no more," Mrs Viggars said, "let me pass on some advice from, let us say, my greater maturity and even greater size." She shook her bulky body in a good-humoured way. "My child," she said, "you have not learned yet to avoid the destructive influences in people. This is most important for someone engaged as you are in exploring human life and reason deeply and sympathetically. More wine?'' Miss Porch covered her glass with her hand. Mrs Viggars filled a spare glass. ''I have come,'' she said, ''to a time in life when it seems that loyalty and responsibility are no longer required. This, for me, is a great sadness. But at this moment it gives me great pleasure to feel and show some responsibility towards you. I have learned this art,'' Mrs Viggars continued, ''I have learned to avoid the destructive elements, and I assure you some people, talkative, intellectual women in particular, can be most negative and destructive. But, can you believe this, though I have learned to avoid, I simply ignore my knowledge and often put myself knowingly and painfully in the path of the very destruction I have warned myself against! To Everyman his poison,'' she announced and drank off the glass of wine. ''The last of the noble Rieslings, Farewell Traminer whoever you are!'' She raised her empty glass and with a magnificent and voluptuous movement of her fat arm she flung it at the stove where it shattered mostly into the black satin lap of Mrs Miles. ''Oh!'' said Mrs Viggars to Miss Porch, ''sorrowfully I must tell you that while my mind was on higher things I unwittingly drank your wine. Do forgive me.''

''Of course,'' Miss Porch said in her most affable voice.

Mrs Viggars studied the grimy notepad which Miles presented discreetly to one side of her.

''Why Miles, you rogue! It's daylight robbery,'' she exclaimed while she cheerfully paid the bill.

''It's not daylight, Miss,'' Miles said.

''No, of course not,'' Mrs Viggars agreed. ''Here,

Miles, help me out of this extremely narrow chair. Thank you so much," she gasped, "yes, you're quite right it is dark. But Miles, it was worth it. Well done! Very well done! Knees Full Bend," she guffawed, "Heaven forbid, Porch, don't even try it, something terrible will happen if you do. Goodnight Porch m'dear. Miles here will help me up the stairs."

"Have you any picture postcards?" Jonquil Castle, on her way to the lemon juice and lettuce breakfast, stopped by the partly open door of Miles' room. "May I come in?" she asked. "I was wondering if you had any picture postcards of this lovely old house?"

Miss Porch, who was having an early morning search for useful props among the rubbish Miles had for sale, thought Mrs Castle looked as if she was approaching the meagre breakfast unwillingly. She felt too that Mrs Castle, being unaware of some of Miles' surprising qualities, was sure that Mr Miles was a perfectly horrible man.

"Oh good morning, Miss Porch," she smiled with her head on one side. Miss Porch could see that her ankle was swollen. No doubt the fall in the courtyard had twisted it badly. Mrs Castle looked like someone who has not slept but is not going to admit this.

I was thinking of writing to my three gorgeous grandchildren," Mrs Castle said, smiling bravely. Miles crouched quickly at her elbow with a lidless cardboard box of dingy, fly-spotted, curled-up cards.

"Oh!" Jonquil said, delicately picking over a few, "but these are all Chrissy cards. Haven't you anything else?"

Miles limped all round the room. The limp was part of his sales technique, Miss Porch had noticed it before. He made an apparently painful journey back to Jonquil's side.

"The old war leg." He rubbed his thigh, high up, affectionately, looking at both ladies with what Miss Porch knew Mrs Castle thought of as a leering grin. "It's the Season of Good Cheer," he said, "well, not so long gone." He picked up a card. "There!" he said, "this one's nice, a robin red titty on a prickle of holly eh?" He nudged them both, first Miss Porch and then Mrs Castle. "A robin red titty on a prickle prick," he said, "prick titty prick titty tit-tit-tit." He nudged them both again with an obscene laugh which Miss Porch could see was offending Mrs Castle. The cards had black fingermarks on them. Jonquil chose three.

"Six dollars," Miles said promptly.

Jonquil paid quickly as unhappy people do pay when they know they are being cheated.

Miss Porch and Mrs Castle strolled together through the courtyard, Mrs Castle giving the impression that they were close friends. Miss Porch, feeling this, wished to unhook herself from Mrs Castle's overfriendly arm. She noticed that the fat people loved large floppy hats. They blossomed all over the courtyard, sugar pink, lemon yellow, orange, mustard, lime and some speckled suggesting scrambled eggs enliven with bacon scraps or a colourful vegetable soup.

"It's still rather too early for breakfast." Mrs Castle

looked at her watch. They paused to gaze at some of the more dedicated students as they lowered themselves gingerly into the Trinity pond to receive the benefits of the purifying properties it was said to have hidden in its uninviting depths. Shuddering, Mrs Castle drew Miss Porch on and they walked to the eastern end of the long house.

"It's so terribly muddy, the water, isn't it," she said. Miss Porch, agreeing, could not help wondering why people felt that they should take part in things like this. Some of them, she thought, were not really overweight at all and surely did not need to do unpleasant things and make themselves so uncomfortable. Slimming diets were popular, perhaps it was fashionable and "interesting" to be on a diet, especially a ruthless one. It often seemed necessary too for those on diets to try to convert those who were not. Rather like people who went to church trying to persuade others. . . .

She looked back at the group hovering on the edge of the pond, their being there was a work of supererogation. She felt pleased to be able to use the word. The Head at Towers always said it was a Killer in Scrabble, perhaps, though Miss Porch would never had said this, neglecting the fact that parts of the word would need to be already in place on the board. She began quickly to work out the possibilities . . . S U P E R to start with — A T. . . .

Mrs Castle was saying something about the roughness of the path. Turning a corner they climbed the broken steps of an old terrace. It was badly built of white stones. The tall windows of the music room faced on to this terrace. Miss Porch, peering through one of the windows, was able to see the grand piano and the harp shrouded in torn tablecloths. She could see too a sofa

126

and some large chintzy armchairs reminiscent of clubroom furniture in the days of the British Raj in India.

"In spite of my painful ankle," Mrs Castle told Miss Porch, "I went for a little walk early this morning. I went through the orchard and, d'you know, the septics are in a fearful state. I rather suspected it, you know, the concrete's all cracked and dreadful black mud is oozing — positively forcing its way out. It can't be healthy can it. The smell was worse than anything I can describe."

They sat on some weatherbeaten cane chairs and surveyed the desolate stretch of wheat stubble with only the prospect, shortly, of a few lettuce leaves for breakfast.

"The lavatories too!" Mrs Castle shivered. Miss Porch felt sure that Mrs Castle would, if given the chance, ask her to have lunch in town one day, "with a small carafe, and we could take in a movie . . ." So intimate, in the eyes of Mrs Castle, did the new friendship seem. "The lavatories," Mrs Castle continued, "are awful, aren't they. I mean, I don't really want to think about them or talk about them but they are a part of life aren't they. Those high-up verandas," she went on, "high-up closed-in verandas, built on I'd say long after the house was built. Perhaps stuck on would be more accurate. D'you know, I feel afraid, in there, to sit down," she confided, "the floor slopes so much and you feel the whole thing will slide away backwards through that really thin wall. Also," she lowered her voice, "also you never know when that dreadful man, Moles . . ."

"Miles," Miss Porch corrected gently. She felt cold and Mrs Castle was a bit boring and, perhaps, there was the pain too of feeling sorry for her.

"Yes, Miles, thank you," Mrs Castle flashed a bright-eyed, red-lipped widow's smile at Miss Porch who felt completely drawn in with sympathy. "You never know," Mrs Castle said, "when he's going to take it into his small horrible head to come in and hose down the toilets regardless of who is actually in them. He hoses them so often there is always water, I'd say two inches of water, on the floors and it drips straight through to the place where we have that awful black tea and the absolutely tasteless fruit."

"Aren't you going to write your cards?" Miss Porch reminded.

"Well yes, I suppose I should," Mrs Castle spread them on her folder and resting it on her knees she began to write:

to dear Bristy   to dear Jonty
to dear Annabelly You would love this big old
rambling house it has attics and a big staircase

"Oh I don't know," she sighed, "I don't know if I can write just now. I keep seeing their solemn round faces in my mind. They seem so far away. I do miss them, I really do. You would love them. Perhaps, perhaps I'll write these cards later." She slipped them neatly into her folder.

Miss Porch, noticing that Mrs Castle's eyes were full of tears, looked away across the stubble. Shading her own eyes with one hand she said; "Perhaps we should go indoors for our lettuce."

"Oh yes," Mrs Castle patted her eyes carefully with a folded tissue. "I'm just being silly. It's my ankle," she said, "that's why I bound it up with my tangerine scarf. I don't want to be a nuisance . . ."

Miss Porch adjusted her stride to Mrs Castle's hobble.

"I don't want to be a nuisance," Mrs Castle said, "but perhaps I could just sit and watch this morning, perhaps by the orchard wall. I don't want to get in the way, you see. Would you mind if I made a few pencil sketches? I love drawing. Actually I am hung in the gallery near my home. I would be quite unobtrusive."

Miss Porch, after her comfortable night, was mellow. "Yes, of course, by all means," she said, "any pictures you care to make will be most useful."

"I'd like the music as soft as possible today, please," Miss Porch said to Miss Peycroft who, with Miss Paisley, was setting up the chairs and the instruments in the courtyard.

"Oh yes! Rather!" Miss Peycroft said, "perhaps you and Miss Paisley can finish the arrangements here, I'll be back in a moment, I must have a word with my Village Maiden."

"Did all this really happen to you?" Miss Paisley asked.

"All what?" Miss Porch placed her files on a chair.

"Why, the things in the story," Miss Paisley said.

"I'm a fiction writer," Miss Porch said, pulling her hat lower over her eyes. "My books are fictitious."

"Oh!" Miss Paisley said, "I didn't know you had written books. I didn't know you were published!"

Miss Porch recalled, for a moment, her pleasure when she had first seen her own book on display at the bookshop. The bookseller had arrange a little row of them just inside the door on a shelf at eye-level. Outside the door on a small rack were more copies. Miss Porch knew that in one of the dark corners at the back of the shop there was a small pile of them. She smiled, quietly pleased, at the memory.

"Oh yes," she said with an easy nonchalance, without explaining that it was one book which had been accepted. Her publishers were not exactly pressing her for her next title. She wished that more effort was made to promote her first book so that people like Miss Peycroft and Miss Paisley would know that it existed. She remembered a fulsome lady encountered not twenty feet from the booksellers, an acquaintance not seen for some weeks. "My dear! Do tell me where I can get your book. I've been looking for it everywhere!" Miss Porch only thought of an answer twenty-four hours later: "Bread from the baker's and books from the bookseller." At the time she had promised to give the woman a copy. Sometimes she worried privately because she had not carried out this promise.

"Josephine," Miss Paisley was saying, "says that I ought not to tell my dreams, she says I ought to write them down. I have wonderfully vivid dreams. They last for ages, last night I dreamed . . ."

Miss Porch could see at once Miss Peycroft — in a frilly white night cap, she thought, sporting inefficient ear mufflers, sitting wearily in bed with Miss Paisley eagerly relating, and including several corrections, her adventures in dreamland. Miss Paisley would perch, she was sure, coyly on the rail at the foot of the bed. The rail might, she began to worry, not be strong enough for Miss Paisley's healthy body. She would have to put her somewhere else in the room. She lifted her from the buckled bed-end and held her hovering, suspended, still animatedly telling, and gingerly placed her on top of the wardrobe. Miss Peycroft would be obliged to suggest writing them down if only to save herself from going mad. . . .

130

"Come along Drama!" Miss Peycroft's rich contralto echoed in the courtyard, interrupting Miss Porch's bedroom scene. Miss Paisley, she was thinking, on cold nights could zip herself into a fleecy-lined sleeping-bag. A tartan pattern would be nice, she thought, big enough to include Miss Peycroft if Miss Paisley should have a nightmare and be afraid. . . .

"Come along, Drama!" Miss Peycroft's voice, in the imperative, rang out once more.

The students gathered in an obedient circle.

"The idea today," Miss Peycroft told them, "is that Miss Porch will read and you, in your little groups, will synchronize the mime with the words. Miss Porch as far as is possible will synchronize her reading with your movements. Everyone," she was emphatic, "will keep time with the music. It will be like a ballet. As expressive as possible. We shall have," she smiled, "the cello and the double bass and the tapping sticks and only change to the heavy beat and the punk rock when required."

Quickly, furtively and even with some reluctance, Miss Porch bundled the frenzied double sleeping-bag out of her mind. There was nothing she could do if the two of them suffocated, she had to pay attention to Miss Peycroft who was actually taking over the arrangements. She picked up her files. The woman was impossible. As she elbowed her way into the circle there was an expectant silence.

"Now!" Miss Peycroft said, "here is Miss Porch. Are the cast ready? Later we shall go back to the dialogue and put that in. I want you all to put on your thinking caps and come up with some really contemporary idiomatic phrases. We'll run through them in the symposium.

"Miss Porch will pause for the scene change.

131

Steadman, that's you, Mrs Viggars, will lead off in the mime. All set? Sandy? Got your hair in a mess? Good! Foxybaby Treatment! Take one — oh! Dash! You there, the magistrate's wife, you've smudged your eyes. Just tidy up the eye shadow there. Here's a tissue. Got a tissue Paze? That's the girl! That's better. Okay? Foxybaby. Take one! Cello — that's me. Tapping Sticks — that's you, Paze. Okay? Porch read!''

"Steadman is an influential man,'' Miss Porch, amazed by Miss Peycroft's intrusion, began to read. It would be useless and undignified to protest. "He has friends who have influence,'' she continued, hoping that her voice was not trembling. "He has money. He has not hesitated to make use of every possible power of influence.

'' 'Dorian's in gaol in Singapore.' He remembers Sandy's thin white face and her imploring eyes. He finds out what has to be done for this unknown young man and makes arrangements which will keep him at a safe distance. Money has to be sent off immediately. He arranges for Sandy to be moved. He tries to put aside all punishing and censorious thoughts and opinions held throughout his life on certain subjects. He banishes for ever from his conversation the cliched and profane remarks made by every member of his circle of friends and colleagues about drugs and their effects.

"It does not occur to him at first that she is pregnant. He takes her back as the child she was rather than the young woman she has become. He sees always in his mind the child with laughing pretty eyes and a sweet face framed in red-gold hair cut square with a babyish fringe.

"Having to see her as she now is, it seems to him that

a birth could never take place. It is as if a baby should not come from her. He even wishes that the child could remain forever unborn so that he could have her back as his child still, close to him and loving.

"He ignores his own sensitivity and the ugliness of her clumsy frock. He tells her it is a nice dress, that he likes it, knowing that it forces him to realize her condition.

"She does not look at him. He repeats his praise and she shrugs her thin shoulders, still not looking, as if she knows he is being false. Both are self-conscious in the presence of the prison officer, the wardress, the one who wept in the earlier scene. She is not dishevelled now. Sexually possessive, she persists in standing very close to Sandy.

" 'Did you make your dress?' Steadman tries again. She glances at him and he seems to see in the glance the big room of benches and sewing-machines and the girls and women, all dressed alike, sewing, never raising their eyes and only speaking when they have to.

"Her body is emaciated. She is like an old woman, a shrivelled stick far too thin to produce a baby. The idea is agonizing, it is inescapable.

"It is better, he thinks, to think and to talk of the future. Making a characteristic small movement with his head and neck he changes his thoughts. He is able to provide the safe nursery, he tells her. All the toys are still there, he says. With a little smile he reminds her of the farm animals carefully put away in biscuit-tins. There is too a train set, he asks her if she remembers the tunnels, the little stations and the signals, the passengers, and the station master. Does she remember, he wants to know, the little brown porter with his tiny barrow?

"Because she is silent he stops talking. He thinks of the books given on her birthdays and at Christmas. These were presents in which he carefully wrote chosen

quotations. He, with pain, remembers them all too
clearly.

    For Sandy — qui remplit mon coeur de clarté
and, *Anyone can find places, but the finding of people*
      is a gift from God. For my Dearest Girl
and, *Since in Nature all is forgiven it would be*
      strange not to forgive. For my Foxybaby
"The ache which started when she left home suddenly
one night leaving him and all her possessions, including
these books and the special inscriptions intended to
accompany her all through her life, is still present.

" 'Perhaps living could become intellectual, an act of
the intellect,' Steadman says at dinner one evening.
He is temporarily at ease with some of his friends.
These . . ."

"May I?" Miss Peycroft interrupted the reading,
"May I make some explanation, please," she asked
Miss Porch. Miss Porch, feeling her mouth to be im-
possibly dry, nodded. "These are people with money
and the privilege of education," Miss Peycroft said,
"they have influence, we are changing the scene. You
will notice in the scenes just read there will be scope for
all kinds of detail for the cameras to pick up — the
nursery, the nursery cupboards, the open books with
Steadman's pen poised to inscribe them. Absolutely all
sorts of things. Miss Porch would appreciate it very
much if you made lists of details to be included in the
scenes. We can study the lists in the symposium — visual
effects for c.u. Okay Alma?" Miss Porch nodded again.

"Okay!" Miss Peycroft said. The word jarred on
Miss Porch. "Okay!" Miss Peycroft said, "it is the
dinner scene now. Ready, Miss Porch? To read?"

" 'Living could become purely an act of the intellect'
Steadman says." Miss Porch read wishing she had a
glass of water or better, a cup of tea. "The friend,
whose house it is, agrees. He pours cognac for his guests
who cradle the glowing glass balloons with contented
hands.

" 'Perhaps,' the psychiatrist says, 'for some people it
is. After all, it could be a way of making life easier.'

"Steadman tells the assembled company that it was
strange that all the places where he had walked or ridden
with Sandy were fenced off.

" 'I mean,' he says, 'someone bought the adjoining
land, searched out their pegs and, quite naturally,
fenced it. Fenced it very thoroughly too,' he adds, 'we
had been taking the horses through there for years.
D'you see, it was as if the time we'd had together was to
be for ever unreachable.'

" 'Oh, you scholars!' the psychiatrist laughs, 'you
pedants of literature and drama, you carry symbolism
too far!'

"The other guests laugh gently. They are sympathetic
though not too much concerned.

" 'But thank heavens,' the magistrate's wife murmurs
to her hostess, 'we are not exactly in the same boat as
Poor Walter with our offspring.' Privately she thinks
that it is a great pity that Walter never remarried and
says so to the successful land agent who is sitting on the
other side of her.

" 'Yes,' he agrees, 'a house needs a woman. Walter
has certainly done his best to be both father and mother,
but a woman is a woman when all's said and done.'

" 'Very profound!' someone remarks.

" 'And fathers,' the magistrate's wife persists,
'fathers do spoil their little girls terribly, everyone
knows that!'

" 'As I said, every household needs a woman,' the land agent nodded wisely, 'if only to prevent all that sparing the rod and spoiling the child.'

" 'Well,' the psychiatrist said, 'Steadman's certainly brought home his spoils now, eh, Steadman?'

" 'Very clever!' someone remarks. There is general laughter. They enjoy their coffee and their brandy. They have, over the years, the same jokes and they all laugh a great deal.

"Steadman laughs too, mainly with gratitude for the companionship and for the pleasure of the enriching comforts of a familiar household. He would like to tell them that it is disturbing to discover that now his daughter is at home with him they find they have lost the harmony of movement they once had. In the house, which is spacious, they are constantly in each other's way and even bump into each other without mirth. He does not say anything of this knowing quite rightly that one of them, misunderstanding on purpose, will say, 'Walter you've Spread! You had better go on a diet!' His thickening body and slower movements provide the evidence.

"He does not speak of the baby either. He does not tell them that the baby is ill. The child is irritable, more so than is normal. He does not speak of his fear. He is afraid for the baby as well as being afraid for his daughter. He is afraid that his fear would not be understood. It has been a shock to him to know that the unborn child can be infected and addicted.

" 'I am going to take you away for a holiday.' Steadman tells Sandy as soon as she is safely at home with him.

They are standing in the cheerful nursery. 'I want to buy you some pretty clothes.' He thinks he sees a flicker of interest pass across her face. 'If you'll let me,' he adds, holding out his hands to her.

"She simply shrugs her shoulders and turns away.

"Cut!" Miss Porch, needing a rest, closed her folder. "We have had the breakdown of the journey," she said, "we can skip the next few pages." She thought with longing of a pot of freshly made tea. "We might have . . ." she began to suggest.

"Could you open your folder at the next marked page, please, Miss Porch?" Miss Peycroft was standing beside her. The students, who, for the purpose of the video, had squeezed themselves into their brightest clothes, pressed closer in their circle of devotion.

"This," Miss Peycroft said, "if I remember rightly, is a scene of direct confrontation. Steadman and his problem. Will he succeed or will he fail? Will the Authorities, doubting his success, follow him and seize both daughter and baby? The next scene highlights the appalling loneliness of the individual. The destructive nature of society as we have created it — it is, above all, a meditation on human wishes . . ." While she was speaking, Miss Porch, quite taken aback, glanced round at the *tableau vivant*, an accidental one of holiday greens and yellows and purples and reds.

"Well," Miss Peycroft was saying, "come along now, gird up your loins, so to speak, give it all you've got! We shall see what happens next. Mrs Viggars, are you ready? And Anna? Good! Tapping sticks okay? Cello — that's me. Okay! Miss Porch?"

"Steadman wishes," Miss Porch read, surprised at her own obedience and at what seemed a renewed strength in spite of feeling tired, "Steadman wishes that instead of chasing after scholarship and fame he was sitting on a sunny corner of a quiet, shabby veranda in the remote township. He feels he would like a life without ambition and without the constant fear of not being able to maintain his progress and position in the competitive academic world. He knows there is no escape. He is committed to his work. He is committed too, deeply, to the idea of bringing his daughter back from her world of terror and starvation to what he believes is happiness. He wants to recreate in her the qualities she once possessed.

"He unpacks methodically putting everything neatly into the cupboards provided. Motels, he thinks, ought to encourage writing and studying but life in a motel simply ebbs. Energy seems to be frittered away. It is not the motel itself. It is the incredible private nature of unhappiness which can be housed in the very private motel unit.

"His understanding of his daughter's unhappiness is limited. She hardly ever replies to anything he says. He has no idea what her wishes or her desires might be.

"On the first evening the baby sleeps and Sandy refuses to eat. She lies down in her clothes. Steadman, thinking she is sulking, ignores her. Later he discovers she is asleep. He looks at her with pity realizing for the first time that her medicines have a power which he does not have. He fetches some water meaning to wash her dirty face and hands, stands for a moment, undecided, and then takes the little basin of water away. He covers her gently with a blanket taken from his own bed since she is lying on top of hers.

"He spends a long time in the shower letting the water wash over him, scarcely noticing it. He eats more bread than he wants and wishes for wine and real coffee, never having realized before how much he depends on them.

"He inspects minutely the squalid history of other lives recorded in the unpleasant stains on the quilt of his bed. He knows that when he sleeps he will wake too early and sorrow will settle on him through the darkest part of the night and stay on into the pale morning.

"Putting off what would be a determined act of going to bed and trying to sleep he switches on the television. It makes more noise than he thought it would. With an anxious glance towards the cradle and the other bed he quickly turns down the sound and watches the silent mouths of a family in a pretty kitchen enjoying a breakfast cereal together; an enthusiastic car salesman helping a happy couple to choose their new car; and some young housewives earnestly discussing an aerosol which will get rid of germs, offensive odours and stop the destructive habits of moths and cockroaches. All the young women, he reflects, are pretty and healthy and have somehow escaped from harm. He allows himself some bitterness towards them and their fathers.

"He watches the beginning of a film in which a girl is walking alone on an endless road. The picture flashes effectively from her tired eyes to her tired feet.

"A van appears on the horizon in a cloud of dust and approaches. It stops and the girl is picked up. The van is crowded with people.

"Steadman sits through five more advertisements; new houses in park-like settings about to be inhabited by clean, pleasant, troublefree little families; swimming pools with similar people enjoying them; some scenes of outdoor living, friends and families happily helping themselves to meat freshly cooked on a barbecue. He thinks the new trousers worn by the husbands are being modelled too. Huge bottles of a summer drink appear on the screen together with a carload of clean children who are about to receive it. Finally a woman cutting an apple and tapping her teeth is demonstrating something to a group of clean children who smile and nod their heads and tap their teeth.

"The girl is dancing in a crowd of other dancers. They seem to have a ceaseless inner energy as if the pulses in their own bodies match the pounding beat of the music. Blue and green and orange lights flash on and off, illuminating haggard, emaciated faces as they emerge from the smoky haze. There is hardly room to move. The men from the van are not dancing. They stand in a silent group at the bar. They have sinister expressions in spite of being young. They watch the girl as she dances.

"Steadman, who has never seen anything like this dance, turns up the sound. The music, with its regular and hypnotic beat, fills the room. There is a song, he discovers, someone is singing, a thin wailing haunting sound as if the voice was pleading from unseen fibres in the singer's body. Other voices echo the singing. All the voices plead.

"The dancers shake their hips and their shoulders, they jerk their heads backwards and forwards. Their thin arms hang lifeless.

"The girl dances separately. She seems to come towards Steadman and then is lost as other dancers converge and cross over; closer and closer but never touching, even in that small and crowded space.

"Steadman turns off the sound. In silence the girl dances still. She twists and shakes and jerks her thin body. Her eyes, which do not seem to see, are half-closed, their heavy lids inflamed with artificial colour.

"Steadman watches the dance. He is unable to stop watching. There is a monotony about the movement, a ritual which is repetitive and forceful. He sits quite still watching the moving bodies.

"The sound of screaming rouses Steadman. He gropes towards the cradle. He picks up the frantic baby. Everything is all right, he tells Sandy. She is standing huddled in a corner of the room. Terrified. He tries to approach her with the crying baby. She holds up both hands as if to scratch his face. Her face, smeared with melting make-up, is like the face of a frightened animal.

"As quickly as he can, using one hand, Steadman fills the kettle and takes the baby's bottle from the refrigerator. He tries to talk softly to the child who is trembling against his chest. He tries to comfort Sandy. His voice shakes and he blunders about in the small spaces between the fixed furniture. He thinks he will make tea.

"In his mind he goes back to the previous night, a scene of horror, during which the girl had torn up her clothes and defaced the walls of the pretty nursery at home. She had smashed cups and plates and mirrors and pictures and bitten her own arms and fingers till everything was bloodstained. He tries now to avoid violence.

" 'It's all right, Sandybaby,' he says to her, 'it's all right, Foxybaby, Daddy's here.' She is suddenly quiet and lies down with one thin scabby arm across her eyes.

"In spite of the peace while the baby feeds greedily, making little, long forgotten but lately remembered noises of swallowing. Steadman is wretched with longing and yearning over his daughter. He is unable to stop looking at her. He longs to hold and comfort her. The baby's fingers curl with surprising strength round one of his own fingers. He continues to look across at Sandy, at her thin white elbows and at the pathetic mess of her hair . . . In the relief of the baby being able to suck . . ."

"I'll just butt in if I may?" Miss Peycroft's voice broke into the reading. Miss Porch looked up from the manuscript. "I just wanted to utter a few things," Miss Peycroft said. "At ease everyone, take a breather! Knees full-bend and down and down and up. Careful there, Mrs Crisp — that's far enough, dear! Once more, knees full-bend! Good!"

Miss Porch could not bend her knees, they were too painful. She bowed slightly from the waist. What did Miss Peycroft want now, she wondered.

"I want you all to think," Miss Peycroft said, "I want you all to put on your thinking caps. Imagine, if you can, this situation. Here is this father who thinks that he can take back his daughter into a relationship which is now not possible. Everything has changed but Steadman refuses to fully understand the change. He refuses to see himself as the world sees him. At the same time he knows he has to bear the opinion of society. An ageing man of sixty-plus, possibly in precarious health — he supposes that he is not ill but at his age one can never be sure — and a young woman, people would not know she is his daughter, and a baby, only a few weeks old, in a motel for a holiday. This whole concept suggests Freudian symbols and inner psychic conflicts. I want you to question yourselves severely" — Miss Peycroft warmed to her subjects — "questions," she said, "can lead to insight especially in the arts. Bear in mind the Freudian slip and the Freudian construction and for heavens sake don't lost sight of the Oedipus and the Electra complexes . . ."

"What is Xerxes doing?" Christobel's shrill voice interrupted Miss Peycroft's lecture, "over there behind the hedge."

The drama class shuffled and jostled each other in order to look towards the orchard.

"There's no one there, Christobel," Miss Peycroft said with endless patience in her voice.

"Perhaps it was only a tree you saw," Miss Crisp said.

Christobel laughed. "Oh yes," she said, "a tree. Xerxes isn't a man is he, I remember now he's a plane tree, he sings in a pantomine. Oh no, wait on, it's an opera, Mozart, we did him at school in year eight."

Miss Porch, weary with years of correcting bright schoolgirls, did not bother to bring Handel as far as her lips. She, while smiling vaguely at Christobel, began to wonder about the problem of an amiable vegetable and how it would be possible to actually make oneself eat it.

"Ready, Miss Porch?" asked Miss Peycroft, rearranging some of the more untidily placed students. "Please continue."

"If only Steadman could," Miss Porch read, "when the baby is asleep again, lie down beside his daughter and put his big gentle hand on her as he had at times not so long ago . . .

Daddy I've got a tummy pain
Never mind, darling, let Daddy make it better

"All his forgotten experience comes back to him. He walks up and down the small spaces between the ugly, useful furniture with the baby wrapped up and held upright to his shoulder. The trusting little head falls drunkenly against his own cheek. He is afraid his face is too rough. Years ago when friends were saying 'Poor

Walter! Managing that Sandy child on his own!' they had no idea of the privately discovered difficulties, like the well-meaning face which would bruise with one attempted touch of tenderness the petal-like skin of a baby.

"He drinks tea. He longs to understand his daughter, her thoughts, her restlessness and her unhappiness. He knows there is no greater grief than to see the lonely unhappiness and the illness of his child. Alone in the night he suffers from inconsolable doubts. He might not succeed. He sees himself in the double mirrors of the bathroom. He is a stranger. He sees his back, as if for the first time, rounded by years of studying and writing and now bent even more by worry. From the side he looks chinless, weak and fragile. His own reflection shocks him. He peers into the mirror more closely. His own face stares back. It is gaunt and his eyes, full of fear, are sunk deep in their sockets. He smiles at himself showing his teeth. He has never seen any man look as he looks. He shudders at his own reflection. He feels he is evil, and that all that has happened is his fault.

"He remembers the film, the various scenes are vividly before him. He knows he is too unaccustomed to watching and following the quick fragments of pictures to understand completely, and he was unable to hear the dialogue.

"It seemed to him that the dancers wore very little clothing. They seemed to be draped in tinselled rags. Their wild hair was patchily dyed giving it a metallic appearance, blue and green and a burnished orange like a burning gas flame. Unreal. The hair was brittle, he thought, and spoiled. When it fell across their faces it was not in any way an added attraction, rather it was sinister, cruel and ugly.

"He remembers the empty expressionless faces with

the unseeing eyes and he remembers the thin arms and the hollow chests and the pathetic shoulders.

"The energy, he suddenly understands, the persistent rhythm and the beat of the dance would all stop abruptly when the scene was over. The thought that the dancers for the scene in the film were all in a kind of artificial sleep and were relying on something taken or given to them to create this hypnotic trance-like continuing movement appals him. He understands for the first time that this forced exaggeration of the senses has made the alteration in his child.

"Thinking over the books and presents which he gave her and shrinking from remembering the ways he tried to cherish her and to bring her up, he realizes now that he has not in any way fitted her for what she might encounter in her life. He, in the darkness, in the quietness with the two sleeping children, tries to speak of this aloud as if some almighty power might exist and, hearing him, help him.

"Steadman wakes suddenly. Someone is knocking on the door. The knocking is not loud but it is steady and persistent. He lies waiting, hoping that the person knocking will realize the mistake and go on to the right place. All the little buildings look alike. It would be easy to mistake one for another though they are clearly numbered and everyone has an outside lamp. Remembering the lights and the numbers Steadman is more alarmed. He listens holding his breath. Waiting. Neither Sandy nor the baby seem to have been disturbed. He lies quietly hoping that whoever it is will go away. The knocking goes on, never louder, never softer. Calling out or going to the door and opening it might cause the kind of disturbance he wants to avoid. Next he hears heavy shoes grinding on the gravel outside. His heart beats violently. He wonders who can be out there and what it is they want. There are many people, he thinks, belonging to Sandy's life. People entirely unknown to him. Three o'clock in the morning might be for them quite a usual time for visiting. The heavy steps seem to retreat, the sound is not so close. Carefully he goes into the small bathroom and, without putting on the light, he climbs on the stool and looks out of the little ventilation grille.

To his horror out there in the night, lit up just enough by the motel lamps, is the prison officer. She is, he thinks, in uniform, unbuttoned. She is standing motionless in the middle of the circular flower-bed. She is looking towards the unit, never taking her deeply shadowed eyes from their door. There is something so horrifying in the unexpected apparition that Steadman hardly thinks of anything which her presence implies. She looks, he thinks, as if she would wait and wait. Reason calms him as he realizes she would not go on standing there in full daylight. She might, he tries to tell himself, be staying in one of the other units. There would be a perfectly reasonable explanation. The officer being there would have nothing at all to do with them.

Groping round the black slippery bathroom, Steadman, suddenly awake, feels sure he has been dreaming. He has never walked in his sleep before. With a sense of disturbance mixed with relief he goes back to his bed where he sleeps at once.''

"In the morning Steadman thinks of pulling back the heavy curtains. He hopes for a view of the sea.

"Driving down from the archway of the office and reception rooms, concentrating on the key with its painted wooden ring, green to match the green door of the unit, he had in the maze of little roads completely lost his sense of direction.

"A view of the sea would remind them of the holidays spent together upstairs in the old hotel, The Neptune — The King of the Sea. He smiles, remembering their spacious shared bedroom with the weathered balcony sloping out over the water. They always ate their breakfast fruit up there, together, after a quick refreshing swim in the clean sea of the early morning.

"He hopes for a view of the sea. He wants to walk to the sea.

"The long windows do face towards the sea but the view falls short into the grey sand track which winds through dismal scrub. From the motel the sea is invisible. This track which widens into the endlessly wide sands is longer than Steadman remembers it to be. The great wide bay known so many years before seems unreachable. And there are the flies. He had forgotten the flies. He makes an effort to not notice them. On either side of the sandy path are ancient peppermint trees. If it were possible to open the windows there would be, at night, especially at night, a fragrance from the long thin leaves.

"As he walks he seems to hear, like some haunting music, her thin little voice as it once reached him. Once, long ago, when he tried to walk away.

Daddy I want to walk the pier
Daddy with you. I want to walk the pier
Daddy I want to WALK THE PIER DADDY

Little girls must go to sleep go to sleep
Little girls must go to bed early and
Wake up with rosy cheeks Little girls
GO TO BED EARLY

Daddy I don't want to go to bed I want
to walk the long pier with you Please
Daddy don't make me go to bed Please
Daddy let me walk the long pier PLEASE DADDY

"Steadman insisting, at the time, because he thought then that children needed sleep, walked alone on the pier and returned to the Neptune in fading dusk seeing her white face, like a crescent moon rising, in the lifted corner of the upstairs window curtain.

"Forgetting all discipline, he quickened his step towards the narrow slip of face.

Daddy's coming, darling, Daddy's coming back

Daddy I want you Daddy Daddy
Where are you? I want you Daddy
Foxybaby want Daddy Foxybaby
Want Daddy
Foxybaby Daddy Foxybaby Play
Foxybaby Daddy Love Daddy Foxybaby
FoxyDaddy love Foxybaby
Love Love FoxyDaddy

Foxybaby darling FoxyDaddy's coming
FoxyDaddy stay with Foxybaby
FoxyDaddy won't leave Foxybaby
Alone again. FoxyDaddy's coming
Back Foxybaby FoxyDaddy love
Foxybaby FoxyDaddy's coming
Love Love you Baby Love Foxybaby

"Hey, Finchy!" The voice of Miles penetrated the concentration in the courtyard. "Hey, Finchy! where you up to?" The raucous voice floated mercilessly over the reading and the mime. "Hey, Finchy! Bet you snatched a bit last night, eh? No need to be shy with me. What room you up to now? Eh? Finchy? What number you in?"

Miss Porch, in spite of the flurry of brooms and mops and dusters shaking a storm of dust and fluff from the windows of the bedrooms above, raised her voice and continued to read.

"The hotel of childhood," she read, "the Neptune of several childhood years is no longer there at the edge of the sea. Now, instead, there is the motel . . ."

"Hey, Finchy!" The voice was directly above the Foxybaby scene. "Hey Hey Hey Finchy! You in number thirteen, hey? Well, I'm up to seventeen. See ya in fifteen. Haw! Haw! Get yor knickers orf sweetheart. Fifteen's the waggon! Fifteen's the lucky bed!"

During the silence following the comment on the bed in room fifteen, Miss Porch, still in command, said, "I'll go back a bit. Just arrange yourselves for Steadman's return to the Neptune. I'll take it from there." She began to read:

*"Foxybaby Daddy loves you Daddy's coming
Love you love you Baby Love Foxybaby . . ."*

A series of throaty laughs and a noisy guffaw mingled with a peal of shrieking laughter fell with a rich sound from the window immediately above. Miss Porch waited with her head bent down towards her pages. *"Farver's 'ealth is much improved/Since 'e 'ad 'is borls removed"* the throaty voice sang, *"Farver's 'ealth is much . . ."* There was a crash of china. "Now see what you been and gone and done!" A female voice, Mrs Finch's, interrupted the song. "Aw gerroff!" she cried with a fresh scream of laughter, "Ooo! Dirty ole man! Ooo! Now just you wait! You ole crab. You! Ouch! Them little pinches hurt more than the big ones. I'll get you for this. See if I don't!

"... *improved*
Since 'e 'ad 'is borls removed

"Pinchy. Finchy. Oo's a pretty birdie!" There followed the sound of a chase with more screams and laughter. There was a crash and a thud.

"Oo the hell left that thingummy there!" Mrs Finch's angry voice turned into a shrill laugh. "Can't catch me!"

"Just you wait my girl!" Miles called out. "Just you wait for it! A kiss, a squeeze and here I am between your knees. How'd you like that for Christmas, eh? Eh, Finchy?"

In the distance a door slammed and all was silent.

Miss Porch raised her head. Steadman was standing quite still on his way back to the Neptune.

"Right, Steadman? I'll continue straight on." Trying to keep her voice level, Miss Porch read: "Instead of the old hotel there is now a motel set back from the bay, a maze of dark brick buildings with dark tiles glazed and fitting neatly in a pattern on the low roofs. Every building is independent of all the others. There are neatly clipped grass plots with white curbs and formal flower-beds. It is discreet, dusty and very private. Dust lies on the furniture and on the uncarpeted parts of the floor. The curtains and the counterpanes are laden with dust as if the little buildings are considered to be still new enough not to require cleaning . . .

"Cut!" Miss Porch, unable to continue, dismissed the drama class.

Miss Peycroft, completely breathless, explained to Miss Porch that the drama discussion in the evening would have to be conducted without the video.

"It's simply has not been made," she gasped. "Sorry to sound so awful," she said, "I've been running round the orchard after Miles. But I do assure you," she managed to add, grasping Miss Porch by the arm, "that tomorrow the equipment will be fully available and there will be a replay, a re-run, I think that's the correct term, before our symposium." She smiled at the students who, while trying not to listen, were politely melting away. "It's every man for himself till tea-time" — she raised her voice. "Miss Porch is, I am sure, eager to accompany the editorial combing of her work — so until tonight you have the freedom of the pen and the paintbrush; the music room is open, I'd like to feel that some of you will go in there and play — what you will! Knees Full-Bend!"

Murmurs and appropriate movements came from all quarters of the courtyard.

The students began to disperse, some to their own rooms, others towards the orchard or to the terrace. Some already had their easels and stools and seemed to be talking with animation. Miss Porch hoped fervently that they were talking about the story so far.

Miss Peycroft measured her tread to suit the rather awkward way in which Miss Porch, because of her painful knees, was obliged to walk.

"Porch, my dear girl I am abject, utterly," Miss Peycroft said. "I had no idea that Miles had sold the video camera before breakfast." She stood still, her frock hanging limp and dirty round her muddied legs. "I've just been trying to get the money back," she continued, "that's why I'm covered in this dreadful stuff. I really must get the septic tanks seen to. Do please excuse this awful smell. Fortunately this dress washes quite well, I've had it for years . . ."

"But," Miss Porch, too tired to mind, interrupted, "who has he sold it to? I mean, to whom could he have sold the equipment? I mean, he's been here all day hasn't he?" She shifted her folders from one aching arm to the other.

"My dear," Miss Peycroft said, "he sold it to Xerxes. That young man must be rolling in filthy lucre." She lowered her voice." Miss Harrow pays. She pays, you understand? She pays Anders, it has a special name, dear. Xerxes must obviously cash in on the relationship. You understand?" She waited for Miss Porch to give some demonstration of understanding. Miss Porch nodded.

"Miles sells everything, But everything," Miss Peycroft said. "He simply only sees things in terms of hard cash. He is a sort of vocational robber. I must say there are not enough people these days with any sense of vocation. And, I do feel it is desirable to recognize and respect true Art in all its forms. Miles is naturally rather a nuisance at times but I must say this for him, he is completely devoted to his art and never ever misses a chance to express himself. And, of course, Porch, I must say this too, he has an excellent eye for a fence."

The two women walked towards the kitchen door. Miss Peycroft paused to allow Miss Porch to enter.

"But this time, thank God, I've recovered the money. He still had it on him. He wears a dreadful calico belt thing," she paused, "my dear, next to his, how shall I put it, next to his skin. Rather awful really but I got down to it. I had to get him down first and for once that disgusting sludge was useful for he slipped, d'you see, and I simply sat on his chest and unfastened his trousers. Can you imagine! You've no idea the fight he put up; kept shouting an obscene word saying that he couldn't breathe because of my, you know what." Miss Peycroft wiped her muddy face with a muddy arm. "I've got the money," she said, "and now I'll have to find Xerxes and Anders, they've gone off somewhere to do things with the camera. God!" she said, "how this mud smells! It's straight from the drains you know. I think my dress is torn too. Oh well, it's years old. Porch, Alma dear, I must explain something. The equipment" — Miss Peycroft gulped — "the equipment," she said, "is not ours exactly, it's hired for your drama class by Mrs Viggars, so you do see, don't you?"

"I do see," Miss Porch said, sidling into the passage. She had hardly stepped on to the first step of the stairs when Miss Peycroft, picking up a package from a small table in the hall, said, "Porch, old girl, I feel embarrassed about this. I don't know whether you've noticed but I've been carrying this around with me on the chance that I'd have the courage to ask you to look at it. It's nothing very much. I feel bashful about it. It's my autobiography, I've done about seventy thousand words so far and I'm only up to the age of twelve." With a quick movement Miss Peycroft placed a thick paper-bag on top of Miss Porch's heavy folder. "I thought," she said, "if you hadn't anything much to do in the evenings after our discussions you might like to read it."

"Oh thank you," Miss Porch murmured, "how kind!"

"Knees Full etc." Miss Peycroft's laugh fell in a cascade of indefinite, partly minor musical notes.

As Miss Porch climbed the stairs she thought she had never, in her life before, felt so drained of energy.

Miss Porch, in the sanctuary of her room, enjoyed the smallness of it and the simplicity. She sipped gratefully the mug of tea she had fetched for herself. It was a luxury to have the room to herself when so nearly she had to share it with Mrs Castle. She was glad she had put aside temporarily her fear of being involved with people and having to talk to them and gone down for her tea. The wish for the tea, even though it was black and unlike real tea, it being made from the plentiful and despicable herb, had been compelling enough to make her dart secretly down the stairs and then, with furtive movements and sidelong glances, to creep back with an almost unbearable longing to start sipping the strangely fragrant drink. Until she started to drink she had not realized how thirsty she was.

No one had tried to speak to her at the ends of the long tables where the enamel jugs of hot water were lined up for people to take what they wanted. Only Miss Harrow, brushing close to her, had said out of the corner of her mouth as if being careful not to be overheard, "We are going to be invited, my dear! An invitation is forthcoming!"

Any question Miss Porch would have liked to ask was silenced before it was formed. Miss Harrow winked one large eye and placed a finger across her lips. "Later!" was all she would say.

In the distance crows called across the deserted paddocks. The monotonous sound of cicadas close by, without challenge, was restful. A flock of screaming black cockatoos with the brilliant flashes of red, like unstopped bleeding, in the partings of their wings, disturbed the tranquility but only for a few moments.

The recently hosed courtyard below, in shadow, was fragrant and deserted. The silence of the courtyard made a pleasant change.

It was easy to be lonely and homesick and unable to work in a strange room. Miss Porch felt grateful that this room did not have this strangeness. She remembered having a room, an office they called it, at the Towers. It was during the time when she was living there. She found it impossible to feel at ease in that room. Later, living in her own house and going to the school every day, not having the office any longer, she passed the door repeatedly wishing that she could be back inside there, knowing that it was an ugly room with a dreary view of the back wall of the gymnasium and the school laundry.

Miss Porch, because of falling asleep with her head on the window-sill, was late for the symposium. There was scarcely enough light in her room as the evening was advanced. Groping for her hairbrush she tidied her hair and straightened her crumpled clothes. She felt she had been dreaming. Something worrying. She was not sure what it was. The invitation was worrying enough. Miss Harrow had seemed so pleased; pleasure bottled up inside. Miss Porch felt, if she had stayed, she would have heard Miss Harrow whimper with suppressed excitement. This in itself was alarming for Miss Porch knew instinctively that what would please Miss Harrow might only disturb and worry her. The secrecy, the mystery of it was alarming too. The actual invitation, whatever it was, had not been given yet.

As she gathered her papers together she recalled an invitation received when she was nine. A girl called Joan Dodds had invited her: "Alma, come round to my place tonight. My mother's going out. We'll draw the curtains and have the fine times. I'll show you something," Joan said, "I'll show you a trick."

Miss Porch's mother was reluctant. Alma did not go out at night as a rule, but since the Dodds lived in the same street she, after much hesitation, agreed, Miss Porch having neglected to mention that Mrs Dodds and Mr Dodds would not be there.

The evening light then had been like this light. A grey dusk full of shapes and mysterious movement.

"Alma, you'll have to take your knickers off." Both girls were crouched in the side garden by a shed. Joan Dodds, because it was her house, gave the orders. There was a ghost upstairs, she said; if Alma listened she would be able to hear it making a grunting noise. If they stayed in the house, she said, the ghost would come down and get them. Too frightened to go back into the house they stayed out of doors. It was getting dark quickly.

Miss Porch unwillingly peeled off her garment.

"Now come near me," Joan Dodds said. "Closer than that." She held a little rough stick like a bit off the apple tree. She put the little stick between them. "You push on that," she said, "isn't that nice, eh? Eh, Alma?

This is what they do in bed'' — she indicated the dark house at the side of them with a quick tilt of her head.

Miss Porch, crouching, felt awkward but tried to do as she was told. She almost overbalanced several times.

"All you got to do," Joan Dodds said, "is to keep this stick in between your legs and do like I'm doing. You'll like it in a minute. Come on," she urged, "don't move away like that!"

Miss Porch found it very painful.

Mrs Dodds, returning unexpectedly, came upon them just as Miss Porch fell over backwards.

"Alma ith duthd teathing me where ickle babith come from," Joan Dodds, in a suddenly cultivated lisp, said. Mrs Dodds sent Miss Porch home, telling her that Joan Dodds was not allowed to play with girls who didn't wear knickers and that she would speak to Mrs Porch first thing in the morning. . . .

Miss Porch, remembering Joan Dodds' little red woollen hat and her ringlet curls, wondered why, as she felt her way downstairs in the dark, uncomfortable memories and people like Joan Dodds should come into her thoughts. She had completely forgotten the incident till this moment. She began to try, against her will, to remember the outcome but was not able to. She hoped that she was not developing an illness. It would never do, she thought, in this place to go down with an infection. She did not think she had a temperature. Of course it could be, how did they say it, All In The Mind. Perhaps a severe nervous breakdown was approaching, or rather, she was on her way to one. The thought was appalling. Hurriedly she went along the passage to the symposium. She could hear the noise of several voices raised in discussion. She must, she told herself, keep well at all costs.

"I've saved a carrot for you," Miss Paisley said meeting her at the door and turning her pocket inside-out to find it.

Some of the students, unaccustomed to having a whole uncooked carrot for a meal, torn between hunger and disgust, were still nibbling.

Above the general hum of voices Miss Crisp was saying, "It's very vivid. I can just see those incredibly boring flower-beds at the motel, absolutely regimental with scarlet cannas. Beats me why those places can't be done up with a bit of imagination. I'd have thought something exciting like man-eating rubber plants would have been the thing. You know, exotic!"

"It's the word *pregnant* that bothers me" — the discussion began to emerge as Miss Porch moved among the students. "You use the word *pregnant*, Miss Porch. Wouldn't it be better to use some other way of saying this! I mean, you could say 'out of town'? For example, you say, 'at the time he did not know she was pregnant' — Would it not be better to say, 'at the time he did not know she was out of town'? Or better still, 'he did not know she'd got a bun in the oven . . .' "

"In Africa, my dear," Mrs Crisp said, "when I was out of town — I spent the early years of my marriage out of town, d'you see — I had a boy who used to hold up the cow's tail . . . a negro, you know, they . . ."

"Yes, mother," Miss Crisp said, "just now we are discussing the novel. You remember? Miss Porch's musical novel?"

"What about," another voice overpowered Miss Crisp, "what about, 'he did not know she had fallen,' or, 'he did not know she was a fallen women?' "

"No, that's not right," someone else said, Miss Porch was not able to see who it was, "it should be, 'he didna ken she'd fell.' "

"Why those awful tapping sticks and that frantically bad cello?" Miss Harrow said, "is that the only music there is? We surely should be having a bit of solid rock or punk rock, and what on earth's wrong with the disco beat? Like at the beginning. Great stuff!"

"Just a minute, please! Pax!" Miss Peycroft's rich contralto rose above the noise. Someone close by bit and chewed a carrot. "Just a minute," Miss Peycroft said, "I shall take the chair. All, and I mean all questions must be directed to the Chair. We can't have Miss Porch battered like this. Questions to me please, and I will pass them, if suitable, to Miss Porch. But first I have a couple of points to make." She paused and waited for the students to be quiet. "My first offering," she said, "is to remind you about Steadman watching the film, remember, the dancers are all hyped up, that is, they are hypnotized — from the Greek *hupnos*, is that not so?" She raised her eyebrows in the direction of Miss Porch who tried to look as though this had been her thought originally. She gave a stiff-necked nod.

"*Hupnos*, Greek for sleep," Miss Peycroft said, apparently pleased with the nod from Miss Porch. "And now my second point, if Miss Porch will not think me intrusive?" Miss Peycroft raised her eyebrows again in the direction of Miss Porch who repeated her stiff and nervous nod. "My second point," Miss Peycroft continued, "is to Miss Rennett. Miss Rennett? Miss Rennett? Are you here?" Miss Peycroft looked round the assembled group. "Are yes, there you are. Miss Rennett, I do not know whether the others will agree, but during Steadman's dialogue with Sandy, you know, about the summer dress, remember this takes place in the presence of the enraptured wardress, could you, Miss Rennett, be a little more demented? Could you look at the Foxybaby, at Sandy, a little more hungrily? Could you devour her with your look, be lascivious, if you like, with your eyes and use a little more Body Language? Remember you are a sex-starved lesbian cooped up in a steamy over-sexed environment and it is more than likely that this young female, the foxybaby, has, in her very un-innocent way, Turned You On? What d'you think, Miss Porch? About my little point?''

Before Miss Porch could reply, Mrs Viggars cleared her throat; "Oomph," she growled, "Madam Chairman, Lady Writer Porch, Fellow Students of Drama, I simply say this, and I quote, *who knows what meat is coffined in a pie before 'tis opened.* If I may," she continued, "if I may put forward my sentiments, I do not think Rennett is properly cast. This, you understand, is not a criticism, merely a statement. Rennett is not properly cast." She blinked behind her thick spectacles, her cheeks quivered. "Obviously," she said, "this is an emotional moment for me, but Rennett is extraordinarily — you don't mind my saying this, do you Rennett, old girl, it is entirely in the interests of Art and all that. Miss Rennett" — Mrs Viggars addressed the whole company once more "is, if I may say so, one of Nature's Gentlewomen, she is extraordinarily naive for a person of her years. How shall I put it more precisely — Rennett is *unschuldig*, that is it, in every way — *unschuldig*. There is no better word. She is without blame . . .''

"Thank you, Mrs Viggars," Miss Peycroft said quickly. She was interrupted again by Mrs Viggars who spoke in a deeper voice.

"Madam Chair," she said, "I am compelled to say something more if you will allow me . . .''

"Why of course, Mrs Viggars, please go ahead. Feel free! Please!''

"Madam Chair, Lady Writer and Fellow Students of Drama," Mrs Viggars embarked, "what I have to say now concerns the first part of the reading. I wish to say that I do agree entirely about the unquestionable usefulness of money. I applaud the sentiments expressed. People have said that I am courageous to travel round the world. It is not courage, I am simply using up the fortune which Viggars made before his death." She gave no hint of a smile and added, "I have often thought that the making of all this money was the cause of his dying — but who can make a statement of this sort and know whether it is true? Before I sit down," she continued, "I would like to say I applaud too the concept of the presentation of what is known as the Drug Scene through the thoughts and feelings of a character who knows nothing — at least that is the impression I have — that you, Miss Porch, intend to show the effects, how shall I put it — well, you are bringing in the innocence of the individual by placing the individuals — one, Steadman; two, a baby; three the baby's mother — a victim; four, the unfortunate lady warder, in juxtaposition with a world that is beyond their comprehension and their present experience." Mrs Viggars paused. "I would like to add," she said, "that I like very much the head and neck movement you have given to Steadman while he is thinking."

"Thank you, Mrs Viggars." Miss Peycroft was gracious. "I think it is perfectly clear," she said, "that Miss Porch is trying to explore the breakdown of the father-daughter relationship and she is looking at and sharing with us the possibilities of complete emotional rehabilitation and the rebuilding of a warm, caring stability . . ."

Miss Porch, drifting away from Miss Peycroft's

voice, could not help reflecting for a moment on the fortune made by Mr Viggars (Roderick) to be used up by Mrs Viggars. Perhaps, she mused, he travelled in plumbing, something always in demand. Perhaps he even took reticulation to the more remote deserts. She could see them clearly, the Viggars in an aircraft, window seat and centre. A jumbo jet Miss Porch thought it was called. She had never travelled anywhere herself by air. She imagined them about two rows in front, in the first-class part of the plane, the greyish backs and tops of their heads clearly visible on the cushioned antimacassars, Mr Viggars with a pinkish scalp showing through the strands of thin, neatly combed hair. He would be in the centre seat with the financial pages of the newspaper opened and held up, blotting out everything. Mrs Viggars would be next to the window excitedly peering down at the frosted-cake appearance of the sunrise, salmon pink and very delicate over the bandit-ridden, rocky mountains of Turkey. Open on her lap she would have the whole world in pictures and maps . . . a colourful travel feature. . . .

"I've got a question." The voice of Miles roused Miss Porch. She tried to look alert and intelligent. She even remembered to raise an eyebrow in the direction of the voice.

"Ah yes, Miles?" Miss Peycroft waved an expressive index finger towards him. "Could you stand up, Miles, so that we can hear you."

"My question is about the Professor here," Miles said. "Being for many years a Union Man . . ."

"Keep to the point please, Miles." Miss Peycroft drew her handsome eyebrows into an amused but elegant frown.

"Well," said Miles, "I don't see what all the fuss is,

why don't the Prof get in a couple of fully trained blokes, nurses, pay them a good wage since he's got the cash and everything? It's just like the nobs to 'ave money and 'ang on to it for dear life repairing their own gutters and drains mowing their own lawns and doing their gardings falling off ladders and busting their boilers so as not to give off some of their cash to someone as needs a job. These days when there's people despritt for jobs I take it as a hooman dooty to give jobs. Take Finchy's yard! With my experience between the bedsheets so to speak I could nail 'er, I could fix 'er up. The little vixen. She'd be no trouble. Have 'er right in next to no time. Take Finchy here, she's great . . ."

"Thank you, Miles," Miss Peycroft said. "Thank you very much." She had to raise her voice as Miss Paisley was playing the tapping sticks with her head tilted to one side and a happy expression on her face, which had the crumpled look of being pressed into a pillow during sleep.

"I shall have to leave you," Miss Peycroft said to Miss Porch, "I have some correspondence to see to. The trouble with Paisley," she added, "Paisley's trouble, one of her troubles, is simply that she has no ears."

"Miles!" a familiar screech sounded somewhere along the passage. "Miles!"

"Hey hey Finchy! My pretty birdie. Miles is a-coming!" The sound of laughter receding indicated that Miles also had things to see to and had left the symposium. "Got a kiss for me, eh? Oo's got a kiss for Miles then, eh?" A distant screech and a door being slammed in some far-off region was followed by a silence.

"To a wolf all mutton is lamb." The resonant growling of Mrs Viggars' voice brought in an entirely new topic.

"I know a delicious way to serve lamb," someone said.

"Have you ever tried tinned oysters?" someone else joined in. "You make a little white sauce, you know, with a knob of butter, the size of a walnut." The lamb was pushed aside for the time being. "And a dessert-spoon of flour," the second cook persisted, "salt and pepper, of course, to taste, and then, my dear, you simply throw in the whole tin — oh — and a squeeze of lemon — the whole thing is done while the bread is toasting. So quick! Quite delicious. Very nourishing and frightfully cheap."

"The perfect midnight snack you could say."

"For myself, I prefer oysters *au naturelle*."

"Well yes, of course, but if you have to consider price . . ."

"Ah! Yes, that is a point."

"Mother and I," Miss Crisp said, "always enjoy our little luxury of the day. It is the famous Black Forest Torte." Miss Crisp snatched off her spectacles while she spoke. She replaced them in order to regard her audience seriously and then snatched them off again. "There's a sweet little café," she explained, "in the New Era Shopping Arcade, our shopping centre," she added with certain pride. "D'you know the Black Forest?"

"Not very well, I'm sorry." Miss Porch hesitated, ashamed that she had not travelled. "I nearly went there once," she began, "or near there . . ." She wondered whether to invent a cousin living in a hunting lodge in the Forest, who was always begging her to visit.

"No, no! My dear," Miss Crisp said with patience as if having to help Miss Porch do something really difficult in the gym, "I'm talking about the cake. Mother, I mean, Mrs Crisp and I . . . don't we, dear? It keeps up the strength you know. It is a deep cake. To make it you need a heap of eggs. It's a luxurious chocolate with thick cream and glacé cherries and a generous spread of apricot jam under the chocolate icing. Very sustaining . . . No! Wait a moment, should it be a red jam? Am I mixing my cakes?''

Miss Porch made little noises of sympathy about the difficulties of knowing one's cakes these days. She was worried because the discussion was slipping away from the prescribed topic. Everyone seemed animated and pleased with the subjects being talked about. She allowed the conversation to continue because there seemed no other way.

"Zzz," Mrs Viggars resorted to her mealtime French, "about that cake," she said, "*chacun à son goût* I always say and fortunately I have good foundations in the circumstances, *ces corsets? Je les ai trouves au Magasin du Printemps. On a tout là! Tout mais toût! Mais ecouté donc!* Mrs Castle is telling us something very enlightening.''

"A nice little dinner which I cook sometimes for Daphne and the children," Jonquil smiled as she spoke, "is a lamb casserole made with a couple of shanks. You see," she said, "Daphne is sometimes terribly busy. She goes to committee meetings and she's rostered for kindy transport. I always ask the butcher" — she smiled again, beaming cosily round her little audience — " 'Have you two nice, really nice, shanks, Mr West?' I ask him. It is an inexpensive meal. Boris doesn't eat shank so, of course, I only cook them when he is away on circuit." She paused still smiling, as if remembering the lovely restful evenings when her son-in-law was away, possibly dining alone at the only laid table in the vast, cold dining-room of a country hotel in a township so remote that it hardly existed in any kind of reality in her mind. "When I cook this little dinner I chop up the onions and the carrots and the celery . . ."

Miss Porch, listening, began to suffer from backache bending over Mrs Castle's kitchen table neatly dicing vegetables with her. Mrs Castle would be wearing, she thought, her frilly peach apron. Miss Porch waited anxiously for Mrs Castle to explain how and when she made the apron and what Daphne said about it. Miss Porch, forgetting the symposium, wondered what colour scheme Mrs Castle and Daphne had in mind if they should decide to have the kitchen completely renovated, perhaps on an occasion when the magistrate had a particularly long absence. . . .

". . . I make sure the dish is in the oven really early. The long slow cooking makes all the difference, it's the secret of its success. I cook," Mrs Castle said happily, "the potatoes and the peas separately and I make the potatoes into creamed whirls. At the last minute I put some very finely chopped mint and parsley into the delicious gravy."

"Oh yummy, yum!" Christobel swallowed, "you're making me so hungry. Do you have sweets as well?" she asked.

"Yes." Mrs Castle's well-shaped smile, if allowed, would have reached her ears. "For dessert with this dinner I usually make Banana Boats." She waited still looking round as if about to hand little dishes of Banana Boats.

Miss Porch, again in her mind, saw Mrs Castle bending even lower over the table, for hours, decorating carefully sliced whole bananas with little strips of angelica and tiny chocolate wafers held in place with minute drops of a perfectly made caramel.

"Did you ever have Banana Boats, Miss Porch?" Christobel asked.

"No, never," Miss Porch said; she could see that the little dinner, the preparation and the serving and the eating were all present in a long sigh which escaped from Mrs Castle.

"That little meal would be more than acceptable just now," Miss Crisp said, giving her carrot, a very thick and woody specimen, a savage bite.

"Oh yes," Jonquil sighed again, "I do rather long to be with my little grandchildren. I am actually quite hungry for them." She gave a shy, self-conscious laugh. "I would so love to have that darling scamp Annabelly in my lap just now." She sighed again. "I never realized," she said, "how much I would miss them, I miss their voices and their lovely soft skin."

Miss Porch, seeing Mrs Castle's eyes redden, looked the other way.

"I made some table-mats," Mrs Castle was saying, delicately patting her overflowing eyes with a folded tissue, "just recently I said to Daphne, 'Daphne Dear,' I said, 'we need new table-mats,' so I worked some in a lovely bright salmon, all by hand with drawn thread and fringes. 'Oh Mumsie,' Daphne said, 'they're lovely!' "

The symposium, having deteriorated, was declared over and Miss Porch began an explanation about reading being a creative process and that it was not necessary for the writer to write absolutely every detail belonging to the characters — for example, their living arrangements and their meals need not be described unless they were an essential part of the story or the novel. Readers, she told them, can piece things together in rapid retrospect. Imagination, she said, in the reader must not be overlooked as endless pictures can fill the reader's mind from what the writer offers. A great deal, Miss Porch went on to say, of understanding comes from the reader, or in the case of a play, from the audience.

Upstairs in Miss Porch's little room Mrs Castle sat down on the wooden chair by the window. It was Miss Porch's place for sitting. Disturbed and tired, Miss Porch sat on the edge of her bed.

"I can't really stay in that other room," Mrs Castle was saying. "I have tried. Really I have. Miss Harrow is a very strange woman. I've done my best." She looked as if she would cry again. Miss Porch, trying to keep Miss Harrow's impending invitation at arm's length, out of her mind in fact, saw the writing materials on Mrs Castle's lap.

"Did you have a question for the symposium?" She asked the question quickly. "I thought you looked as if you had something to say."

"Well, yes," Mrs Castle said, "I did write out a question but it seems silly to ask it now. But I will — if you really want me to." She read aloud in a soft, self-conscious little voice: "My Question, by Jonquil Castle. 'How can Dr. Steadman go out to dinner when that girl and her baby are in his lovely home? I mean, she could wreck the place. Some of her friends could easily turn up and wreck everything. I have heard of things like this happening. Shouldn't he have heard of things like this happening? Shouldn't he have a baby sitter? Perhaps there are nice ladies living alone quite near to his home and one of these ladies might love to be Nana for one night. I mean is it wise to leave that little baby alone with that girl. How could he!' ''

Miss Porch nodded and smiled encouragement. "A good point," she said, bring it up tomorrow, will you?" She gave a square yawn into the palm of her hand which was not quite capable enough to hide it.

Mrs Castle, not noticing the yawn, said, "Well yes, I will mention it if you insist. But, you know, I must tell you, I don't feel at all up to the high standard of the others. They are all so clever aren't they?" She paused wth her head tilted to one side in a manner which struck Miss Porch as being wastefully flirtatious.

"Oh I don't know, I mean you are the same as they are." Miss Porch was embarrassed. "You're very good," she added, feeling more entangled.

Mrs Castle fluttered her blue eyelids. "I've never before," she said, "thought about what a writer actually does. The idea of the writer," she regarded Miss Porch with widened eyes, "actually exploring, I think that was the word you used, characters and their relationships is very frightening. Where does it all end?" She did not wait for an answer but continued: "What if I, little old Jonquilly Castle . . ." Miss Porch shuddered; memorioo of the imagined Daphne's repeated protest, "But Mumsie you can't!" flashed in her mind. Mrs Castle did not notice Miss Porch's shudder as she was, for a different reason, enjoying one herself. "What if I," she said, "tried to explore in my own writing the character of my son-in-law! The whole idea makes me feel vulnerable, so exposed." She gave a self-conscious little laugh; her eyes search Miss Porch's face. "What if you were studying me now, I mean, the way you are looking at me now — I feel you could be writing about me, using my life." She clutched her white vinyl compendium close to her neat bosom as if threatened by Miss Porch's presence.

"Before the end of the symposium, I mean your lecture," Mrs Castle went on, "I simply had to realize that I understood for the first time in my life the meaning of the words subjective and objective. I don't know what you'll think when I tell you this" — Mrs Castle leaned forward still clutching her spotless folder — "there is," she said, "something not quite nice about those words. They seem dreadfully, well, sexual — don't you think?"

Miss Porch, at a loss for an intelligent answer, gave a half-hearted little smile which became, without her intending it, another yawn.

"I was wondering," Mrs Castle said, "if you would like to hear a few of my poems some time. They are my new babies. I mean, don't you think writing poetry is like giving birth?"

"Actually, I haven't any children," Miss Porch said, offering an apology. She wondered if she should quickly invent a child or two or even three, while she was about it, and with equal speed dispose of them. Clearly she saw them, two boys and a girl, making their way bravely in the cruel world earning a modest living being paperboys and working in Woolworths. She sighed.

"Aw!" Mrs Castle spoke as if nothing could make up for this deprivation. "I've got some photos of the children, perhaps you'd like to see them? Here's Jonty, only nine days old. He's nine now of course. We used to call him our Pet-petty-pet. He was always so serious. See his little round face? This is him at three months.

170

He's just a teensie bit eager and do you see his big little knees. We hope he'll be a Soccer Team. If you look closely you'll see he just wee-wee-d his nappy while Daphne snapped him. Don't you think his eyes look thoughtful and deep?"

There was no escape from the cascade of coloured photographs. They spilled from the white vinyl.

"Here's Annabelly, this one is Jonty again. Here's one of all of them together. Can you see the family likeness? They're all Castles — definitely. Ah! here's Annabelly again. Isn't she a little charmer! Here she is in her third birthday party dress, sugar pink organdie, a dream. I made thirty-six little pink satin roses and thirty-six little pink bows and sewed them by hand — see the hem . . ."

"Mrs Castle," Miss Porch said, her nose turned towards the window, "can you smell garlic bread?"

Both ladies sniffed.

"I distinctly caught," Miss Porch said, "the unmistakable smell of hot garlic bread."

Mrs Castle sniffed again. "I can't really smell anything very well," she confided, "not since I had my sinus trouble last year. I'll tell you about that later. I had a pretty bad time . . . Here's one of Bristy. I suppose I shouldn't say this, promise you'll never tell?"

Miss Porch promised.

"Well," Mrs Castle said, "Bristy is Nana's favourite!" She paused and frowned. "I think I do smell something cooking. But," she added, "my nose is rather unreliable these days — though I have been able to catch that dreadful drain smell out there in the orchard."

Miss Porch, with a sly movement slipped the heap of photographs to one side.

"Excuse me," Mrs Castle said as she began with deft fingers to put curlers in her hair. "D'you know," she gave a genteel little laugh, "I've still got half a carrot! It would have been better, wouldn't it, to have the carrots grated. I mean," she added, "if that was all the meal was to be, which it was, surely someone in the kitchen could have grated them. Perhaps we could all volunteer to be graters and be on a sort of roster. Yes, that's what we ought to do!"

Miss Porch, in her mind, saw Mrs Castle in the twilight of dawn leading teams of sleepy recruits, a regiment of non-combatant graters, to the kitchen in search of innocent vegetables.

"Oops!" Mrs Castle was on her delicate knees picking up her spilled hair curlers.

"Let me help." Miss Porch picked up one or two which were near enough for her to reach. Her own knees were too painful for scrambling about on the floor.

"What time is it?" Mrs Castle exclaimed. "I promised Daphne I'd phone her this evening. She'll be waiting for the call."

"I think there's one of those red phones on the landing," Miss Porch said, "completely ugly and out of place there, but useful."

"I'll not be long," Mrs Castle promised as she went, giving her carrot a lady-like nibble, to find the telephone.

Quite soon Miss Porch heard her voice, eager and strained, asking about the children, naming them one by one, in turn. Trying to relax and not think about either the symposium or the Harrow invitation, she suddenly remembered the occasion some days after the Joan Dodds apple-stick invitation when her knickers, washed and neatly ironed and folded, had arrived in a small flat parcel by post. (Her mother, Miss Porch recalled now, had never said anything about that evening visit to the Dodds house.)

"Oh Alma, these are your lost knickers," Mrs Porch said when she unwrapped the parcel. She had not said anything else except to suppose that some gipsy must have stolen them from the clothesline. "They get hungry like the rest of us," she said.

Miss Porch remembered that her mother seemed to be seeing in her mind the tormented, guilt-ridden gipsy woman hurriedly washing and ironing the knickers secretly in her caravan or outside her tent (she may not have been one of the fortunate ones with caravans). A poverty-stricken gipsy, humbled by remorse, making the little parcel and walking at least five miles to post it to Mrs Porch.

"How would the gipsy know our name?" Miss Porch had asked unaware then of her own innocence.

"Gipsies know everything," Mrs Porch had said, "remember that one who told me I'd get varicose veins?"

Miss Porch sighed, remembering her mother's painful swollen legs resting on the sofa cushions. Her own legs were swollen. She longed for the sofa. . . .

"I mean Daphne dear . . ." Mrs Castle had been telephoning long distance with reversed charges (I'll pay later dear) for nearly three quarters of an hour. It was impossible for Miss Porch, lying on her bed, half-asleep, not to hear all that Mrs Castle was saying.

"I mean, Daphne dear, raw carrots are truly good for you, especially for the kiddies." Mrs Castle's voice seemed to be in Miss Porch's pillow. She woke with a start. Mrs Castle had come full-circle back to the raw carrots.

"I mean, Daphne dear, that there are ways of making them attractive. Once could be cut to resemble a battleship, that would be nice for Jonty. Bristy, now what would he like, a carrot gun? And for Annabelly a lovely little girl carrot dolly. Perhaps we could find one with a bit of green left on for hair. And Daphne, I must tell you about Mrs Viggars, dear, she is all zeddy with French pouring from her corner of the dining-room — well, you could hardly call it that, it's a sort of darkish closed-in veranda place open on one side to the court-yard. Terribly hot and full of flies. Must be freezing in the winter. There are some trestle-tables and you would agree with me, Daphne dear, that these and the chairs need a thoroughly good scrubbing. Well, this evening Mrs Viggars, Daphne dear, was rumbling away saying she hadn't got teeth in the right places for an uncooked carrot — I don't remember my French very well, dear, but is *merde* a naughty word? A no-no? Never mind if you can't remember either. And dear, when Miss Rennett got up suddenly to leave, Mrs Viggars jumped up in the middle of a sentence saying the most awful things — 'Exeunt Rennett pursued by a Bear, Exeunt Rennett pursued by a Bear — It's only Shakespeare,' she said to us and she went after Miss Rennett, positively ambling, you know how bears walk with their paws up waving in front of them. I've never seen anything like it and I couldn't help wondering what she was going to do . . . I mean, Mrs Viggars looks just like any one of us, though a good deal older and she is very stout of course. She wears a lot of make-up, dear, violet pancake, I mean it makes it hard to know just what her age is and though she is like us she isn't if you know what I mean."

Miss Porch sat up. She was fully dressed still. She could not stand being in the place another minute. She had made up her mind earlier to put up with anything for the sake of the money and for the chance that there might be more opportunities ahead if this one succeeded, but she had had more than enough. That money she had been persuaded to pay to Mrs Miles earlier, she would probably never see that again. There were other things too. Another five minutes of Mrs Castle and she would go mad. In a short time Mrs Castle would come back into the room and start describing the whole telephone conversation, boring word for boring word. Miss Paisley could and should have made other arrangements about the room. There was something dishonest about it all. If Miss Harrow was shutting Mrs Castle out of their shared room there was no reason at all why she, Alma Porch, should have the endless company of this perfectly harmless, even quite kind but dreadfully irritating woman.

It was all too much. She pulled her case from under the bed, pushed her books and papers and her spare dress into it and made for the backstairs. A few cars, having managed to avoid the back of the Trinity College bus, were in the College carpark. She would use her nail file, as heroines in films did, and steal a car. Possibly Vladimir's car was not even locked. Foreigners, when travelling, were often unreliable and had things happen to them like having their unlocked cars stolen. The newspapers often had little paragraphs. For a moment she saw, perhaps on page three of the paper, a rather blurred picture of Vladimir and a dramatic account in broken English, reported speech of course . . . She hoped Vladimir's car had petrol. The thought was worrying. She knew just how unreliable foreigners, especially artistic ones, could be.

"But that Foxybaby. The whole nasty problem, Daphne, is something surely for other people to think about and to worry over." Jonquil Castle, with the heavy red receiver held close in her two hands, had her back to the escaping Miss Porch.

"I can understand, Daphne dear, about the father" — Miss Porch was, for the first time, grateful to hear Mrs Castle's voice going on and on. "After all, Daphne, a father wants to do all he can for his kiddies. I mean, Daphne dear, your father and I had no worries ever about you. You were such a sweet good girl — topping your year always and winning all the races and being in all the plays and concerts. Your father was always so proud of you. But this girl — she's beyond me — but you know me — I wouldn't dream of saying that in the symposium. Yes, dear, symposium — it means a discussion in the middle of a banquet — so I'm told. I think some of the others are actually sorry for this awful girl. Well, I'm sorry for people in trouble. I'd be the first to help anyone, but this girl . . ."

Mrs Castle's voice faded into a buzzing whimper as the distance became longer. Miss Porch, having reached the foot of the kitchen stairs, crept along the passage towards the door which opened into the courtyard. A bewitching fragrance hung about the unlighted passage and a pleasant, familiar noise came from the kitchen, the door being wide open. Miss Porch tried to slip by, resolving not to be tempted by the agreeable notice scrawled in coloured chalk across the Growmore Pellets For Calves and the Pregnant Mare Cubes.

TONIGHT SPECIAL
WHOLE CRAYS WITH
GARDING SALLAD
TRAYS EXTRA

The happy sounds of knives and forks, the moving of plates and glasses and the well-bred hum of the kind of conversation which accompanies food and wine were almost too much as she glided by trying not to let her awkward case knock against the walls of the narrow place. It would never do to be Mrs Viggars' guest a second time and she had not the money to afford the meal for herself.

"Hail Porch! Ah Hail!" Mrs Viggars appeared at the other end of the passage. "Sweet are the uses of adversity, Porch." Mrs Viggars was drying her hands on a little paper towel. "In the middle of a meal too. Such bad manners!" She growled a laugh. "Come on in, Porch. I was hoping you'd show up. You'll come to dinner?"

"Oh rather!" Miss Porch said, holding her case as much behind her as she could. "I'll just pop back upstairs and fetch Mrs Castle," she said, enjoying suddenly one of those rare moments of unexpected inspiration.

"Good idea!" Mrs Viggars' voice, booming, filled the passage. "See you anon Porch, with or without the Castle."

Miss Porch found Mrs Castle in the enormous bathroom. She had wrapped her swollen foot in her tangerine scarf and was sitting on the edge of the bath running cold water over her feet.

"I'm too tired to write anything tonight," she explained to Miss Porch. "My foot, ankle rather, has come up again. I'll just hobble back to our room and go to bed. Please don't worry about me. Just you get on with your work, your own writing," she said, her voice full with tears. "I'm not really overweight," she said in a rush of words, "I can't think why my son-in-law thought I should have this diet. The exercises too are awful, too extreme, with my ankle hurting like this I can't do that KFB all the time. The diet really is for fanatics. It's impossible here. Not your story, I don't mean that, it is upsetting but that's not . . . Oh dear! I am so sorry. I didn't mean to break down like this. I feel so depressed." Jonquil began to howl.

Miss Porch, as gently as she could, led her along to their room. "You're hungry," she said in her kindest voice, "that's all it is. Just plain hunger I . . ."

"Yes. Yes, I know," Jonquil interrupted, sniffing and searching for a tissue. "There isn't a shop anywhere near, is there. I haven't a thing in my luggage, not even the rusks I usually have in my handbag for the children. Children gets so impatient." She smiled at Miss Porch through her tears and dabbed at her cold-creamed cheeks.

"Come on," Miss Porch said, "is this your dressing-gown?"

"Why, yes," Mrs Castle said, "it's a housecoat. I made exactly the same pattern for Daphne only hers is a lovely shade of plum, a beautiful colour in velvet, gentler than this cherry or cerise as it is sometimes called. Oh my! But velvet is difficult to work! I had to use special tacking thread and I had to put sheets of tissue-paper ever so carefully between the panels of the material . . ."

"D'you think you can make it down the stairs?" Miss Porch tried not to show her impatience.

"I think so, if I don't hurry too much," Mrs Castle said, "but where to at this time of night? It's like a mystery tour. I love anything mysterious."

178

"Follow me," Miss Porch said, "and, er, bring your handbag. We shall need it."

"There's a nice boiled fowl for them as don't fancy shellfish." Mr Miles, at Jonquil's elbow, had his pencil poised over his dirty notebook.

"I like shellfish but shellfish don't like me," Mrs Castle simpered. A few people looked up from their plates but immediately went on eating. Miss Porch noticed a remarkable increase in the number of guests.

With a plate on which a generous breast and a shapely mountain of diced, parsley-speckled vegetables had been arranged Jonquil Castle approached the over-crowded table.

"Will yers all hootch up," Miles said, "and let the lady sit down. There! That's the girl. Under yor bum!" He pushed a wooden stool into position and Jonquil sat down gratefully. Miss Porch, following, carried an oval dish on which a handsome crayfish, nestling in bristling lettuce, gave off an exquisite fragrance of lemon juice and garlic.

"Catches you somewhere between the nose and the mouth." Mrs Viggars nodded with understanding as Miles pushed a second stool into place for Miss Porch.

"What about a glass of Rennett's choice?" Mrs Viggars held up her glass. "Tonight she has suddenly, for no apparent reason, gone all out on this Bubbly, pure soapsuds if you ask me but," she gave a thickset shrug, "but there you are *zzz chacun à zzz son goût zzz*. Be my guests. Both of you. Come along, tuck in!"

"Oh thank you." Jonquil's good manners almost deserted her as the scent from the herbs in the golden broth mingled with her face pack. She was able to disregard completely the fact that she was in public in her dressing-gown, with her hair in rollers and her face and neck smothered in cold cream.

"Don't let little old me interrupt the conversation," she said, trying to be slow and delicate in her attack upon the tender breast.

"What was it you were saying just now, child?" Mrs Viggars turned to Christobel.

"I was saying, Mrs Viggars, what do you do?"

"Do what, child? When, child? What do you mean, dear child?"

"I mean," Christobel broke off and sucked at a bit of shell, "I mean, what do you do, you know? What do you work at?"

"Nothing child. Absolutely nothing. Dear Christobel I am retired." Mrs Viggars paused. She turned to Miles, "Yes, Miles, thank you, please do fill up. It's an exceptionally good Semillon, crisp and dry," she said nodding with approval. "The first few mouthfuls of this wine," she said, "are particularly delightful." She waited for Miss Porch to drink. "You will notice," she said to Miss Porch, "the wine has a herbaceous character like fresh grass." She watched Miss Porch as she tasted the wine. "It is matured in American hogsheads," she explained, "oak of course. Thank you, Miles. Have another bottle yourself. I eat," she continued to Christobel, "I sleep and then I eat again and from time to time I try to get rid of what I've eaten. It's quite simple. Dull, incredibly dull but simple."

"But," Christobel persisted, "what did you do before — before you retired, I mean." Mrs Viggars gave a shortsighted and generous smile in the direction of the girl. "Nothing," she said, "absolutely nothing. I have always been like this."

Christobel, snapping the crayfish legs, continued to suck them one after the other.

Miss Porch glanced round the crowded kitchen. The midnight meal was in great demand. Trays were being prepared and carried off swiftly to rooms upstairs. It was clear too that some sort of celebration was being held in the courtyard.

"I think it's an eightieth birthday," Mrs Viggars said, "perhaps Mrs Crisp?" She was resplendent in manure-coloured brocade. "How do you like my caftan," she asked Miss Porch. "You know," she lowered her voice, "I thought, I really expected this cloth, this dress to smell because of the colour." She gave a rumbling laugh. "I must tell you, Porch, and I quote — " Mrs Viggars tossed off the remains of her wine, " 'Action like Virtue brings its own Rewards' — big letters for Action, Virtue and Rewards, for emphasis," she said. "I might be misquoting. Have you not noticed, Porch, that being hungry turns one off things? It's all nonsense about having to starve in a garret before being able to write or to compose. Hungry in an attic one would merely wish for and try to get food. I'll tell you this. I was far too hungry to be lecherous but once hunger is satisfied who knows what I might do to Rennett!" She laughed again. "Rennett has fallen asleep over her meringues," she added kindly. "You understand Porch, I hardly need to explain to you, I am giving Rennett *raison d'etre*, a life mask, assuming a mask myself in order to serve Rennett with one. It is something by which men live. What do you writers call it? The life lie? In reality, Porch, I am no huntress, it's all a pretence. Your book, Porch, the story so far has given me a reason for being, and for this I thank you. Do you understand? From the bottom of my heart, I thank you. You do understand?"

"I think so," Miss Porch, feeling deeply moved and grateful, spoke in a hoarse whisper. Someone in the courtyard was making a speech. It was followed by applause and the sounds of rattles and whistles.

"Miles is selling them party hats," Christobel said. "I think I'll go out there. They're having an ice-cream bomb!"

"I am looking forward to the rest of the story," Mrs Viggars said to Miss Porch. "My part as Steadman has given me the wish to cherish and to nurture. Perhaps a young woman and her child. I have the necessary wherewithal, the money." She spoke in a modest way. "Viggars," she said, "worked too hard making money for me to spend." She paused. "But I have known great tenderness . . ."

"Oh of course, I am sure . . ." Miss Porch began. She was soaking some soft bread in the golden garlic liquid left on her plate.

"I have known it from Viggars." Mrs Viggars paused, watching Miss Porch with approval. "He was a man," she went on, "who cherished me and for this I am grateful."

Miss Porch sat back a little. She had intended to slip away with her case, which was ready at the foot of the kitchen stairs, to look for Vladimir's bright little car. Escape, she thought, seemed easier when she was no longer hungry. But Mrs Viggars was saying things from which it was not easy to escape. Things which changed the idea of escape. Perhaps running away was not the answer. Mrs Viggars, it seemed to Miss Porch, was actually saying that she needed the Foxybaby.

"That girl," Mrs Viggars said, "who is she?"

"Christobel, I'm afraid I don't know her other name."

"No. No. The other one who is and is not, Sandy."

"I don't know her either, but I gather . . ."

"I heard that she has no home, no one."

"So I believe." Miss Porch realized she had not listened properly to all the things Miss Paisley talked of.

"And those two small boys?"

"They seem to be her children," Miss Porch said. "I did overhear something," she added, "that she is about to have another child." She did not offer Miss Paisley's earlier gossip about the absent Mr Peycroft. For a moment Miss Porch seemed to see Miss Peycroft's brother, perhaps an unmentionable relation, perhaps wearing a pale blue or a pink silky rollneck body shirt and stepping lightly across the courtyard, a clipboard of poems held close to his slender chest. He would be pleasantly surprised by a cheeky greeting from a hand-some, naked to the waist, gardener's boy as he rose from behind the heap of leaves he was sweeping with all the grace and beauty of the healthy labourer. Miss Peycroft, Miss Porch thought, would have advertised in the Cheathem West News for an outside man, an offsider for Miles who . . .

"Most suitable!" Mrs Viggars said.

"What d'you mean?" Miss Porch was startled from a further thought that this image of Mr Peycroft would hardly be the cause of Anna's triple motherhood.

"From the point of view of the mime, the coming of the baby," Mrs Viggars said, "but not so good for her. I gather there is no husband."

"That is correct," Miss Porch said, dismissing the pink poet before he had time to laughingly fling himself into the bed of careless leaves. "She is very young to be on her own with three small children. She seems to have no one, though I know very little about her, naturally. I expect the father has, as they say, shot through. At least that is my presumption.''

"Oh, I see." Mrs Viggars was thoughtful. "I do not know," she said, growling as she lowered her voice, "I do not know anything about sexual love. Viggars did not go in often for that sort of thing, but when he did he always apologized handsomely. The fur coat, the little silk dress or the brooch, and the diamond ring and pearls, of course there were always pearls, a milky sunrise — a reward of daylight. . . . But tell me — is there a Mr Porch?''

"Well there was," Miss Porch replied, "but he was my father.''

"I see, naturally of course. Is it true," Mrs Viggars sipped her wine and changed the subject, "is it true that Miss Harrow has published an embarrassing book?''

"I don't know of it," Miss Porch said cautiously.

"I rather think, from what I have heard, that she is an actress and not really a writer.''

"Actresses often want to write," Miss Porch replied, "I suppose people do want to write their own experiences. Sometimes these are interesting to other people.''

'More wine, Porch?''

"I don't think I should — I've had more than enough!" Miss Porch almost giggled.

"You do understand, don't you, how I feel about your book.''

"Yes," Miss Porch said, "Yes I do, thank you very much.''

"Tomorrow," Mrs Viggars said, "tomorrow will yield some further episode. You, of course, know what it is to be already!" She began to get up from her chair. Miles ran, on bent legs, to her assistance.

"Miles! Have done! Miles!" she growled at him in a good-humoured way, "just see me to the top of the stairs there's a good fellow! Your bill makes me quite faint even before I see it. It's the thought of your bill, you wicked thief! Porch here will see me along the passage. You, the stairs."

"I am just a teensie bit embarrassed," Miss Porch heard Mrs Castle's voice immediately behind, she was following accompanied by Christobel, "it's about the, um, that Foxybaby" — she said the word as if it had an improper meaning — "because," Mrs Castle went on, "because we are discussing intimate things and we are all different ages. You know what I mean, dear, our ages are all so very different. I am a grandmother, you see, and you are a schoolgirl."

"I'm year twelve," Christobel said.

"Yes, year twelve, dear, I have always felt this about television," Mrs Castle said, "showing all sorts of things, not knowing who is sitting with who in the T.V. room. I mean T.V. goes into all our lounge-rooms without a thought as to who is in them watching, I mean all different age-groups with all different experiences." Mrs Castle dropped her voice as she spoke. "Experiences," she said, "looking at, well, you *know what* and everything." She paused. "All at the same time," she added.

"You mean sex and all that jazz?" Christobel smoothed her full hips with both hands. She wriggled her shoulders and then her buttocks, glancing over her plump shoulder to see the effect.

"Well yes," Mrs Castle said, "I feel embarrassed." She gave one of her noisy little shudders. "Silly old me," she said, "I'm just an old-fashioned Nana." She gave Christobel one of her brave-widow smiles adding her kind-Nana twinkle to her eyes which, in spite of the enormous meal, still held their ever-present hunger.

Mrs Viggars, squashing Miles flat on one side and Miss Porch on the other, reached the top of the kitchen stairs.

"Made it!" she gasped, "never thought I would. Bravo, Porch! Ditto, Miles! Oh and Miles, pop down for Porch's case, there's a dear! I think you'll find it just at the bottom of the stairs."

They waited together on the landing. "The thing about Miles," Mrs Viggars said, "is that he has such remarkable talents. Did you know," she added with a look of incredulous admiration, "Miles actually sews on his own buttons."

"It is very interesting," Mrs Viggars said from her squatting position to Miss Porch who was, with difficulty, rising from hers, "to observe all sorts of things about people when we are all together in the circumstances as they are. We have all come here for our own reasons. We came because we have chosen to come. And here we are exercising, dieting, feasting, receiving intellectual stimulus and communicating. Oh!" she shaded her eyes with both hands, "this morning sun is too bright for me! Also this exercise! I am sure it is not wise to try to bend the knees like this at my age. I shall be in agony and there is the added predicament that I shall not be able to straighten them." Miss Viggars gave a shy laugh.

"But for you Miss Porch," she said, "there must be great advantages." She paused. "For example," she said, "over there are Mrs Crisp and Miss Crisp, so clearly mother and daughter, endlessly together, their movements, their wishes, their voices matching, because of the years, exquisitely. And in this case they are the best of friends, not so usual in relationships of this kind, especially if the daughter feels that life or, in other words, a husband has passed, so to speak, her by. For you, Miss Porch," Mrs Viggars continued, "the opportunities for observation are numerous. The writer needs to be boiled up, as it were, with people."

Miss Porch, agreeing, struggled to an upright position.

"Oh excuse me! Pardon!" Mrs Viggars said. She turned towards the house. "I have," she said hurriedly, "an attack of the mulligrubs. I never could handle a cray!" As she made for the house she called back to Miss Porch: "Don't start the class without me. I'll only be five minutes."

"Oh there you are Miss Porch!" Miss Paisley hurried across the courtyard, "shall you mind awfully having the Pop Art Sculpting students in Drama? Vladimir Lefftov has left us!" Miss Paisley was breathless, her slack mouth happy with gossip. "He left last night," she continued, "he had his own car here, you know. Miles missed him with the bus. It was like this, he came up last night, Josephine and I were rehearsing, in her room, and there was this loud knocking on the door and he came straight in before Josephine had time to throw on her gown or her dressing-gown. Oh my! Miss Porch, that man's handsome when he's angry! After he'd gone I couldn't help saying to Miss Peycroft, 'Josephine, he is a good-looking man isn't he,' I must have said it several times as Josephine suddenly snapped at me to shut up about him. As you might have gathered she doesn't like men. I mean most men are awful aren't they. Male chauvinist pigs — I think they are anyway. I think Josephine's glad he's gone. Of course he won't get paid. He won't get a cent."

Miss Porch remembered various agreements and various sudden terminations in her own life. "Did he say where he was going?" she asked, moving her folders from one arm to the other.

"Oops a daisy! Mind your books!" Miss Paisley almost caught one folder as it slid to the floor. "Well, you know," she lowered her voice, "he complained about everything, but everything. Right from the food, which he said was disgusting, down to the Greek chorus behind the barn. Miss Peycroft had, you see, asked Miles to put the men's toilets there completely forgetting that she had another aspect of drama in mind for that place. And d'you know," Miss Paisley's round eyes gazed at Miss Porch, "d'you know, he said grey hairs and cardigans were an insult to his art and his teaching and then after stamping round glaring with those truly magnificent, beautiful flashing eyes, he said, he positively shouted, that in the miserable room provided for him there was nowhere for him to hang his things. I must say that stand-up collar with the metal studs is very handsome, don't you think, Miss Porch, that Russians are romantic? I mean I could have listened to his quaint English for hours. He went then and d'you know what? He clicked his heels and bowed from the waist, first to Josephine and then to me. I suppose he would have kissed our hands had we held them out in the way foreigners do. Such a lovely idea! I almost wished I had, just to feel his handsome lips, but there I'm a silly old thing, sentimental too I suppose. Miss Peycroft, Josephine, says it's post-menopausal. Everything gets explained that way, doesn't it. Ah! I see Mrs Viggars over there. She's probably coming over to the class. I mustn't hold things up — I must away as the Great Bard said . . ."

"Just a minute," Miss Porch said quickly, in her mind rehearsing on the spot her words of complaint about the shared room, that she could not tolerate another night with Mrs Castle — this apart from all the nonsense, yes it was nonsense, being made of her work with this stupid mime and the video which was so badly handled. The class was not as she had envisaged it — she wished to make a formal complaint. Knowing it was a mistake to say all this to Miss Paisley, Miss Porch continued to complain.

Miss Paisley blinked behind her round glasses. "We do have a policy and a precedent here at Trinity College about the bedrooms," she said in a flat voice as if reciting something prepared and learned. "It simply is not possible to make any changes at this late stage . . ."

"But I did have the room to myself," Miss Porch began, "and as a Tutor in the School I would have thought . . ."

"Miss Peycroft," Miss Paisley said, "never offers a post to a tutor, that is, she never re-appoints a tutor who makes complaints. You may have had some success with a book, as a writer, but that will not hold water with Miss Peycroft. With the best will in the world," Miss Paisley drew breath, "there is nothing we can do for you here at Trinity College. As for a tutor walking out because of some obstinate holding on to preconceived ideas, you just don't do that sort of thing in Schools of this sort." Miss Paisley puffed out her self-important chest. The sight of her and the stuffy smell which hung about her disgusted Miss Porch. She could imagine the garbled account of the conversation which would be reported to Miss Peycroft in the seclusion of the shared apartment upstairs. She turned abruptly to walk away from the self-created annoyance and almost bumped into Mrs Viggars.

"What was all that about, Porch old fellow. You look a bit white about the gills." Mrs Viggars, still drying her hands on a paper towel, did not wait for a reply. "I don't think there was anything wrong with the crays — though I suppose they could be 'not above suspicion', as the saying goes. I suspect really it's one of my old troubles. I should have stayed with the boiled fowl. But before we start the class, Porch old man, I feel a bit shy about this but I have written something and I would be very glad of your opinion. Here it is. I have written it out in two ways and I cannot, for the life of me, decide which is the better." She handed Miss Porch a sheet of paper. "I'll read it out," Mrs Viggars said, clearing her throat, "I have this other copy:

The Roses	*The*
On my wall	*Roses*
Have their mouths	*on*
Wide open	*my*
Wide.	*wall*
	have
	their
	mouths
	wide
	open
	wide

Mrs Viggars finished reading the page. She looked startled. "Roses! Oomph! Is it a poem d'you think?"

Miss Porch studied the page unable to make a comment. She was saved by the arrival of Christobel.

"Has Vladimir Lefftov beating his wife?" she asked. Her plump face was shining and pink, bursting with smiles. "And wait," she said, "Mrs Viggars and Miss Porch, have you seen Vladimir?"

They both said they had not seen him. Miss Porch remembered, with sadness, his bright, noisy little car. She might have been nearly home by now if she had only had the sense and persistence to steal it during the night.

"No?" Christobel tried not to laugh. "No! He . . ." she almost choked, tears filled her eyes," he lefftover the garden wall!" She shook with laughter. "There's a whole lot of Vladimir jokes going round," she said. "Listen! Why is the fridge so full of butter?" She gazed at Miss Porch and Mrs Viggars who said they had absolutely no idea. "Because," Christobel managed to gasp, "Vladimir Lefftov eating it! Also," she said, "I've had a super idea. I'm going to write to Mummy and ask her to post a fruit-cake and some hard-boiled eggs and . . ."

"There doesn't seem to be a posting-box anywhere here," Miss Porch said, "also there is the diet . . ." she began, but on seeing Christobel's face she stopped.

"Oh!" Christobel cried, "it's so awful being too fat. I hate it! I want to be thin like the others at school. But I get so hungry and I can't seem to lose any weight at all. Look at me! I'm squeezed into this huge overall thing — Mummy had to make it specially." She burst into tears. "I'm so ugly!" she wailed.

Miss Porch looked at Mrs Viggars in dismay.

"Dear child," Mrs Viggars said, "don't cry like that. We are supposed," she said, "to be doing our exercises, the knees full-bend. Help me to do the exercise. There there, don't cry.''

"Oh yes, of course, Mrs Viggars." Christobel dried her eyes.

"Just once I'll do it with your help," Mrs Viggars said.

"I'm awfully sorry for crying just now, Mrs Viggars, Miss Porch, please do excuse me."

"Knees Full-Bend!" Mrs Viggars made the announcement. Miss Porch pretended a part of the necessary movement. Her knees ached at the idea. "Here, child! Help me up!" Mrs Viggars said, "I should never have attempted something so extreme!"

Miss Porch, trying to stride, crossed to the other side of the courtyard blowing her whistle. The ache was not only in her knees, it was also in her heart. She looked back. Mrs Viggars and Christobel were collapsing in helpless laughter. Miss Porch felt better. She would soon have the dramatic reading and the mime started. She supposed that they all might be feeling guilty because of the midnight feasting. Better to get the class started at once.

"Oh Miss Porch!" Miss Harrow, in black tights, came out of the house. "Miss Porch, we have at last received the invitation,' she said, "it's here. It was pushed under my door just now. It's for this evening after the symposium. We are invited, just the two of us. You and I. Remember I told you we were going to be invited?"

"Oh really? How nice!" Miss Porch let her thoughts rush to the glowing comfortable midnight kitchen. She wondered what Miles would have scrawled on his piece of board. "Who has invited us?" she asked.

"Here," Miss Harrow said, suppressing a yawn,

"you may as well read it for yourself." She gave Miss Porch the invitation.

'Moozychatte *ma chère Maybelle*' — the note was written in violet ink — 'please to come *avec* your charming friend Miss Porsche please poossychatte to come to a nice little *déjeuner* we are preparing up-ladder for you both Xerxes and I yr. ever loving Anders. Après *le* drama *naturellement*.'

"Thank you," Miss Porch handed back the note.

"You will come won't you," Miss Harrow said, "it is sure to be fun!" Her handsome face did not show an expectation of fun, Miss Porch thought, rather she seemed a figure of tragedy, even more so than before.

"Thanks, I'd like to come with you," Miss Porch said, regretting her words as she said them.

"I missed the morning sports and the dip in the pond," Miss Harrow confessed, "but I'm looking forward to the drama, to the next instalment. As a prison officer I gather there is no part for me today, but I am happy to observe points for the symposium."

"Let me see," Miss Porch consulted her files, "Christobel will be the waitress in the restaurant at the motel. Steadman and Sandy, Mrs Viggars and Anna as usual, let me see . . ."

"*Tableaux Vivant* on video could, if properly done, be very forceful," Miss Harrow said. "Did I ever tell you," she said, "*pardon* if I change the subject, that I published a book? A sort of novel, autobiographical of course. I'm an actress and have had a remarkable career. I think I told you. Anyway the book was dismissed by reviewers who were very unkind about it and I have to bear the shame of this daily — especially as I have to pass a book exchange on my way to the shops, near my flat, you understand, where the book, my book, is tossed on to trays marked Rubbish Boxes.

Being remaindered and sold off at fifty cents is a particular sort of disgrace." She paused and Miss Porch, in spite of herself, gave a shudder which bordered on despair. It could so easily be her own book.

"Very humiliating," Miss Harrow said. "I hope," she added, "that it does not happen to you. However, no one at Trinity College knows about it or, if they do, I don't know that they know. But," she brightened, "there is this lovely exciting invitation to look forward to. Isn't it sweet of them to ask us. I was feeling utterly dejected and then this note came and transformed everything. I am so looking forward to it and it's sweet that they've invited you too." She squeezed Miss Porch's arm, unfortunately on a bruised part. Miss Porch did her best not to cry out with the pain.

"I shall watch," Miss Harrow said, "and take part energetically in the symposium later. Meanwhile — until this evening then!"

"Till this evening," Miss Porch replied trying to put some kind of excitement into her voice. "Don't go away," she added, "we shall possibly get to the prison scene, the flashback from the scene in the motel — back to the prison. You will be required . . ."

"I'll be here," Miss Harrow promised.

Miss Porch, blowing her whistle again, hurried on across the yard. She assembled the group quickly. The deserted Pop Art students, stranded, formed a rather sullen half-circle on the edge of the class.

"Miss Porch has conceived," Miss Peycroft's voice rang out in the stillness, "and is producing," she continued, "a drama which integrates conceptual performance, art, contemporary music and the theory of human communication through a series of statements created through the coordinated efforts of the participants. We are all being videotaped so put your best feet forward and don't hold your horses!

"The story so far," she said, "to put you all in the picture" — she smiled in a motherly way at the disgruntled Pop Art students who were doubtless missing Vladimir — "Dr Walter Steadman has undertaken to rehabilitate his daughter, Sandy, to bring her back he hopes to happiness and to health after a nightmare existence at the hands of heroin addicts. Steadman has paid for the release from a prison in Singapore of Sandy's boyfriend, the father, he thinks, of her baby boy. He has used his money and his influence to keep the boyfriend as far away as possible from Sandy. Money and influence have enabled him to take Sandy and the baby to his own house instead of her having to go back with her baby to the women's prison. The baby is only a few weeks old and is tainted by his mother's condition. He is irritable and not thriving. They are all three at present in a motel on the edge of a remote seaside township. And now read on!" Miss Peycroft's laugh cascaded. "Miss Porch," she said, "will narrate. I shall, with Miss Paisley here, present the music, double bass and tapping sticks respectively. The action will, as before, be in a series of little groups of mime. Divide yourselves! Newcomers," she smiled, showing her bottom teeth, "perhaps you would like to watch to start with and then attach yourselves. The dialogue, what there is of it, will be in the reading at this stage. Okay?

Miss Porch? Miss Paisley? Foxybaby Treatment. Take one . . ."

"When the ordered cereals and poached eggs are pushed through the serving hatch," Miss Porch obediently began to read, "Sandy tells her father that she is not hungry. Steadman feels the accusation in her empty expressionless stare. He wants to tell her that her complexion will improve if she will only leave the sores alone and eat properly.

> *"Just to please Daddy — there's my sweet Foxybaby . . .*
> *But I don't like it Daddy . . . Daddy I don't want to . . .*
> *Just try to please Daddy. Just to please Daddy. Try.*
> *But I don't want to Daddy No and No and No!*

"He remembers her little-girl voice.

"Sometimes, he thinks, there is a greedy look in her eyes. But not greedy for food. He is unable to define the look. He wishes that she would eat.

"His anger is only partly suppressed. He tells her if she would stop chewing gum she would eat. 'That incessant chewing,' he says, 'of that awful rubbish. Stop it! Can't you! The smell of it!'

"Her jaws, continuing their endless slack circular movement, pause at his words only for a moment. Immediately he suffers from remorse, wishing he could take back the words. He thinks of explanations and is unable to offer them.

" 'Any coke?' she asks, 'any coke?'

"He tells her, yes, in the refrigerator. He knows he is giving in. He feels irritated and tired. To feel so tired at the beginning of the day makes him feel afraid.

196

"His own breakfast, eaten without the accustomed pleasure of newspapers and the knowledge of the actions of a discreet and competent housekeeper, seems indigestable . . ." Miss Porch, without raising her eyes, was somehow aware of ludicrous movements as Miss Peycroft, with her double bass, tried to show the nearest group how to mime Steadman's indigestion and a flashback of longing for his housekeeper.

"He suggests a walk by the sea," Miss Porch read as quickly as she could to bypass this very difficult scene. "He wishes he had not eaten so heavily. He hopes the sea air will make Sandy eat.

"The girl sits at the fixed table and makes no reply." That one is easier, Miss Porch thought with relief. She paused and saw a row of fat Sandys sitting and not replying. The effect was satisfying. Miss Porch waited and then went on reading.

"Irresistably he is drawn to the jetty, the old long pier. At one time it had reached for a mile out to sea. The other one, the long curving one with railway lines is still as it has always been. He walks between the metal rails, stepping with care, lifting his feet high, lightly, between silent men, who, concentrating on their fishing lines, do not seem to notice him.

"He feels dizzy on the narrowness.

"He tries to recapture something of the wonder of walking out over the sea. He leans on the last remaining stump of railing, not trusting himself beyond it. He looks at the clear green sea. The water breathes lightly below him, moving imperceptibly in unknown depths. He has made a bad mistake in showing anger. Instead of seeing the sea he sees her unhappy white face.

"It was made clear to him at the prison and in other places of consultation that he was attempting something incredibly difficult. Something which required more than fatherly love and guilt and that there was no room for mistakes. *No man alive is free from error,* he remembers something consoling from Sophocles.

> *No man alive is free*
> *From error, but the wise and prudent man*
> *When he has fallen into evil courses*
> *Does not persist, but tries to find amendment*

"As he repeats the words to himself he moves his lips to form the words, a secret praying whispered across the quietly moving sea. He remembers copying the quotation into one of the books chosen for Sandy and left behind with other possessions, discarded ornaments, clothes, toys, pictures, many of them gifts and many of them symbols, he understands now, of a young girl's loneliness.

"It is not an error, he tells himself, to be in this remote place with his own daughter. He is only doing what he has always done. If she had a mother, mother and daughter would be on holiday quite naturally with the baby. Father and daughter. He knows there is a difference. If only there could be no difference.

"Of course she should be out by the sea with him. He can see in his mind a little picture of the three of them, he could carry the child, making a happy little family together. He hurries from the jetty stumbling in his eagerness to get back to her.

"There is a slight movement in the dark folds of the heavy curtain behind the thick glass of the motel window. Steadman thinks he sees her face, a narrow white half-moon, peering before the curtain drops back into the dust-filled folds.

"She is screaming. The baby is screaming. The table and the floor are littered with combs and curlers. The mirror is smashed and Sandy's hands are bleeding. Steadman snatches up the frantic child. The real tears on the baby's face check his anger. He holds the child close, feeling the quivering of the subsiding agitation as if it is in his own body. He tries to reach with his other hand, to draw Sandy to him, but she flings herself on the bed. He kicks aside a heap of torn-up clothing, remembering for a moment a little scene of real pleasure recently, during one of her better days, when they bought the dresses together.

"He tells her they must attend to the child. He shouts to her to be quiet and to help him.

"She shouts that she is going out and spells the word. He sees that her insolence makes her ugly. He shouts at her that she must wash herself and clear away the mess and that she must help with the child. He tries to prepare the child's bath and to fill the kettle. She screams that she is going out.

"Steadman, unable to control his anger, tells her she is ugly. 'You're ugly,' he says and immediately regrets his words. She stops screaming and stares at him. He tries to find ways to unsay what he has said. He agrees that she should go out. She tells him, 'I want the car.'

" 'My car? The Mercedes?'

" 'Well of course, what else is there?' her laugh is shrill and sinister. 'I'm going down town. I want the car.' The screaming, Steadman thinks, was better than the hard unhappy laugh.

"They stand regarding each other. The baby, placed on the bed, lies as if exhausted. As Steadman looks at the child and at his daughter he seems to see Sandy as a baby, pretty and smiling on the bed in place of the little grey infected one.

"Steadman slowly puts the keys on the table, releasing them unwillingly from the palm of his hand. He looks at her and hesitates. He remembers being told that she must feel that he trusts her completely. In a meeting with one of the prison psychiatrists he was told that in being with him she was trusting him. The vivid memory of this comes to him. He puts some money beside the keys telling her to buy some fruit while she is out.

"She grabs the money and the keys looking at him fiercely. He starts preparing at once to wash and feed the child.

"Looking at him quickly and defiantly she puts on green fluorescent eye shadow and a vivid red streak of lipstick. The next minute she is gone. Steadman takes off his jacket and, rolling up his sleeves, starts to unwrap the child.

"There was a time, Steadman remembers, after his daughter left for Europe so unexpectedly, when everything he did reminded him of her. The memories of her loneliness are the worst. He understands now that there is no greater sadness than this, to see his own child suffer.

"The foxybaby game started, he could not remember exactly, perhaps when she was very young. In the unused wardrobes, in among the silences of heavy fragrances, there were the softer scents of old leather and tarnished buckles, there were caressing cloths of light coats and dresses, the elegance of silks and sables left from an earlier time.

"Whenever he opened the doors of these cupboards it was like hearing again the husky-voiced conversations before he was required to light cigarettes for them both when, laughingly, his sexual achievements would be compared with former lovers, favourably.

"That this frail red-gold foxybaby girl should have

emerged from one of those wayward nights remained forever a mystery. Steadman's beautiful and ageing wife never knew her child and the only feelings the child could have for her unknown mother came from wardrobes which were never emptied.

"The little girl had his bluish-white skin, like diluted milk in a glass, and her eyes were light blue, perhaps perplexed like his own.

"Farther inside the wardrobe among the expensive and sweetly scented scarves and stoles, between the velvets and the woven things was the smoothly lined fox fur with its sharp-nosed alive head. The once powerful brush dangled helplessly as did the four pretty little feet and the tiny gold chain with its broken clasp.

"Between them, the lonely father and his tiny daughter, it was the foxybaby game.

Foxybaby Foxybaby where are you?
Here Foxybaby

" 'Foxybaby,' she called.

" 'Here,' he replied. She climbed into his bed early in the morning. She climbed astride him as if he could be ridden.

" 'Foxybaby!' raising his voice, falsetto, to make her laugh.

"Along his strong arm the light foxyfur ran and ran, alive, covering her wriggling childish laughter.

" 'Foxybaby. No!'

" 'Yes. Foxybaby.'

"And still she laughed. Tormenting. And when she cried, shrill, delight and terror, he comforted her and himself.

"Every time Steadman knew it must end. He told himself, 'It must end.'

Foxybaby. Foxybaby where are you? the voice at daybreak waking him. 'Foxybaby!' She asked him for a cigarette.

"He knew it was time and he stood fully dressed ready to leave the house before the sun had risen; before the appointed time.

Foxybaby is gone and will never come back

"Steadman remembers all the holidays spent together, all the loneliness written with a stick in the sand on remote beaches. He knows that the crooked messages in the sand, although addressed to some unknown and hoped-for friend, looked for in an unreal world, created by those celebrities and personalities who have made spectacular flights, overnight, to glamour and fame and wealth, were for Foxybaby every time.

"And every time the sea, washing up the beach sometimes curling in lazy ripples, sometimes slapping from the edges of a storm, washed away the hopeful words.

"Steadman, while completely absorbed in washing the baby, even delighting in the bad-tempered baby's temporary pleasure at being put in warm water, does not think of his daughter and her drive to the little town. Something about his occupation prevents him from worrying. He has been taking care not to knock the vulnerable little head on the taps. He has to concentrate on the order of events which are part of the child's bath and feeding.

"It is with surprise that he greets her on her return knowing at once from her shrivelled, white, unconsoled face what the answers to his questions will be.

"Outside someone is shovelling, sliding a spade back and forth on the brick path, without pause, scraping and sliding with great force. The abrasive sound matches the unharmonious return. The noise is as if someone busily, and with intention to destroy, is removing weeds and grass from the path. Momentarily there is a penetrating smell of disturbed earth and bruised grass.

"Steadman remembers the wardress, the prison officer, in the moonlit flower-bed. An apparition, a spectre, but only a dream he reminds himself. After all he did wake up in the bathroom after what must have been a bout of sleep-walking. He hopes that he is not ill.

"Sandy does not speak. She does not look at Steadman or the child. She stares at her own face in the broken mirror. To Steadman, the mirror distorts.

" 'It's shithouse down there,' she says. 'It's dead! Crap! A dead hole.' Her voice is calm. She moves stiffly as if made of badly jointed wood. She sits down and tries to push away the table.

"Steadman reminds her that, like the bench, the table is a fixture. He tries to console her. Still holding the baby he suggests the drive-in cinema — 'you used to like that.'

" 'Aw sure! Sure! Like hell! *Tarzan. Sound of Music. King Kong!*' she spits, '*The Return of King Kong*,' she spits again.

"He continues to try, he suggests that as soon as she is better they can move to other places. He wants her to walk and to swim, he tells her, and to eat well. He hurries his words in a soft voice as the baby is asleep. 'I brought you to this place,' he tells her, 'because we used to have happy times here together . . .'

" 'Like hell!' she bends forward, turning her face away. He notices that large tears, overflowing, are smudging her make-up. He gets up quickly and puts the baby down in the clean sheets of the cradle.

" 'Where the hell!' she shouts, 'all the goddam places are the same! They're all fucking shithouse!' She sobs.

"He sits beside her on the bench and puts an arm round her thin shoulders. The pain is the worst he has ever known. The action of comforting her comforts him. He promises her a nursemaid, new clothes and more new clothes, he tells her they will travel, 'to Paris, to Rome and to London.' He promises her a new life. He tells her she will get better but, at present, she is not fit to travel. 'Your ill health,' he tells her, 'makes you . . .' he pauses, 'makes you . . .'

" 'Go on!' she struggles away from him, hurting herself on the fixed table. 'I'm ugly!' she beats the table with her thin hands. 'You think I'm ugly and disgusting,' she cries, 'that's why you're hiding me here. I can't help these sores and things. It's not my fault! It's not my fault! Why has all this happened to me! These sores, they hurt!' She sinks down on the bench crying bitterly. Her thin arms with their bruised places are stretched out on the table as if they do not belong to her.

"Steadman pauses, hesitating. He bends down and raises her in his arms saying her name in a low voice. He carries her to her narrow bed and sits on the edge holding her across his lap. He rocks to and fro holding her and singing to her in a soft low voice:

> It's all right Foxybaby
> Everything's all right my Foxybaby

"Gradually she is quiet. She puts her arms round his neck and nestles against his chest. He bends his head so that his lips are in her hair and, still crooning, he rocks her to and fro.

"Steadman notices a small brown paper bag on the table. He is preparing some food for them. In the bag are three apples. She must, he realizes, have chosen them and paid for them. He tells her to wash her face; they must eat something. He tries to hide the shakiness in his voice. He peels and cuts up the apples and spreads biscuits with butter. A fragrant steam rises from the two cups of instant bouillon. He places a carton of chocolate milk on the table. Washed and neatly dressed she sits opposite him. Like a lover he feeds her with his spoon. Laughing, she tries to eat the apple pieces and the biscuits. Suddenly she pushes the food away. 'Isn't there any coke,' she wants to know. 'Isn't there any coke' — her voice rises.

" 'Oh God! Yes of course there is, if you must have it.' "

"In the afternoon, misery, trapping them in the dark rooms of the motel, forces them out of doors. With Steadman carrying the child they walk towards the beach. The track is long, the soft grey sand is tiring to walk on. Because of the flies neither of them speaks. Steadman has a headache. He finds the baby heavy to carry. The flies cling and crawl. Steadman thinks the flies will drive him mad as he tries to keep them off the child's face.

"He walks behind. His daughter's thin stern back

makes him think of one of the visits to the prison. It is vivid in his mind, the unlocking and locking of the doors, the hollow-sounding footsteps as the officer strode ahead. The girls were going to the kitchens to make pickles, the handsome wardress said. He had to wait. He tried to look at their faces but they all kept their eyes averted. Mostly they looked at the ground, not as if they were searching for something but simply as if to avoid the eyes of other people. As the girls passed he was unable to recognize his daughter though he guessed she was among them.

"He reflects, as he walks, that the prison officers were either calm, well-bred and aloof or large and homely and easily flustered. He remembers the moon-silvered wires and the dark shapes of two unknown women consoling each other quickly during a few snatched minutes of privacy. One of them had spoken about a little bitch, was it? A vixen? Their obscure grief was no less, he supposed then, than his own.

"He follows his daughter as she plods ahead of him.

"The long evening, settling along the coast, shrouds the motel. Steadman reminds his daughter cheerfully about her pills. He finds consolation in looking forward to the peaceful time when both mother and child, suitably sedated, will be asleep and he will be able to read and write in peace. With a growing confidence after the walk, during which there was only one outburst of anger, he tells her he has ordered dinner in the restaurant. He has booked a table for two, 'nicely secluded,' he adds, seeing a look of fear cross her face. She frowns angrily and shakes her head. He tells her the baby will be quite safe asleep in the motel room.

" 'What restaurant?' she interrupts.

" 'Here in the motel, just across the path and the flower-bed.' It is time, he tells her, that they had a properly cooked meal. Probably it will be fish of some sort.

" 'I don't want to go in there,' her voice, strained, rises sharply.

"He tells her it will be quiet and clean and comfortable and that she must get dressed at once. His voice is loud to hide any indecision. He continues to dress himself and sees, with satisfaction, that she is pulling one dress from the cupboard and not all of them. He moves smoothly across to her and puts an arm round her shoulders telling her that he was hoping she would wear that particular dress. 'The blue is lovely,' he says.

"She twists from under his arm. 'Big Deal! Any band? Any Group?'

" 'Good heavens! Silly of me! I never thought of asking!'

" 'That waitress,' she says, 'that waitress, that's the one that doesn't like me.' She moves the shining cutlery about on the polished table. 'She hates me. She'll never bring anything I ask for, you'll see.' Her little white face twitches and jerks as she, like a frightened animal let out of its cage by mistake, looks round at the other empty tables.

"Steadman tells her that she has never seen the waitress before, that her being uneasy is all nonsense. He offers her fruit juice and tells her to choose which soup.

" 'I know, I just know she hates me. I know what

she's thinking, how she's thinking, she's . . .' Sandy gets up from the table and walks with nervous little steps, dropping her shredded paper napkin all the way to the curtained door and out of the restaurant. The bits of torn-up paper look like badly made, misshapen confetti.

"Steadman, who has the key, thinks he should go after her. The waitress on unthreatening flat feet brings a menu encased in thick clear plastic.

" 'I expect my daughter will return in a few moments.' Steadman smiles up at the good-natured face which is too simple to match the elaborate foods described in the ornamental curves and flourishes of someone's best handwriting.

"He orders the soup, a lobster bisque. Breaking some bread into small pieces he settles back in his chair determined to wait for Sandy's return. Determined that he will not go out after her. He even calls the waitress back and, with another handsome smile, suggests that a dash of sherry be added to the soup.

"Sandy does not return. Steadman, drinking a whole carafe of an unnamed and slightly sour white wine, eats more than he wants. The food is greasy and the service depressingly slow. No other guests have committed themselves to the restaurant. Looking at the sham opulence Steadman is not sure whether it is better to be there alone or with people whose happiness or tranquillity might make his own indecision worse. The thought that she is somewhere by herself and unhappy is entirely intolerable. This thought, becoming an irrational fear, makes every mouthful harder to swallow.

"Always he avoids images which persist. Sandy alone and frightened and unhappy and Sandy intimate with some other person, yet not, in his mind, as a grown woman. It is as if the sexual encounter or encounters she must have had are only games played in the sand or on some innocent grassy bank. That is all. In his thoughts he sees her simply as a child, always, laughing and tumbling in an everlastingly pleasant place. He refuses to see her as being spoiled or bruised or infected. It is as if another person cannot exist in any relationship with her. Not even the father of her child. He even refuses to acknowledge any re-enactment of the foxybaby game. He refuses to admit his own desire.

"Sternly sitting with an eggshell of tasteless coffee he resolves to find her. He will wait for her endlessly.

"He will walk the whole curve of the wide bay with her even if it is shallow and dull and no longer beautiful, spoiled by other people. He dislikes the tents and the caravans, squalid human arrangements, partly hidden in the scrub, along the beach, at the edge of the sand.

"He knows the sky will be overcast with unbroken cloud and the sea, without brilliance, will be trimmed with dirty foam.

"He knows too that when he walks he will be unable to lift his mind from the immediate surroundings which reflect his cares.

"Like the waves meeting over the rocks his ideas could meet other ideas. Usually when he walks his thoughts, following the thoughts of scholars and writers, can bury him in a paragraph or a chapter which, during his walk, he can analyze and understand more clearly simply by going over it in his mind. This self-healing habit might, he hopes, be retrieved in time. Occasionally where the apparently lifeless sea meets the sky there is a line of light, a gleam of a hidden promise.

"He will carry the child in his arms, everywhere, so that she can walk easily. . . .

"Cut!" Miss Porch brought her reading to an abrupt halt. "Cut!" She frowned in the direction of Miss Paisley, who had not noticed that the reading had ended and was still, without any sustained rhythm, tapping her sticks.

The characters, in the various positions of the attempted mime, remained as if frozen in the *tableau vivant*.

Mrs Viggars, sitting at the table, stared across the courtyard as if she did not see the enormous coloured shapes of her fellow students. She seemed unable to move.

Gradually the students stretched themselves and began to disperse in the direction of the black tea.

"Come along, Dr Steadman!" Gently Christobel shook Mrs Viggars to rouse her.

"Oh this place!" Miss Harrow said to Miss Porch as they moved slowly together across the courtyard. "It's so hideous," she moaned lightly as if keeping something back for a dramatic shriek later on. "I know," she continued, "that Miss Peycroft says it's beautiful here. Beauty must be in the eye of the beholder, as they say. She actually said to me that she found that barren desolate paddock across the road, know where I mean? so beautiful that she wanted to pick it up and write on the back of it and send it, like a gigantic postcard, to someone who has never seen a wheat paddock. The woman's mad!" Miss Harrow seemed to tear her hair but, in fact, did not. Miss Porch noticed that it was freshly washed and combed and arranged.

"Do not forget," Miss Harrow hissed before Miss Porch could reply about the impact of what Miss Harrow felt to be ugliness, 'we are to go up to Anders and Xerxes this evening, a little later on." They entered the dark veranda place where the evening lettuce decorated the badly washed tables. "How d'you like my dress?" She turned herself round. "It's a kind of Spanish moo moo. I love it. Makes me feel so free! I've got some lovely perfume too, at least it was absolutely ravishing but it's gone off. D'you know anything about the habits of perfume?"

Miss Porch shook her head, saying she did not.

"Well, sniff this." Miss Harrow pulled up her thin loose sleeve and presented a plump white arm. The arm invaded that private place, the space immediately below the nose. "Don't you think it's just like an anaesthetic? Like ether? well, perhaps ether mixed with pine disinfectant. It's revolting! My body acids," she said as if making an announcement, "are all disturbed and this has affected my perfume. Perfume sometimes does this, you know, mixes with a person's body acids and the result is awful. There's only one thing to do and that is to change perfumes. But this is all I have here in this Godforsaken-Place. Not a shop! Not even a shop in the house, a sort of sophisticated school shop."

Miss Porch thought for a moment of a Trinity College tuckshop, quite small, stacked with cans of coca cola, cream matchsticks and vanilla slices. Immediately behind a mountain of jam-filled doughnuts an anxious mother would be trying to impose the vitamins and roughage of an Oslo lunch on the fallen standards of a customer about to buy a Mars bar and a packet of salt-and-vinegar potato crisps. Perhaps the shop, her thoughts began an immense flowering, perhaps the shop could occupy a part of the entrance hall to the right of the once noble staircase . . . It was hard to know, at this stage, whose mother . . . there would have to be a roster . . . perhaps Miss Paisley could . . . Also there would have to be, though unknown in ordinary tuckshops, a small part of the counter given over to cosmetics and perfume. . . .

"Not a damned shop!" Miss Harrow was saying.

"What about Miles?" Miss Porch, meaning to make a funny remark, said. She wished at once she had not said it. Miss Harrow's puffy eyes filled with tears.

"Don't!" her moan was heavier, "you see perfume's so necessary at my, at our age," she included Miss Porch. "To get a young man started we need something exquisite, very heady, provocative and sweet. In Paris once, *ma chère*, I had the most wonderful time all because of a wicked but perfect perfume. Oh! wicked! wicked!" she sighed, tears overflowing.

"But I thought we were going for a meal," Miss Porch began as they made their way with the others towards a tray overhung with limp greenery.

"Oh, but you are so delightfully innocent!" Miss Harrow whispered. "You are still a virgin, yes?" She gave Miss Porch's arm a squeeze. "Oh, but my dear! How I envy you this evening. A first time! Of course a woman has many 'first times' but tonight you will discover truly for the first time the delights of youthful passion. You see, my dear, though it is over quickly with an ardent young man who cannot wait, he is, afterwards, so sweetly penitent. He weeps immediately, here on the breast. One consoles him, stroking the bowed head, quieting the pounding heart and embracing him gently at first with subtle movements and then *mon Dieu*! what a tower he becomes, an edifice! So! He is yours! And not just once, my friend, but several times. You will see!"

Miss Porch placed a little bundle of leaves in her mouth. She looked across at Miss Harrow and tried to chew calmly.

"Ah! My friend, do not look so worried," Miss Harrow said. "It is fortunate to be a virgin though there are difficulties perhaps when one is no longer young. But, *ma chère*, think of the Mona Lisa! There is absolutely no need to be afraid or ashamed. Look at the Mona Lisa! She was not a young woman, and that satisfied smirk on her face is, you see, obviously the 'Helen of Troy' smile of the morning after. Be lighthearted," Miss Harrow said, "there is much pleasure in anticipation. Look forward to our evening. Maybe," she seemed struck by a thought, "maybe we shall change partners. Oh! that will be fun!" She began tearing her lettuce, looking round at the other people as she did so. "Did you ever," she continued in a low voice, "*ever* see so many stout, middle-aged, middle-class women in your life before! Did you ever!" her voice became an excited whisper. "Their lives are absolutely predictable," she said, "I can't help imagining them in over-furnished bedrooms, rattling about on their hands and knees, frightful grizzly hair all over the place, searching for reading glasses belonging to husbands silenced forever by an incredible boredom." She paused. "I'm an actress," she said, "an actress whose ambition and exceptional talent hoped for Phèdre — yes I'll admit this to you, I long to play

Phèdre, but, as you see, I find myself in an everlastingly embarrassing play which has the ultimate degradation of being episodic. I am," she added, "cut out for the climactic." Miss Harrow chewed some lettuce and, with difficulty, swallowed it. "I am also," she continued, "as you yourself are, an observer of life. I am a listener too," she added, leaning towards Miss Porch who, because she had a very tough stalk, was crunching noisily and so was unable to hear properly.

"You are very fortunate," Miss Harrow said, "you are lucky to be able to chew this stuff, this tough roughage. You obviously have all your own teeth." Miss Porch was surprised at this very personal remark. "I," Miss Harrow said, "have my teeth but they have been sewn back into my gums."

Miss Porch, taken by surprise even more, made suitable noises of sympathy. "I do hope they're not painful," she said, feeling that her remark lacked originality.

"I was Privates at the General." Mrs Finch brought a replacement tray of lettuce to the table. She put it down with the same pride which would have accompanied an offering of freshly baked scones. "Ooo!" she said, "it was beautiful. I'm Radio Active see, so I was kep' private. Little tea-pot, tray clorth, double knives — the lot and curtings ever so nice and private little butter-dish little toast-rack little pats of butter ever so purty . . ."

"Don't!" Miss Harrow moaned, increasing the volume of the previous moan till it became a groan, "do not speak of butter now!" She was able, Miss Porch could see, because of looking forward to the meal being prepared by Anders and Xerxes, to enjoy complaining about hunger and could give way to mouth-watering images. "Toast," Miss Harrow said, "toast dripping with butter and golden honey."

"And are you still radioactive now?" Miss Porch felt she should ask. She hoped, while speaking to Mrs Finch, to escape the frightening thoughts about the later part of the evening. She wanted to hide somewhere. Perhaps Mrs Finch had a pantry, a place where glasses were washed in wooden sinks and where silver could be polished on peaceful afternoons. Perhaps Mrs Finch was in the habit of asking students and tutors to drop by for a chat. If there was such a place Miss Harrow need not know, at once, where it was.

"Lord Hisself knows and He won't split." Mrs Finch leaned over the table to rescue, between capable thumb and finger, a straying leaf. "Mr Finch," she said "sez I give orf electrickitty, sez he can feel it . . ."

"Ah! My trusty village maiden there you are!" Miss Peycroft's voice broke into the radioactive condition of Mrs Finch. "My serving wench of long standing," she said.

"Too right," Mrs Finch muttered, "I've stood it too long!"

"Mrs Finch" — Miss Peycroft, Miss Porch noticed, was able to ignore anything she chose to including discontented mutterings — "Mrs Finch, can you find Miles for me? I think we did get something on video after all," she seemed excited, "even if only a little bit of the mime, it will make all the difference to the opening of the symposium." She smiled at the dutiful lettuce eaters.

Mrs Finch, at the hall door, drew breath. "Cooo — ee Miles! Miles cooo — eee! Miles you're wanted. Miles you stupid crab!" Her deafening shriek grew fainter. "You rotten old turnip, where the hell are you!"

215

The moon above
My thoughts on love
Lover come back to me

Mrs Viggars, in a purring voice, sang her love song. "Ah! Rennett. There you are!" she said. 'I have been looking for you to bring you in to lettuce, but I see you are in the trough already! And, good evening, Miss Peycroft, I hope I am not late for the symposium."

"No of course not, Mrs Viggars, we would never start without you." Miss Peycroft was gracious. "Perhaps you would like to lead the discussion while we wait for Miles and the video."

"Well, yes, thank you," Mrs Viggars said. She turned to Miss Porch. "First I must tell you," she said, "that I am deeply moved."

"Thank you," Miss Porch said.

"I am reminded," Mrs Viggars went on, "of the Tissot, 'The Widower', perhaps you know it? Jacques Joseph, I think it was, Tissot. What we have heard in the reading is shown in this painting. Dependence, need, sorrow, protection and possession; the father forced to accept the great hurt — the death of his wife and then to be aware of the ultimate loss of his daughter. In the painting he is shown holding the child, no longer a little child, she has long silk-stockinged legs mysterious and unchildish. His hands hold her firmly, she has flounces of petticoats which could still be the frilled clothing of the little girl but also they belong to the young woman. The whole mixture of child and woman is covered by a babyish pinafore. The little round head of the child rests against the father but her solemn and wayward face is turned from him looking upwards. One plump arm reaches up to pluck blossoms? fruits? from life?" Mrs Viggars paused. "That is all," she said.

"Thank you, Mrs Viggars." Miss Peycroft bestowed one of her more generous smiles. "Any comments?" she asked.

"May I, with reference to the housekeeper," Miss Harrow said, "in recent scenes there has been mention of a housekeeper, may I ask, should we have had some knowledge of her offered earlier?"

"Yes," Mrs Crisp said, "one simply cannot be too careful about servants, especially in the choice of a housekeeper. It is so very personal a service. It leaves the way entirely open to immorality. I have known an innocent family employ a housekeeper only to find the husband hidden away in her bedroom at weekends. Dr Steadman may well have a problem of this sort." She paused. "And in South Africa, dear," she said, "they are black you know . . . they are very sweet when little babies . . ."

"Mother!" Miss Crisp said in a loud whisper, "do remember . . ."

"Dr Steadman might be very lonely all on his own." Mrs Castle tried to use her kindest voice. She gave a knowing smile, passing it round the group. "He might need company and they do say, don't they, that a house only becomes a home when there's a woman in it."

"Naturally he will need relationships," Miss Crisp interrupted in her sensible voice, "I would have thought he would have acknowledged this need and made suitable arrangements to satisfy it."

"Well," Mrs Viggars said, "is not that just what the Foxybaby game was and," Mrs Viggars paused, she looked at Miss Porch, "and is?" she said.

"Perhaps we should all bring our underwear, so to speak, into the open." Miss Peycroft spoke bravely into the silence which followed Mrs Viggars' remark.

"Perhaps," she said, "we should take an honest, a complete look in the direction of our own sexuality, at sexual freedom and at the directions our own sexual requirements are taking. Though there is nothing in the text to suggest a liaison between Steadman and his housekeeper." She raised an eyebrow in the direction of Miss Porch who pretended to be searching for Steadman's sexual needs in her folder. Miss Porch shook her head at Miss Peycroft and pretended to make a note in her file.

"I would like to ask," Miss Crisp's gymnasium voice rang out as if echoing and rebounding from oiled floorboards and golden beams, parallel bars and ribstalls, "I would like to ask if it would be possible for Mr Miles to shoot the crows and the galahs. Mother and I," she said, "simply cannot sleep. And perhaps he could knock orf a few of those pigeons while he's about it. It literally is impossible to get any rest. All that pouting and preening along the gutters just outside our window . . ."

"Make a note, please, will you, Miss Paisley." Miss Peycroft waved her long fingers in the direction of Miss Paisley. "Just a note about the birds, Paze old girl. Next? Next comment? Any comments? Come along. Surely there must be something to say about Dr Steadman and the girl in the motel scenes? Or in the restaurant? Surely you have some questions? Nothing at present? Well, let's have some suggestions for the dialogue. I think Miss Porch will want a repeat performance with dialogue. Let's have some suggestions now in colloquial speech, some contemporary idiomatic phrases. I'll remind you that contemporary idiom has a wide span and people of different ages have different colloquialisms. Let's start off with the language of the street and the Drug Scene." She made little inverted commas with hooked fingers held up on either side of her head. "I'd like to share the language with you." Miss Peycroft signalled to Mrs Finch to remove the remains of the lettuce. "I'll lead off," she said, "with Fuck Fit and Junkie, has anyone anything to add?" No one said anything. All faces were turned solemnly towards Miss Peycroft and Miss Porch.

"Come along!" Miss Peycroft encouraged, "come along!" she began walking backwards and clapping her hands as if inviting her kindergarten to march with Schubert or Grieg. Miss Porch stood with a forced smile causing her dry lips to stay hooked, as it were, on her teeth. She tried to somehow undo the smile.

"Come along!" Miss Peycroft said again. She looked round the anxious faces. "What about Junkie? Oh, I've said that one already. Well, perhaps you'll correct me if I'm wrong, Miss Porch, there's gig — snort and smack." She paused. "Surely," she said to the group, "you are aware of the language? What about shit? Shit, anyone? Surely you must know some of the words!" She raised her eyebrows.

"Hm, well," Mrs Viggars said, her chins quivering, "the only word which comes to my mind is a word, a strange word. Viggars used it occasionally, but only on occasions, you understand. He never said this word in the bedroom." She paused. "Actually," she said, "I don't think I can remember him ever using this word in the house."

"Oh, do tell us the word," Christobel cried. "Mrs Viggars, do please be a sport, tell us the word."

An excitement seemed to stir and ripple through the tired drama students. Miss Porch wondered, even though she was longing for tea, what the word could be.

"Strange that this word should come into my mind,"

Mrs Viggars said as if pondering and reminiscing. "The word in question," she said, "is snaggers. Snaggers, is that of any use?" she asked Miss Peycroft. "I believe," she said, "it has two g's in the middle. But someone, perhaps Miss Crisp? might like to verify that."

"Thank you, Mrs Viggars," Miss Peycroft said graciously, "actually I think snaggers belong somewhere else. It is a specific word. It is certainly contemporary idiom but it has a more, how shall I put it, a more ordinary place in our society." Miss Peycroft smiled, "Ordinary," she said, "but valuable."

"Well yes," Mrs Viggars said, "the barbecue, now I come to think of it." As she spoke her mouth watered. "Viggars," she said, "used to enjoy a barbecue. He always did the cooking. Delicious! He seemed to know just when the dripping fat would revive the fire."

Excited buzzing conversations broke out in various parts of the group as the choice of thick or thin, curried or plain, beef or pork sausages came under discussion.

"Of course if preservatives are added . . ." Mrs Castle seemed to shine with experience.

"Mine always burst over the years," Mrs Crisp confessed.

"Come along!" Miss Peycroft interrupted the animated descriptions, "come along," she cried, "we must get back to Steadman and the restaurant scene. Mr Miles has the video ready. Lights out. Please, Christobel, if you would just switch off, thanks."

The scene in the film was, unexpectedly, the lawn and the grassy edges of the Trinity pond and not the improvized imagined motel room or the track to the beach. Suddenly someone or something bounded across the squelching grass and flew into the pond in an awkward mixture of a dive and a jump.

220

The audience gasped and someone screamed. Miss Porch thought it was Miss Harrow's moan finally reaching the scream. There was a second scream.

"Who is it?" Christobel called out. "Whoever it is has got nothing on. She's quite undressed, did you see, she's nude! Did you see, everyone? She's nude."

"Hallo noodle!" the voice was unmistakeably old Mrs Crisp's. She began to cackle uncontrollably. "Noody. Nuddy. Nuddle."

"Mother!" Miss Crisp was indignant. "Mother!"

"Oh look!" Christobel cried, "it's coming out of the water. Look! Look! It's Miss Harrow with no clothes on. It is Miss Harrow, isn't it? All undressed. All covered in mud. Coming out of the pond. Miss Peycroft! Miss Peycroft, it is Miss Harrow isn't it? What is she doing Miss Peycroft? What's Miss Harrow doing?"

"Good heavens!" Miss Crisp said, "come along, Mother. Come along at once. We'll go up to our room. Mother! Do come along!"

The audience made way reluctantly as Miss Crisp edged by, pushing and pulling old Mrs Crisp to the door.

"Just when I was enjoying myself for once," the old lady complained. "Nancy! it's too bad, just when I'm having a bit of fun. Oh Nancy!" she began to laugh, "Nancy, I am reminded of Aunt Madge at your wedding, you remember your wedding Nancy and Aunt Madge . . ."

"Mother! Nancy died years ago," Miss Crisp hissed. "I'm Yvonne, remember? I'm Yvonne and I'm not married." But Mrs Crisp was cackling again, "Aunt Madge!"

"It must be Miss Harrow," Christobel persisted,

"and that's why she screamed just now. What is she doing? Christobel asked. "It's some kind of dance isn't it? Miss Harrow? The Flashdance, is it? Look, it must be a dance the way she's twisting her legs and holding her bosoms like that. I never ever saw a dance like it before. What's the dance called Miss Harrow? Ooo!" Christobel giggled, "the way she's jiggling around. I can't help laughing. It's weird! Really weird!"

"I feel rather faint," Mrs Castle said, "I think I really am going to faint."

"Oh don't faint now, you'll miss the show," Christobel said, "Oh look!" she gasped, "whatever is she doing with her hands?"

"Miles!" Miss Peycroft called across the darkness. "Miles! stop the video. Turn off that thing at once! Stop the film Miles, at once!"

"Aw Gawd," there was another scream. Not Miss Harrow this time. "Aw Gawd! Just get a gander willya." Mrs Finch's screams blended with throaty appreciation expressed by Miles;

"Keep still, Finchy! My Birdie! My Beauty! Aw Beaudy! Hey watch it Finchy! Just you watch it!"

"Surely the French have a name for this." Miss Crisp had reached the door and was bundling Mrs Crisp into the passage.

"How perfectly frightful!" Miss Harrow grasped Miss Porch on her painful arm. "It must be," she said in an angry whisper, "it must be a blue movie; those terrible creatures have made it. I didn't know," she said, "that they were filming me. Come on, let's go. Quick! before the lights come on." She helped Miss Porch to gather her folders and together they squeezed through the enchanted audience and found the way to the side door and out into the passage.

"Miles! turn off that thing!" they could hear Miss Peycroft's voice calling, "Miles! turn off that thing!"

"How humiliating!" Miss Harrow said. "I am used to all sorts of undignified situations," she added, "but this one is worse than any. It is only the thought of the evening which makes it bearable. I shall simply look forward to the evening upstairs with Anders and Xerxes. All the same this has been humiliating. It is always like this for me, Alma, I am forever being humiliated, I will tell you some time, my experiences with . . ." Miss Harrow was hurrying ahead of Miss Porch and her words were lost.

Miss Porch thought about Miss Harrow's book described so cruelly by the critics. She wondered why critics were so cruel. Many of them, she noticed, were one-time teachers now called freelance writers. She realized that she herself almost belonged in this category. She was never sure of her position at The Towers. One could never be too careful she told herself. One was always at the mercy of someone else. No position could be more precarious than her own. Suddenly she too could be 'freelance'.

"I haven't read your book," Miss Porch caught up with Miss Harrow, "but I'd like to very much," she lied.

"Oh you are a dear!" Miss Harrow said, "but then you are a writer and writers are a bit like actresses, though of course writers are quite unable to act, to perform or shall I say, put on an act. I am both actress and writer," she announced.

"Yes," Miss Porch said in a low voice. Really the woman was impossible. She wondered where Mrs Finch had her secret pantry. A hiding-place was needed badly. She welcomed the thought of a corner somewhere just off the kitchen. The prospect of Miss Harrow's evening did not appeal to her. She walked with little steps.

"Oh come on!" Miss Harrow called, "you look as if you're trying to hold your knickers up with your elbows and your knees." She waited for Miss Porch.

Slowly Miss Porch followed Miss Harrow up the stairs. The appalling evening was ahead. Miss Porch was frightened.

"Come to my room for a bit," Miss Harrow turned back to whisper. "We have an hour to kill. It is bad manners to be early and Anders, who knows my ways, will expect us to be a little late."

In spite of herself Miss Porch accepted Miss Harrow's invitation. As she followed Miss Harrow she wondered at herself and why it was she seemed unable to resist people. So often she found herself either doing the most extraordinary things or yawning through long evenings because she had no reason to put forward as an excuse for not being there. An invalid mother would have been so useful; she often wished for one; not in too much pain of course, but someone who was demanding and tiresome so that people could be full of pity and understanding.

"Oh yes, Alma dear, we do fully understand, so sorry you can't be with us — I've brought a little something, a remnant from the feast for you and Mother — it's just a little bit of apple-pie, homemade. Careful! that's the cream in that little plastic jar, it's whipped with a pinch of sugar and a dash of rum, the teeniest dash. All right for Mother? The rum? Oh good! And the others sent you this — a delightful Rosé, a *Spätelese* — you'll love it — must dash Alma darling — must get out of my pinny before they start arriving . . ."

Miss Porch, not having any sort of mother and no

other excuses, not even a disagreeable and forbidding cat, had no imagination for reasons. Such rescue always came to her too late.

"Quite frankly," Miss Harrow said, wading into her room, "this place simply is not big enough. I ask you," she tossed an armful of clothing into a corner which already had its heap, "I ask you," she said, "these rooms are like prison cells, aren't they. Thank goodness that widow, that Daffodil, an awful woman . . ."

"Jonquil," Miss Porch corrected with that primness which is associated with acute boredom.

"Oh yes, a flower, a bulb, I wasn't far out, I knew it was something like that. I think of her as a container of polyunsaturated." Miss Harrow laughed. "She's utterly impossible! I was pleased when she left this room. I do, however, feel the teeniest bit guilt-ridden." She narrowed her grey eyes." She hasn't told you anything?" she asked.

"Not a thing," Miss Porch said.

"Thank heavens!" Miss Harrow moved to the window. "Ever since I arrived I've been meaning to leave," she said, "but it's not possible is it. No car, no transport — that disgusting man, Miles, has the bus stripped down, as he calls it, the wheels are off and it's on wooden blocks. Vladimir," she pronounced the name with a suitable foreign accent, "Vladimir was fortunate to get away. I had my eyes on his car I can tell you — but I am so hampered by those two young men. They are insufferable, d'you know, I drove all the way here, well as far as the accident, with those two holding hands and worse in the back seat. All the same, you see, I do feel thoroughly responsible for them. Also," she dropped her voice, "I can't bear the thought of leaving Anders, I simply can't do it however awful he is

225

sometimes; you see," she laughed, "you my dear friend, Miss Porch, Alma, you will have to take on Xerxes tonight. You will have to have Xerxes."

"I?" Miss Porch stepped back, "but I thought we were going to a meal . . . Really I must go . . . I have some work . . . some urgent writing I must . . ."

"A Feast my dear," Miss Harrow interrupted her. "Oh!" she cried, "just look out there." She drew Miss Porch to the window, saying again, "just look out there!"

Unwillingly Miss Porch moved forward and stood beside Miss Harrow. "Aren't they just beautiful!" Miss Harrow pointed across the courtyard to the old garden at the side of the orchard. Anders and Xerxes were wrestling on the grassy slope below a solid wall of agapanthus. In spite of her feelings of uneasiness, Miss Porch had to admit that the two young bodies, one fair and the other dark, were graceful and slender and, at the same time, powerful and vigorous. The two young men pretended to punch each other, prancing and sparring like boxers, ducking first to one side and then to the other, shielding themselves with one arm raised in turn, and then bending over, they seemed to break in half, bending doubled over in laughter. The golden head shone and the dark one gleamed. Suddenly both bodies disappeared as if in a wild entangling ecstasy into the green fleshiness of the agapanthus. The long frail stems rising from the thick green leaves quivered and swayed violently. The light blue flowered heads, as if shocked, dipped in frenzy and then, seriously vulnerable and exposed, regained their tremulous balance.

"Oh, think of the cockroaches!" Miss Harrow said in a voice which showed that tears were not unthought of. "When I was a child," she choked, "the cockroaches lived in the dusty clumps of agapanthus. Terribly suburban!" she said, "I can't think why people grow them."

Miss Porch was thinking that the broken leaves and stems might contain harmful sap. She remembered, from her childhood, that some flowers if picked and held in bunches were said to cause dreadfully persistent skin eruptions. She felt it would be useful if she could remember a suitable treatment. A cold compress came into her mind, perhaps a compress of cold tea. She was about to offer the idea when Miss Harrow laughed.

"What a messy bed for passion," she said, "well — for a messy passion, you know, young men are extremely messy, you can have no idea! Furthermore they seem absolutely not to notice their own messiness. D'you know I've been meaning . . ." she stopped. "Oh!" she cried out as if in pain, "this is too much! They're still down there. It's so — so unsuitable!" She made an effort to laugh again and sat down on the only chair by the window. She glanced down at her own legs, taking care, as always, to sit in such a way that they were displayed to advantage. Miss Porch noticed that she let her skirts slip to one side with the kind of nonchalance which accompanies confidence in one's own legs.

"Do sit down," Miss Harrow said, "I'll be better directly. It's just that I've had too much to put up with lately. And now that" — she nodded towards the trembling agapanthus. "That's right, sit on the bed if you can find a flat space, we might as well be comfy." She smiled with a kind of handsome bitterness. "You know," she continued, "if my unhappiness could only be written down it would be described in terms of catharsis. I wrote a villanelle once, you know, nineteen lines on two rhymes. Sometimes the formal approach appeals to me, it somehow takes the grief and accepts it and makes it into something beautiful." She gazed at Miss Porch; her eyes, in spite of being filled with tears had a shrewd expression. "Tell me, Miss Porch," she said suddenly, "why do you put yourself in this ridiculous, forgive me, ridiculous is right, position? I mean, why have you come to this place? And why have you put an unpublished manuscript at the disposal of a group of people who, quite frankly, are really only interested in getting away from here able to pass the pinch test. All that rubbish today about contemporary idiom. How can those people offer you dialogue for your characters? There's no such thing, no such single thing as contemporary idiom. Speech spans a man's life and he speaks in his own phrases. If you listened to speech as I do you will hear how people speak — not just in one place or in one layer of society but in several."

"I . . ." Miss Porch tried to speak but Miss Harrow continued: "Tell me honestly," she said, "d'you really think this school and the so-called drama course you're giving is a good thing for those fatties? How many of them, for example, have actually asked you how your story ends? Don't you think the whole thing's ridiculous and that Miss Peycroft is — well, too awful to be true? I spotted her for what she is as soon as we arrived."

Miss Porch tried to stand up. She felt the pulses beat in her neck and her temples. Anger and a kind of weakness made her tremble. She knew that she could recognize truth when she heard it. She remembered her own needs, her intention to earn money, her hope for further employment. She supposed Miss Harrow must know that people had to earn a living. Having her own doubts about the success or the value of what she was trying to do made it more difficult to offer some kind of defence. Defence, in her nature, rose to her aid, as a rule, too late. She thought of Mrs Viggars. The large friendly shape of Mrs Viggars offered support.

"Of course I think the School's a good idea," she said, "if I didn't I shouldn't have come, I shouldn't have agreed to come . . ." She sat down suddenly, her legs shook. "Mrs Viggars, she . . ." her voice shook.

"Oh my dear," Miss Harrow said, "please do forgive me. I'm sorry. I shouldn't have attacked you like this. I am not really myself. I'm very jaded at present. It's that lemon juice and that awful lettuce, it doesn't suit me, it gets me down. Let's change the subject. Tell me," she said with a pleasant smile, "who is your publisher?" She crossed and uncrossed her legs. "I copied out some lines written by John Dryden to his publisher. He must have felt as mad with him as I do with mine. I feel I can use Dryden's insult, as a quote of course, when I write my next letter. I write to him every week. Naturally he never answers." She pulled a piece of notepaper from her handbag. "Here it is," she said, "I'll read it to you:

with leering looks, bull faced, and freckled fair,
with two left legs, and Judas coloured hair
and frowzy pores that taint the ambient air . . .

"Oh, what's the use!" Miss Harrow pushed the page back into her bag. "It's too awful!" she cried, "all that awful physical culture, the diet — I hate diets, especially this one, and I hate doing exercises in public — there's that terrible terrible video — I was only massaging myself, a little body massage that was all . . . Your story interests me, but the students are so stupid and there's something crafty, wily, really *vulpine* about that — that girl Anna, Anne or whatever her name is. The one who is playing Steadman's daughter, the addict, she certainly fits the part you've given her — but she can't act!" Miss

Harrow seemed to spit out the words. "That girl," she said, "is out for all she can get. Oh!" She took Miss Porch's hand, "Oh, I am sorry, there I go again," she tried to force a smile, "it's my temperament, the *prima donna* in me and," she paused, "and it's those two out there." She indicated the now fast darkening ridge of agapanthus. Evening was settling over the house and the courtyard and over the orchard and gardens. "Neither of them," she said, "neither of those two young men will be fit for anything tonight! But *ma chère* I am being altogether too terrible. I must pull myself together and apologize. Tell me," she rearranged her attractive legs, "how are you going to solve the problems you put forward in your piece?"

"My niece?" Miss Porch blinked. "I haven't got a niece."

"No, not niece, I said piece, I mean novel, on the boards we speak about a piece or a part. How do you propose to resolve the fearful problem? I can see the situation perfectly but I can't see any way out of it."

"Oh, I see what you mean, sorry. I don't think a writer needs to necessarily solve the human problem." Miss Porch knew she sounded pompous as she tried to reply. "The Norwegian poet, Ibsen," she said, "is supposed to have said 'A writer's work is merely to ask questions, not to answer them.' "

"Ah!" Miss Harrow stood up. "I like that very much, it fits in with my own sentiments. Now," she became brisk, "we must do our faces. I like to get my eyes in early . . . and then we will go up. I could eat a horse. I'm absolutely starving."

Miss Harrow busied herself mysteriously in the bathroom for half an hour while Miss Porch sat contemplating the black outlines and shadows of the sheds at the side of and beyond the orchard. She thought of the forthcoming visit with the hopeless wish that she would wake up and find it was all over.

"Wherever," she said to herself in a voice very like Miss Harrow's, "wherever can those two young men find any food to serve."

"But Anders darling! How on earth will I get up that ladder and how will I get through that terribly small hole at the top? How will Miss Porch get up there too?"

From the landing at the end of the passage both ladies contemplated, with their heads thrown back, the way they must take to gain the place they were about to visit. Miss Porch, unwillingly dressed in one of Miss Harrow's Arabian costumes, felt more ill at ease than ever. She would have liked to tear off the clothes. Having refused to part with certain undergarments she felt hot.

"Oh Alma! You're like a schoolgirl going to bed in your hockey jumper and your knickers," Miss Harrow, in good spirits after her deluge of sorrows, said. "Now Anders," she turned to him, "how on earth do we manage?"

"It has no worries *ma chère*, Maybelle, *ma vielle* Moossychatte, I will push — oops — from your underneath and Xerxes is pulling off your head."

"Oh that will be delightful, Anders. Thank you so much. Shall I go first Alma?"

Miss Porch was surprised at the smallness of the attic room. There was scarcely room for one person let alone four. They were not able to stand upright. A large, not very clean, bath towel was spread over the low folding bed. Miss Porch, with misgivings of a very private sort, looked at the bed. Suddenly she remembered the lump under the mattress of Joan Dodds' mother's bed. She seemed to see that bed, private in the married Dodds' bedroom. Joan Dodds said it was, the lump was, the baby Mrs Dodds was going to have soon. She could not recollect ever seeing a baby . . .

Miss Harrow and Miss Porch discovered quickly that they were required to squat on pillows, one each, on the floor at the side of the bed. With embarrassed smiles all four managed to sit down. Little noises of hunger mingled with conventional greetings. Miss Porch could see that Miss Harrow's legs did not bend at all well at the knees, rather like her own present problem. Chairs, she thought, would have been acceptable.

"But Anders! Beloved Pet. If I get down there on the floor, how on earth, dear boy, will I get up?"

"It has no worries *ma chère, ma vielle*, Maybelle Poossychatte, Xerxes he have the muscles and will lift you up."

On the bath towel were some lettuce leaves secreted from the black trays downstairs. The brownish remains of a cooked chicken, a very small one, lay on the torn foil bag in which it must have made its journey from Cheathem West to Cheathem East.

"If you please, Moosseychatte, to help yourself. It is *modeste*, as you will see, our little *dèjeuner*." Anders placed a badly opened tin of pineapple rings in front of Miss Harrow.

"Anders, have you perhaps a fork up here?"

Anders and Xerxes looked at each other in mock dismay and made signs to show that they would use their fingers. "It is quite *comme il faut* have no worries." Anders, in a playful movement, tweaked Miss Harrow's garment where it was possible that a nipple lurked. Miss

Porch looked hard at the lettuce. Her face ached with a stiff smile.

All round the tiny room, which had the smallest, most horrible gable window, was an assortment of paintings. An arrangement of hastily splashed reds and yellows and blues glaring from pieces of cardboard, one was even on a sheet of folded newspaper.

"You like our leetle exhibition, yes?" Anders was quick to notice when Miss Porch turned from the lettuce to look with what she hoped was not ill-concealed horror at the pictures.

"Oh yes. Rather! Don't we Alma." Miss Harrow helped herself eagerly to a desolate chicken wing. Miss Porch noticed that she ignored the lettuce. She noticed too that Miss Harrow was uncomfortable, having no alternative but to waste her legs, either cramped in an impossible contortion under her too heavy body, or pushed straight out to be hidden immediately under the squalid canvas bed. The grey blanket under the towel did not look at all clean either. Miss Harrow seemed to shudder as she nibbled the chicken bone.

"Some salt would be nice," Miss Harrow said in a low voice to Miss Porch, "but I don't see any," she added.

Xerxes and Anders, in the small space, moved about with surprising agility. They kept moving the paint-splashed boards into different positions. There was only one light bulb and, with their heads tilted first to one side and then to the other, they studied the effects of this one light on their work. They seemed to keep moving the pictures so that different ones were in front of Miss Porch and Miss Harrow, one after the other. Neither Anders nor Xerxes ate anything.

"Oh for heaven's sake!" Miss Harrow, laughing,

ducked to avoid a picture, not the soft one on newspaper, "for heaven's sake Anders, dear boy, do sit down and have some of this lovely meal."

But Anders, taking another picture, displayed it with graceful movements. "Gouache, *ma chère*," he said in a seductive tone, "gouache, a method of painting with opaque colours. I got from him," he indicated Xerxes, "we grind the paint in the pond and mix with honey and . . ." he seized another picture and planted it in front of Miss Harrow. "How do you like this one?" he asked. Miss Porch averted her eyes from what looked like a carrot in a mop.

"Of course," Miss Harrow said in a low voice to Miss Porch, "we really need some wine. In ordinary circumstances I would bring some wine as a gift. Of course," she said with a laugh choking in her throat, "in ordinary circumstances I should have provided the meal and it would have been a Meal."

Miss Porch could feel Miss Harrow's unhappiness.

"It's not just this tasteless fleshless chicken," Miss Harrow said, "it's only a bone, probably the one I bought in Cheathem West on the way here. How awful! I am sorry, Alma, to get you into this. In the ordinary way of things I would entertain you in my comfortable apartment or in some fashionable yet secluded restaurant. Somehow I suddenly have a ghastly vision of my fast disappearing capital. I never think about things like that, there must be something wrong with me." She gave a harsh laugh. "Oh come along, Anders," she said, "do come and sit down and share this meal, this refreshment. Alma and I cannot eat alone, can we Alma. And do tell Xerxes, for heaven's sake, to stop prancing about so madly."

Miss Porch was aware, all at once, that both young

men were crouched on the other side of the low bed. She saw the expression in their eyes. Both seemed suddenly to have small glittering eyes, set too close together. Their noses too seemed more hooked, beaklike and threatening. The handsome young faces were smaller as if shrivelled with some mean intention. Xerxes frowned and his eyebrows met in a heavy fold of flesh just above his nose.

Both men seemed to stare rather than look. Miss, Porch, glancing quickly at Miss Harrow, saw that she was tired of pretending to enjoy the meal and she saw too that Miss Harrow had realized, as she had herself, that Anders and Xerxes, in a sinister way, were intending that they buy the pictures.

"Anders darling! I shall have to reprimand you and remind you of your position and that you have other duties to perform this evening." Miss Porch was horrified to hear the suggestion of 'other duties' and even more horrified as she heard Miss Harrow's imperative drawl lose confidence. Anders stood over the little bed straddling its smallness. If Miss Harrow was unable to protect herself, Miss Porch thought, how could she, Alma Porch, manage to look after herself?

"Which will you choose Mabel?" Anders seemed to bark, "and you, Miss Porch? Which pictures will you choose?" The coloured cardboard flopped forwards or fell back crazily as a final threatening attempt was made to display them all at once. The carrot in the mop one was clearly, Miss Porch could now see, something else. She felt very uncomfortable as though violated in some way. She did not want to consider the possibilities though found herself, against her will, wondering whether the purple-red vegetable was protruding from the bushiness or whether it was being pushed into it. She tried to draw back from the violence of the painting. There was no room to recoil.

Miss Harrow was struggling to her feet. She gave a long-drawn-out cry of anger and pain and she clutched the part of her where her heart would probably be behind the folds of the generous garment she wore. "Oh!" she cried again, "help me up, Anders before it is too late!"

Anders left the paintings immediately, letting them all collapse showing their dirty, shabby backs. He struggled behind Miss Harrow and, putting his hands under her arms, lifted her up. It was not easy, Miss Porch could see his face flush darkly and sweat formed beads on his forehead.

"Oh!" Miss Harrow gave a cry. "I am so utterly humiliated and so angry. Anders, you shall pay for this." The last words were like a hissing whisper. "Oh, Miss Porch," Miss Harrow's voice wailed, "Miss Porch, Alma, I do apologize!"

"Please," Miss Porch managed the words, "it's nothing."

The two ladies were helped down the ladder by the two silent young men. Miss Harrow did not look at either of them.

"Moossychatte!" Anders trembled at the foot of the ladder, "have you perhaps a cigarette, please? I, I, we, need a cigarette." His hands shook. "Please?"

Miss Harrow opened her handbag and threw an unopened packet at him. He caught it, holding and opening it with pathetic eagerness.

Slowly Miss Porch and Miss Harrow walked in the courtyard and Miss Harrow recalled in detail, for Miss Porch, the deliciousness of some enormous handmade chocolates she had had once.

"They were so smooth and creamy," she said, "and the exquisite taste of the rum in the rich fudge centres is unforgettable. Eating just one of these chocolates," she said, "was like having a whole box of chocolates, but perfect quality of course. I suppose," she added, "the skill in writing depends heavily on being able to make use of adequate metaphor." She sighed. "The trouble is," she said, "I'm hungry."

Miss Porch thought that perhaps the best thing to do would be to make for the kitchen. It might be possible that there would be the late-night specials offered by Miles which would take Miss Harrow's mind off the sufferings of the Trinity Pond movie and the subsequent disappointment in the attic.

There was no chalked board outside the kitchen and no familiar good-humoured sounds of people eating. Only Miss Peycroft was there boiling kettles and tearing up sheets.

"It seems," Miss Peycroft said to Miss Porch and Miss Harrow, "that Anna is having a baby in one of the attics. This is what they always do in novels, well cheap or old-fashioned novels" — she indicated her preparations. "As a writer," she said to Miss Porch, "you will know about this sort of thing. Apparently," she went on, "Miss Rennett is the only person here able to do anything and you know, I mean, you have seen for yourself what an extraordinary shape she is. It wasn't at all easy getting her up into the attic. We had to hoist her up the ladder with a rope and, as you will have realized, she doesn't seem to have any neck to speak of.'' As she spoke Miss Peycroft went on tearing up the soft white cloth. ''I hadn't any old sheets,'' she added, ''these are practically new. You do realize don't you,'' she said, ''we'll have a real baby for Foxybaby. This is an exciting breakthrough. Apparently Anna is in the second stage. Miss Rennett says the head is on the perineum and that she, Rennett, expects to be down for rehearsal tomorrow as usual. Miles has a winch up there and will lower her out of the window if they can get her through. Those attic windows are awful, ridiculously small. Dr Black is on his way from Cheathem West. So useful to have him. Even if he has been struck off, he still knows his childbed and being unlisted doesn't charge so much. Mrs Finch, our trusty village maiden, will attend to the immediate needs of the mother and child.'' She smiled. ''So you see, we at Trinity House can take care of everything.''

Miss Peycroft filled another kettle and sat it on the stove. ''It's so useful about Miss Rennett,'' she said, ''apparently her brother used to be a vet. I am not at all sure what all this boiling water can do — or this heap of what is now rag,'' she added, ''it does seem, however, to be a necessary part of an emergency. Miss Rennett was emphatic that I should leave the attic and prepare all this.''

Miss Porch was still in bed after the troubled night when Mrs Finch put her head round the door. ''Mind if I do yours first?'' she yelled.

Miss Porch sat up quickly saying that yes of course it was perfectly all right. During the snatches of sleep she had only partly enjoyed, a dream invading repeatedly brought a street van, a mobile coffee stall, within reach and twice she asked the attendant if he had something with bacon and egg. Yes, he said and twice handed her a greaseproof, warm package, just fitting nicely into the palm of her hand, but both times the deliciously fragrant prospect disappeared when Mrs Castle, who had come back to share Miss Porch's room, announced, first, that she had decided on her little lemon for rehearsal, and, second, that it was such a shame that the cogs, or whatever they were, of the winch prepared for Miss Rennett's descent, had slipped and Miss Rennett's subsequent arrival in the courtyard was rapid enough to have her, in front of the dismayed eyes of the people gathered there, suddenly in a fat heap of flesh and clothing on the well-washed flags of the yard.

"I don't think she was too badly hurt," Mrs Castle said, "but Miss Peycroft said it rather looked as if several of her bones were broken. Fortunately Dr Black was, as he knows the matron rather well, able to have her admitted to the General in Cheathem West."

Mrs Castle, during the night, had been very talkative, telling her unwilling listener, "she's a lovely little girl, the baby is, a sweet little sister for those two young monkeys. I must say the little boys were very good, and d'you know, one of them wanted to hold the baby, and while he nursed his new little sister he didn't breathe! His face was quite blue when they took the baby off his little lap." Mrs Castle sighed. "Two little boys," she said, "and a little sister. Like my own grandchildren, two boys and a girl. I am," she insisted on telling, "going to run up some little gowns and Mrs Crisp, who always has bootees on the go, is giving a dozen pairs of pink ones as a gift. Isn't that cute?'' Mrs Castle, Miss Porch had known without seeing in the dark, was blinking her eyes and patting her rollers. "Mr Miles," Mrs Castle went on, "imagine that man! He thinks of everything! He had some disposables, you know, snugglies, in his room — I mean, his shop. Also — ", this after a pause during which Miss Porch had dozed off " — also," Miss Porch woke again to the voice, "also it's very lovely for a woman to have her very own daughter," followed by a long sigh, "I remember when Daphne was born," she said, "her daddy said she looked, promise you'll never tell. . . ." Through gritted teeth Miss Porch promised. "Well, her daddy," Mrs Castle continued, "her daddy said she looked like a poached egg but I knew she was truly beautiful."

Dinner, during the night, because of the emergency of the childbirth and Miss Rennett's spectacular drop from the gable, had been a simple affair. Cold sideboards with emphasis on veal and ham, cheeseboards and a selection of little known Hungarian wines followed by fresh fruit. Miss Harrow, Miss Porch had noticed, was visibly cheered by the meal, going off before everyone else to sort things out with Anders.

"So wise of Miles" — Mrs Viggars, moved by the turn of events had made a speech — "to have a simple repast of this nature. I have always held the Hungarians in deep respect for their various uprisings and the cold collation is generally acceptable especially if it spares human effort in times of stress."

Mrs Finch seemed to fill the room. Mrs Castle, clutching her white compendium, stood pressed closed to the wall, both feet together on the worn boards leaving the little floor mat free because Mrs Finch's hands were poised to pull the mat from its accustomed place in readiness for sweeping.

"I like yella." Mrs Finch, on her knees, paused to approve Mrs Castle's nocturnal choice.

Miss Porch flopped back on her pillow. She felt sure Miss Paisley could have done something about the rooms. They were not all occupied, she knew; for one thing there was the room Vladimir Lefftov had so recently vacated. It would be simple, she thought, to put Mrs Castle into that room all by herself. It might even be possible, she let herself go, to lock Mrs Castle in the room, not for the whole time but perhaps for a selected number of hours every night. In this way one could be absolutely sure of being in a room, of having a room of one's own. It was essential — Miss Porch continued her thought which was accompanied by a smothered growl — to have the complete privacy of a room to oneself in these circumstances.

She knew she was going mad. I am going mad, she told herself several times during the night. As for all that rubbish from Miss Paisley about Miss Peycroft having to observe the strictest precedents and having to standardize their methods of accommodation, it was all self-important nonsense. It was unpleasant to recall Miss Paisley's obvious enjoyment in reciting the refusal and puffing out her boring chest as she did so.

Miss Porch, pretending to rest on her pillow, pressed her lips into a thin, far from restful line. She would have her own word, if she could get it in, with Peycroft.

"I like yella." Mrs Finch made the announcement once more in clear tones as if to reach from one end of the long house to the other. "Nice and bright and cheerful but if I put on yella, doesn't matter what it is — if it's yella, I'm seck. There's sumpin about yella brings up everything I've ett. Wunst when I'd had a steak and fried eggs and a nice bit of kidney for me breakfast, Miss Peycroft lent me a yella pinny. I'll fetch up I tode her. But would Miss Peycroft listen not on yor life, so I fetched up . . ."

Miss Porch, trapped in bed, and Mrs Castle, pinned by invisible forces to the wall, unable to escape, waited unwillingly to hear the terrible result of Mrs Finch's day in yellow.

"Finchy Pinchy my pretty Bird. Where are you? Oo's a pretty Birdie then? Where's my Finchy? Tweety Pinchy tweetie tweet?" Miles, whistling and calling along the passage, came nearer.

"Finchy Pinchy?"

"Number fifteen, where d'you think I am you bald-headed goof!" The pretty Bird's roar travelled back through the partly open door.

Undaunted Miles called once more, "Hey hey hey Finchy, what did — wait for it Finchy — what did — oh this is killing me! You there, Finchy?"

"Course I am you stupid crab!"

Listen to this, Finchy. Listen to this willya. What did Vladimir do when they said 'don't stop?' "

"Oo said 'don't stop?' "

"Them, they say 'oooh Vladimir don't stop!' Heh, heh, heh! What would you say, Finchy? You'd say 'don't stop' now wouldn't you? Come along, Birdie. Heh? You'd say 'don't stop . . .' "

Miss Porch rose awkwardly in her bedclothes and Mrs Castle pressed back even more closely against the wardrobe.

"What did Vladimir do when you told him 'don't stop?' " Miles repeated. "Come on, Finchy. What did he do? You can tell me."

"For Gawd's sake how should I know." Mrs Finch thumped at the tiny rug with her little brush.

"He lefftov! Haw. Haw. Haw. Get it? He lefftov! Haw!" Miles and Mrs Finch spent a few minutes in noisy mirth. "Vladimir lefftov! Wah! Haw!"

"Aw Gawd! Look what you've gone and made me do," Mrs Finch struggled up from her knees. "Wait on. I'll have to go to the toilet."

"Have I time to phone my daughter, Daphne, before class?" Mrs Castle asked Miss Porch when the double presence of Mrs Finch and Miles was reduced to a series of thumps and screams heard from some distant place. "Thinking that there would be nothing to spend money on in the country and my son-in-law having paid everything for me in advance," she continued, "I haven't brought much money with me. I arranged with Daphne that she should bank my pension cheque; such a good way to save, don't you think? I'll need money, won't I," — she paused, her head bobbing to one side — "for our little midnight-you know what."

"Yes, yes, you'll have time to phone," Miss Porch said. "I'm not even out of bed yet, they can't start without me." She pushed back the blankets. She supposed she should hurry. If only the woman would get out of the room and leave her in peace. If only the cogs, the mysterious little wheels of machinery, could have slipped for Mrs Castle; nothing too painful of course, but something which would bring about instant removal. Why Miss Rennett? she wondered, someone who never uttered a word. . . .

"I've made my bed all nice and tidy," Mrs Castle's

voice interrupted, "I'll just slip out here to the phone. I mean," she gave a little laugh, "to look at my bed you wouldn't know, would you, that I'd been in it all night — so smooth and tidy!" She gave another self-conscious little laugh. "I do like to leave everything neat and tidy. Well, I'll just slip to the phone then. I really can't allow Mrs Viggars to shout me treats if we're going to dine in style every night, even last night, with poor Miss Rennett's dreadful fall, we had a nice meal, but what I mean is it isn't exactly cheap, is it. And after I've phoned I simply must pop up to see the baby."

"You'd better hurry to get your telephone call," Miss Porch said with an increasing sharpness of impatience. She knew only too well that Mrs Castle had been in the other bed all night.

Mrs Castle was still telephoning when Miss Porch returned from her shower. Down below, under the row of upstairs windows, the students were assembling in the courtyard.

"Mrs Viggars is altogether too generous" — Miss Porch could hear Mrs Castle plainly. "You know, Daphne dear, I don't understand how Miss Rennett can allow such generosity, or could allow I should say, poor dear. She never seemed to say 'thank you', not in public anyhow. We can't know, can we dear, what people do in private. But I have never heard her shout Mrs Viggars, not ever. Also dear, if we are going to dine in style as I've been telling you, could you post my dinner dress? Please? No, dear, not the one with the little fruits on it, could you post the champagne silk? Yes, I know it's got a plunging neckline and I haven't worn it for simply ages but it would be most suitable. And, dear, could you pop in one of my more subtle lipsticks, something mauve dear, not red, no not red dear. I've got the *Midnight*

Beetroot here. I am sorry to give you this trouble. I never thought I would need extra clothes and more money. As quick as you can dear, thank you. Yes, I am enjoying the course though I must confess I missed the exercises again this morning. Naughty little old me! My room mate, Alma, and I had a lovely little chat instead. We're very cosy. No dear, there's no need to bother with shoes. I'll be able to wear my sandals — yes — I did bring them. They're a mushroomy wine if you remember and will go perfectly with the champagne. Yes, yes dear I know you have to go, so much to do — Bysie Byse — Bysie Byse to Jonty Bysie Byse to Brissty and Bysie Byse to my very own Pet Annabelly love love Daphne dear.'' Mrs Castle hung up.

The act of choosing is a narrowing process. Miss Porch rubbed cold cream into the wrinkles of her neck and wondered again why she had chosen to offer the novel, the Foxybaby, in this way. She had chosen to come to this place and discovered at once that it was not possible to choose to leave. There was Mrs Viggars before Miss Rennett's fall and there was Mrs Viggars after Miss Rennett's fall. Miss Porch found that she was with small actions putting off leaving the room which, because of Mrs Castle, she found it hard to stay in. She knew she was longing for familiar voices, her father's voice from years ago making a statement about the weather, her mother's reply, which was often a question having nothing to do with the statement. There was the nasal resonance of an indignant aunt and now, lately, the risings and fallings of the voices from the Senior Common Room at The Towers. There was the Headmistress there too; because of her voice, Miss Porch often went for short walks.

However one might feel about Miss Peycroft, there was nowhere to walk here. The empty street, the even emptier paddocks — all were unfamiliar places where one would not be welcome and where there would be this incredible longing for the sounds of particular voices.

Miss Porch knew that she was putting off the meeting with Mrs Viggars after the events of the night before. She knew it was because of Mrs Viggars that she did not set off blindly to try to walk away on to some distant and hoped-for place which, she felt, must exist beyond the horizon which was visible but would retreat as progress towards it was attempted.

Slowly she made her way down to the courtyard. She could hear the muffled sounds of excitement as the students gathered in readiness.

There are times, Miss Porch thought, in life when one might be walking towards oneself. Either the child towards the adult or the other way round. Either way it was a passing confrontation, not recognizable until it was over.

The sound of the sea, the steady all-embracing sustained roar of the sea, the sound behind the immediate splashing sound of the waves running up and falling and running back was like a returning to consciousness. It was as if the sound carried something, bringing it nearer and nearer, and yet, as in the partly conscious, half-waking dream whatever is being brought stays as part of the background. The sustained roar suggested limitless depths, untouched and mysterious.

The wind blowing from the sea and across the wide expanse of sand was unbelievable. Words were snatched from their mouths.

"Unusual weather for the time of the year," Miles managed to say.

Most of the school were huddled out of the wind sheltering behind the great slabs of rock which were strewn and piled along that part of the coast. Miles, who had brought a small and ancient donkey on a trailer behind the bus, was unpacking baskets of thick cheese sandwiches. There was a supply of lettuce for the Faithful. It was a relief to Miss Porch to hear that the usual lemon juice had been left behind by mistake. Instead, a steaming potion was being stirred in a container strongly resembling the inside of an old laundry boiler suspended on three stout sticks over a remarkably substantial fire.

The first thing they had done on reaching the coast was to clamber down from the bus and rush down at the side of and in front of the brave, heavily laden little donkey as she, on dainty hooves, picked her way down the uneven path to the sands. Once on the sands and feeling the cold wind they busily collected driftwood and built a fire. Now they stood in good-natured, colourful groups warming themselves. A few people helped Miles. They poured the claret into the copper. Some threw in the lump sugar and the broken cinnamon sticks and others, with cold clumsy fingers, cut up the fresh lemons, adding the pieces cautiously to the simmering dark pool. At exactly the right moment Miles added a fortification of hospital brandy and several handfuls of raisins.

Because of the unexpectedly bleak circumstances the mulled wine was very acceptable. They warmed their fingers on the battered aluminium cups (wherever did Miles find mugs like these!) and blew into the steam in between the little sips of appreciation.

Miss Porch had forgotten the proposed excursion to the coast and was surprised on reaching the courtyard at breakfast time to discover that the prevailing excitement was not in anticipation of a further instalment of her novel, but came from the preparations, the repeated running back upstairs for things which might be needed, for the outing. The expedition, the word *picnic* naturally was not used, to the sea was about to start.

Miles, dressed in a pirate's cast-off clothes, drove the bus, off its blocks for once, Miss Porch noticed rather sourly, with a flourish of gears and brakes and horn-blowing into the yard.

In no time everyone was seated. Leaning her forehead against the cool window of the bus Miss Porch wondered what the day would have in store for them. The sea, she thought, must be quite a long way away. She supposed the bus would manage the rough drive. Fortunately she was not sitting near Mrs Castle. Jonquil's voice could be plainly heard above the rattle of travel. She was describing, to someone who had hitherto escaped the telling, her grandchildren.

"Jonty is a lovely child," Mrs Castle was saying, the passing reflecting rose-coloured sky and stubble meaning nothing to her. "He has written some novels," she said, "we, Daphne, my daughter and I, published them in a little set of six books. We made such pretty covers. One I did in Venetian needlepoint and two are knitted, no, I'm a liar — one is knitted, moss-stitch, beautifully firm, you know one plain, one purl — and the other I did in finger crochet. I had some lovely wool . . . leftover wool from . . ."

Miss Porch could see Mrs Viggars sitting farther down in the bus. She was on a seat, taking it all up, alone. Miss Porch wondered if Mrs Viggars was thinking of Miss Rennett. Miss Peycroft was not present. It was clear that with the admitting of Miss Rennett to hospital and the arrival of the new baby in the attic there would be administrative things to be done.

Being in the bus was once more an arrival. Miss Porch remembered the absent Potter. She wondered how she was managing without her teeth. Without teeth, Miss Porch realized, it would not be possible to accept invitations, even for morning tea they would be needed, especially if the hostess was providing exceptionally well baked rock cakes. Perhaps at this very moment an assiduous surgeon was groping with long, strong, beautiful fingers in the secret regions of the Potter's alimentary system searching for the missing dentures. Miss Porch did not care for the word but thought if the Potter knew that she, Miss Porch, was thinking about the Potter's teeth, she, the Potter, might prefer dentures as some people definitely thought the word less crude, a more conventional way of mentioning false-teeth. In fact, Miss Porch began to enlarge on the subject, in the English language, she told herself, common usage was often a choice made by the people. She was sure the Potter, if she knew, would choose dentures. "I have mishlade my denchoos" she might at this moment be explaining with difficulty But no, the surgeon would have insisted that an anaesthetic be given. He would require silence and privacy for his exploration and certainly would not want to chat with the patient . . . Heavens! her own knees ached but how could she complain when the Potter had both knees broken? Her own knees, whenever she looked at them, seemed more swollen and more discoloured. Bruises have to come out. It was consoling to recall an old wise saying remembered from childhood.

Thinking about the accident she was not able to remember a fourth car. Yet the unknown Potter, the valuable moulder of clay, must have been in a car in order to be flung from it and injured at the roadside. There was another car surely, one like her own, but that had been at another time. Now when was it!

She reflected how unreliable she would be if asked to give evidence after an accident on the road.

"Yes, Your Honour, the bus reversed into my vehicle. Yes, Your Honour, the bus driver was reversing at a hundred kilometres per hour. He had red hair. His hair was black. He was bald. Your Honour! the man was a woman. Also my car was followed, Your Honour, followed, with emphasis, by another car. Both cars became very excited. I am wondering, Your Honour, if the Potter knew this thing about our cars, their obvious attachment, the same dents. Funny isn't it that the Potter and I should have identical cars, that is possibly the reason why I am not able to say where the Potter's teeth are since I am not sure about the cars at the accident . . . All I know is that this woman . . ."

She knew she could not have identified the other people involved at the time, only from seeing them later. She felt this to be a great lack in herself, that she should rely so much on the unreliable qualities of supposition, of imagination and invention; on fiction, she supposed that was what it was.

"Miss Porch! Miss Porch!" Christobel's cheeks were bright red in the cold air. "Miss Porch," she said, "what did Vladimir want?" She laughed. "Can you guess?"

Miss Porch muttered aloud as people do with riddles. "What did Vladimir want? I thought we'd heard them all," she said, "what did Vladimir want! I give up, Christobel!"

"Vladimir wanted to Gopak," Christobel spluttered. "This is positively the last Vladimir joke," she said. "What did Vladimir want? He wanted to Gopak!"

"Oh I see," Miss Porch said. "It's very clever," she added kindly. "Very clever! Thank you, Christobel."

They stood in little groups devoting themselves to the bread and cheese. In spite of the fresh wind and the pleasure of being at the edge of a wild sea Miss Porch let her thoughts wander to less pleasant things. Unwillingly she remembered looking through some new journals before leaving The Towers. New writing, new novelists, new dramatists and new poets so many of them, all young and handsome and clever . . .

"Here I am in grief, trying to lose weight and, like everyone else, feeling ravenously hungry and eating as if I had been starving for weeks. Eating enormously!" Mrs Viggars was beside Miss Porch who, wanting to say something wise and comforting about Miss Rennett, told Mrs Viggars instead about the hundreds of literary journals, the plays, the poems, the novels and, unable to restrain herself, she added something about all the very young and very successful writers.

"There are so many of them," Miss Porch was surprised at the mean-sounding words and the spiteful discontent evident in her own voice, "that I feel it is not worth anything at all to try to go on writing. I mean, if so many writers are writing what is the point of adding to the great quantity of words?" She did not want to go on with the stupid conversation she had started. Miss Rennett should be talked about. She waited for Mrs Viggars to dispose of the last crumbs and said so.

"My dear Miss Porch," Mrs Viggars said, "oops! I almost called you 'child' and that would have been quite wrong."

Miss Porch, agreeing, felt old and tired. "I am not young any more," she said inside herself.

"Fontane," Miss Viggars said, "often considered by the Germans to be the father of the novel, was fifty-eight when he published his first novel. Schopenhauer," Mrs Viggars continued, "is supposed to have said that novels should be written only by ageing authors." She paused. "But to get back to numbers," she said, "think of the supermarket or the airport." She turned her ample back to the wind. "All those people! What do you do about them? If you apply the attitude you have just expressed you might as well, in the face of all those crowds, decide to end it all. Too many people, you could say to yourself and bang, with a pistol, shoot yourself. And, if you miss, you could step off a jetty where you know the water to be deep with savage under-currents. There are plenty of ways. Possibly," she added, "best to do the shooting when already standing or sitting on a suitable jetty. But allow me to remind you that you are probably suffering from an inadequate supply of the excellent mulled grape. To me your symptoms are all too clear." She turned round. "Miles!" she bellowed into the teeth of the gale. "Fill us up, Miles," she bawled. "Ah! there's a good chap!"

"I'm sorry," Miss Porch began, "I really meant to ask, Miss Rennett . . . is she? . . . I am sorry I spoke of other silly things."

"Think nothing of it, Porch old man," Mrs Viggars said. "I am pleased to be able to tell you Rennett asked for champagne and I was able to supply it. I was glad to see her powers of selection improve. Rennett, d'you see, has very little taste. Her recent choice of champagne, not a cheap one either, was a breakthrough." Mrs Viggars gave a little laugh which was more of a choking cough.

"Chekhov," said Miss Porch primly, "asked on his death bed for champagne. He, like Miss Rennett, was far away from home in an unfamiliar place. He was with his wife, she was an actress, on holiday in Germany. Of course he was a very sick man. He told the German doctor '*Ich sterbe*' and then lay down with his face to the wall and, full of champagne, he died. His body," she added, feeling ashamed of her pride in her knowledge, "was sent back to Russia in a railway waggon marked *oysters*."

"Oysters," Mrs Viggars sighed, "but what more could one wish for! Well," she said, "Rennett is certainly full of champers." She sighed again. "It remains," she said, "to be seen what her future, if any, will be." She paused. "Perhaps a heart attack before the winch slipped would have been infinitely more satisfactory, but then we simply cannot make choices or requests in matters like these."

They moved away together from the sheltered places by the rocks and walked, side by side, heads down into the wind.

"Very bracing," Mrs Viggars said. She tied her metal cup, now empty, to her belt, a loose sash arrangement which passed round her body like a slipped decoration. A displaced garter, Miss Porch thought. When people were invested, she supposed, the garter did not really sit with coy little rosettes on the fat white thigh but straddled the recipient's chest; a diagonal smooth ribbon of colourful honour. Worn thus outwardly there was no need for the honoured person to undress in order for people to see that he was honoured.

"Rather!" Miss Porch uttered a sound which did not fit. She was trying to bring herself back from an unknown person's instant ceremony, an investiture, the honoured one kneeling on the edge of a precipice about to be tapped on the shoulder by a graceful sword, the gorgeous ribbon poised to be flung with precision across his brave . . .

"The truth is," Mrs Viggars said, raising her voice above the sustained roar of the sea, "I am not at all bothered really about losing weight. I do not dread the end of School weighing session. I try and do as my doctor tells me, a little gentle exercise twice a day. Best to walk, he says, and to buy a book or a picture or something nice to wear. He says to walk to the post-office occasionally and send a postal order to some deserving cause. He says to try to do one thing every day which makes me feel better. He is right, of course. And to cut down on the endless cream cakes, especially the noble eclair which I love.

The truth is, Porch, I don't come to these Schools to lose weight. I come to these Schools because I am lonely. I don't suppose you know what that means. I expect with your thinking and writing you do not feel alone, in fact you want to be alone for a good deal of the time. I am alone too much. I have no one to belong to and no one belonging to me. Certainly not Rennett, though, as you see, I did keep up something there. All on my side, I expect you noticed. A sort of wild goose chase. Stupid. So that she should feel chosen. I don't suppose anyone has ever chosen Rennett — mothers do not choose their children. I wanted Rennett to feel chosen and I wanted a reason, however slight, for being. Viggars, d'you see, died before they could be any sort of explanation. I did not even know that he felt ill. It turned out to be the old ticker. A bit rusty, you know.''

"Oh I see," Miss Porch let the wind carry away her small shaky voice. She wondered whether to catch hold of Mrs Viggars, her arm perhaps, or would it be better to pat her gently somewhere? On her shoulder? Not knowing what to do Miss Porch did nothing. "I am sorry," she said.

A lid of heavy clouds settled above them. The sands reflected the melancholy. The sea boiling darkly now along the beach seemed heavy with dirty foam. The water, slapping, rose, washing endlessly, from both sides, over the rocks. It was as if two oceans were meeting in some kind of passion at this place. Like the meeting of ideas — Miss Porch managed to put the thought together somewhere inside herself. Far out along the horizon there was a shining strip of light. It looked like a strip of metal joining the sky and the sea.

"I like the wild gleam out there," Mrs Viggars said, stopping and waving an arm in the direction of the sky. "It must mean something." She walked on. Miss Porch plodded in the sand beside her.

The wind rushing, as it did every evening across the wheat stubble, brought the fast-growing waves higher up the beach.

"Schools," Mrs Viggars said, "don't mind if you're a person on your own. That is one of the delights. You don't need to be a couple or a triangle as you do in ordinary life.''

Miss Porch nodded. Mrs Viggars, in her usual way, made the school seem entirely worthwhile. Uncertainty faded. Miss Porch thought about the Foxybaby girl. She thought about the girl's father and about what he was trying to do. She wanted to sit and write somewhere, quietly, without distraction of any sort.

''You know, Alma,'' Mrs Viggars said, leaning towards Miss Porch so that her voice seemed to sing in the wind. She drew closer as they walked. ''I am not able to see into the future like the prophet, Teiresias. He, though blind, was able to make predictions about the future but was not able to change it.'' She paused. ''I am looking,'' she said, ''into the future and feel that I am able to make some changes. I've heaps of money;'' she paused and then said quickly in a gruff voice, ''I'm sorry to sound so naive but I want to make myself clear. I want to take that girl home with me.''

''What girl?'' Miss Porch spoke sharply. ''I can't let her go, I haven't finished . . .''

''Why, that girl, the one who is and is not Sandy, of course.'' Mrs Viggars gave an embarrassed laugh. ''The one who is pretending to be my daughter while I am pretending to be her father. I don't want to go on pretending, I want the real thing. You may or may not believe this, Alma, but your book has made a great difference to my life, perhaps more so because it is not finished. I want to take that young girl and her three children.'' She gave another embarrassed little laugh. ''I know,'' she said, ''there's a lot of talk about rôle-playing these days and that people, especially women, should not be cast into certain expected rôles — it goes right back into kindergarten games, I'm told. But, as a woman, I dearly long to play the rôle I might have had. If I had had children, Alma, I would have made their beds for them every day. It seems to me to be a privilege to be able to prepare the place where someone will sleep. I have a huge house,'' she went on, ''and gardens and stables and a pool — everything that a little family could need. I would like to provide food and clothes and to choose suitable schools, in short, I want to give them a home. What d'you think I should do? Would I be misunderstood d'you think? It's your novel, I know, but I'd like to make my offer. I've thought about it a great deal.'' She paused. ''I do hope that you don't think I am vulgar,'' she said.

''Of course I don't.'' Miss Porch would have liked her voice to be stronger in the wind. She cried again in her thin voice, ''of course I don't think you are in the least vulgar. But,'' she said, ''what about Miss Rennett? What about Miss Rennett?''

''Plenty of room for Rennett,'' Mrs Viggars replied. ''Plenty of room for Rennett if she chooses and is able, in the end, to make a choice. I have been asking her for years to come. Now I must simply wait to see if she, well, I must wait to see how she . . .'' Mrs Viggars gave a helpless shrug to which there was no immediate answer.

''You know,'' Miss Porch said quickly, ''when you talk, it all sounds so simple, I mean your idea about a nice home and choosing schools and so on.''

''Well, yes,'' Mrs Viggars replied, ''if one is not the parent I suppose it is more simple, much more simple. If I were Anna's mother the girl might well tell me to get lost, I think that is the phrase. But because I am only Mrs Viggars she might be willing to listen and to see the possibilities of choosing what else to do in her life, as

257

well as being mother to her children of course. I would like to offer her opportunities."

"I see," Miss Porch said slowly, "but what am I to do? The predicament is, as I have it, insoluble." She put her hands up, cupping her ears in order to hear Mrs Viggars better. The noise of the wind seemed to be increasing. "Do you think it is hopeless? That there is no solution?"

"No, not at all," Mrs Viggars said, "a father does not give up just as a mother never gives up, though both may lose heart and both, as the child suffers, suffer." She paused. "You do have," she said, "others on the page, so to speak — the prison officer, for instance, in a situation of a different sort her qualities could provide . . . but look, Alma!" Mrs Viggars stopped suddenly. "Look!" she said again but Miss Porch could not see anything.

"When we get back," she said, standing still only because Mrs Viggars was, "Why don't you tell them what you would like to do. Speak to Miss Peycroft only a little. It is not really any concern of hers. Ask the girl, ask Anna and find out about her, what she really wants and needs. Ask the little boys . . ."

Mrs Viggars raised one arm, its huge size seemed to catch and hold up the rushing wind.

"Look, Alma! Look there along the beach," she said, her voice gruffy with excitement. "Can you see them?" Miss Porch felt herself held close to Mrs Viggars in the cold arms of the wind.

"Look there! Alma! There ahead!" Mrs Viggars said again. She pointed to something in the blurred distance.

"I can't see anything," Miss Porch began, "but wait a minute, there is something. I think there is something."

In the distance in a patch of sunlight from between the parted clouds Miss Porch thought she could see two people stumbling in the soft sand coming towards them. Slightly in front there seemed to be a thin girl. The slowly emerging light from the sun shone for a moment on the red gold of her hair. Behind her, close to her, was the well-preserved, middle-aged, well-dressed man.

"What is he carrying?" Miss Porch's whisper was devoured immediately by the wind.

"See for yourself," Mrs Viggars said. "He's carrying a baby," she said. "Go on!" she urged. "They belong to you. They are yours. Don't let them go now. Go on! Go!"

Miss Porch thought she felt Mrs Viggars' hand in the small of her back pushing her forward. Then she seemed to be holding her, preventing her from going on.

"I hope to see you at Easter," Mrs Viggars put her face close to Miss Porch's ear. "I don't imagine Easter makes much impact on your particular life but could we make it a deadline nearly achieved? What do you think, Alma?" They were walking forward again.

"The idea of some sort of awakening? Is that what you mean?" Miss Porch, still whispering, strained to make herself understood.

"Yes," Mrs Viggars said, "that's what I had in mind." Mrs Viggars seemed now to be falling behind. She was no longer keeping up. "Go on!" she said, "don't let me hold you up. Don't stop now. There they are. They are still coming towards you. Don't, whatever you do, turn away from them now. They are coming towards you. Make the most of it. Till Easter, then."

Like the waves, the two figures, the man and the girl, were coming closer. Carefully the man held against his chest a baby.

Miss Porch, pulling her feet steadily out of the wind-blown drifting sand, kept on slowly walking towards them.

The bus seemed to be stopping. There was the feeling of moving forward and being held back at the same time. The rhythm of travelling had changed. Miss Porch raised her head from the window where her forehead rested on the soothing glass. She felt dazed as she always did if she slept during the day or on a journey. Her knees ached.

The other passengers were leaving the bus. The elderly woman in black was the first to get down. She stood on the remains of an old pavement, a little to one side, and watched the passengers disembark.

The driver, Miss Porch remembered he had said his name was Miles, was pulling the luggage from the various parts of the bus where it had been stowed. He stacked the boxes and the bags and cases at the side of an archway through which could be seen a spacious yard. From the corners of the walls tall sunflowers tipped their bright heads towards them. Miss Porch was glad to see the flowers. In spite of their straggling appearance they were bold and brave and, because of this, their shabbiness did not matter. Something she had learned long ago came into her mind:

Ah, Sun-flower! weary of time,
Who countest the steps of the sun;
Seeking after that sweet golden clime,
Where the traveller's journey is done.

The few passengers, strangers to one another, exchanged little smiles of embarrassment and surreptitiously rubbed their bruises.

"Miss Peycroft expects youse for afternoon tea in her rooms," Miles said, "in about a hour I should think. Would that be right Mother?"

Mrs Miles said she thought that would be about right.

"So," Miles said, "you've got nice time for a lay-down and a wash and a brush. I'll get youse and your bags up to your rooms in next to no time."

"Yes," Mrs Miles said, "he'll do that."

Miss Porch, glancing up at the windows, thought she saw behind the slight movement of a curtain being lifted a slip of a white face, like a crescent moon, pressed to the corner of the window-pane. Perhaps, she thought, Miss Peycroft was keeping watch to see that the recently employed, part-time, outside man was not wasting all his paid time with Edward unexpectedly returned . . . Quickly, in her own words, she pulled herself together, wincing at the profane phrase. She followed Miles upstairs. In mounting anticipation, and with a curious feeling of excitement, she almost asked him if he had a little table for sale. Pausing in the doorway she said, "I'll need a table, something quite small will do."

"I'll see what I can find," Miles said, "there's sure to be something up in the attic. If I remember right I think I've the very thing for you."

A NOTE ABOUT THE AUTHOR

ELIZABETH JOLLEY (1923–2007) is one of Australia's most celebrated authors, critically acclaimed and read worldwide. She was born Monica Elizabeth Knight in England, grew up in a strict, German-speaking household, and attended a Quaker boarding school. During the Second World War, she left school to become a nurse in a military hospital. Later, she married Leonard Jolley, a university librarian, and, in 1959, with three children, they immigrated to Western Australia.

Although Jolley wrote all her life, it was not until she was in her fifties that her first book was published. Over the next twenty-five years, she published twenty-three books, of which fifteen are novels, and won every major Australian literary award. Since then, her work has been translated into every major language. In the United States, her novels were selected as *New York Times* Notable books, excerpted in *The New Yorker,* and prominently reviewed, including on the front page of the *New York Times Book Review* several times. She is best known for her masterful, semi-autobiographical *Vera Wright Trilogy (My Father's Moon, Cabin Fever,* and *The Georges' Wife)* and for her blackly comic novels *The Sugar Mother, Miss Peabody's Inheritance, Mr. Scobie's Riddle,* and *Foxybaby.* These and others are now published by Persea Books in its ongoing series of Elizabeth Jolley revivals.